FREEDOM'S
Island

SABRA WALDFOGEL

For Clark, who never did find the citation

Table of Contents

Prologue

The One-Eyed Man

On a humid August day in 1876, the year that Mississippi was redeemed by the Democrats and their associates in the Klan, two men dug a pit in the wet loam of the Delta soil. It was bright daylight, but they didn't mind who saw them do it. They were unashamed of what they'd done, and they wanted to strike fear in whoever might think about crossing them. The dirt was easy to lift and to turn. They didn't need to dig deep. They had a big hole to dig. They had fifty corpses to bury, men, women, and children.

The man wielding a shovel, who was short and stocky and flushed in the heat, grumbled, "Don't know why we're burying a bunch of niggers. I wouldn't bury a dead dog."

The man who watched was tall and fair-haired—he went hatless, despite the summer sun—and he wore a black patch over one eye. He said sharply, "You'd bury a dead dog if the buzzards were likely to make off with the remains."

The bodies were two and three days dead. In the August heat of the Delta, the corpses had already begun to putrefy. The men didn't talk about the smell.

The stocky man leaned on his shovel. He looked at the bodies and turned pale. "I don't feel good," he said, and leaned over to vomit into the hole. Finished, he wiped his mouth and gestured at the heap of corpses. "We done right here. But it's still ugly."

After they dumped the bodies into the pit, and covered them with a foot of earth, the stocky man looked at the mass grave with distaste. "I reckon we're finished here."

The tall, one-eyed man stared at the horizon. "I don't think so."

Chapter 1

A Speck of a Place

When the train pulled into the station, Ambrose Byrd rose from the hard wooden seat of the colored section. He reached for his carpetbag and grimaced at the ache in his back. His friend Joe said, "You ready?"

Byrd said, "How will Ben know you?"

"I sent him a photograph."

Byrd and Joe had soldiered together in the 25th Infantry out West. When Joe was wounded and mustered out, he decided to visit his brother Ben in Mississippi. Byrd was tired of soldiering. He quit the Army and left with Joe.

Joe was a big man, strong enough to carry his trunk onto the platform, where Byrd followed him. As Joe scanned the crowd for Ben, Byrd scrutinized the town. Across from the depot were two general stores, one a little weathered but bigger, and another with a newly-painted sign that said "Levy's". A ramshackle saloon stood at one end of the street, and the church—the only brick building in sight—at the other. Everything a soul might need, Byrd thought. He watched the people stream from the depot. Almost all black. Used to the West, where white, black, and Indian mixed together, he was reminded that he was in the South again.

Byrd shivered. He had been so long in the dry heat of the West that he'd forgotten about the Southern damp, hot in summer, cool in winter. He put his hands into the pockets of his greatcoat to warm them.

A big man, broad of shoulder, muscled of arm, used to heavy labor, came towards them. Dark of skin, as Joe was. Big in the belly, like a man who'd gone a little soft, Byrd thought. "Joe! Is that you!"

Joe hugged Ben and introduced Byrd. Ben said, "I've got my wagon ready. Do you have much stuff?"

Ben grunted as he lifted Joe's trunk into the wagon. "Good Lord, man, what have you got in here?"

"My uniforms, regular and dress. And my coat made from a buffalo hide."

"Did you shoot the buffalo?"

Joe laughed. "Bought it from the man who shot it."

Next to the tracks was a row of big sheds roofed with tin. Byrd asked Ben, "What's in there?"

"Cotton. Bring your cotton to the depot, store it in those sheds, and it goes right onto the train to them mills up north. Ain't you ever grown cotton?"

"No, sir, I'm from Virginia." In slavery times, he had lived on a tobacco plantation, but he hadn't been a slave for a long time.

A white man, short and rotund, with a rosy, smiling face, stopped beside Ben's wagon. He wore a suit of checked wool and carried a gold-topped cane. He asked, "Ben, who are those boys with you?"

Before Ben could answer, Byrd said pleasantly, "I ain't a boy. I'm a grown man." He held out his hand. "I'm Sergeant Ambrose Byrd, lately of the 25th Infantry, U.S. Army. Who are you, sir?"

The man stared at Byrd's proffered hand and began to

guffaw. "Certainly you don't expect me to call you Sergeant? Or Mister?"

"Most folks do," Byrd replied, still holding out his hand.

The man raised his cane and pushed Byrd's hand away. He said to Ben, "Where's this nigger from?"

Ben rested his gaze on the man's shoes, which were new and highly polished. He said, "Marse Little, he ain't from around here, and he don't know our ways."

The man said, "You'd better school him, then." He laughed again. "Or I'll have to." Still laughing, he turned and walked away. Byrd had never heard a laugh with so much malice in it.

"Who was that?" Byrd asked.

"Marse Little. Owns ten thousand acres of cotton land. Has two hundred folks as tenants on it. Wasn't wise to cross him."

"Didn't mean to cross him. Just to act courteous."

Ben stared at Byrd. He said, "Don't you know you're a nigger?"

"I surely know I'm a black man," Byrd said, stretching out his hands, which were fair enough to show a freckle. "I ain't a nigger, and I ain't his nigger. I've been free since President Lincoln said so, and I conduct myself that way."

Ben shook his head. "What have you got to put in my wagon?"

Byrd lifted the little bag. "Just this."

Trying to lift the mood, Ben said, "No buffalo coat?"

"Got a clean shirt, my discharge papers, and any money I still got left." It wasn't much to show after twenty-five years of soldiering. He also had his sidearm, which he hadn't expected he'd need to brandish in a peaceable place. He was glad to have it, because he now knew he'd been wrong.

They climbed into the mule cart, Joe next to Ben on the driver's seat, Byrd on the plank behind. Byrd had no love for a mule cart—as a soldier, he'd always had a horse to carry him— and today his bones ached from the pleasure he'd bought last night after they stopped in New Orleans. His wallet was lighter than yesterday, but his head was considerably heavier.

They drove past a field where last year's cotton plants had been stripped of the bolls. Wisps of cotton lint littered the ground. A man was plowing, his mule straining to pull through the dirt to bury the dead stalks. He waved as the wagon went by, and Ben waved back. Little houses, their boards weathered, their windows covered with cracked oilpaper, sat back from the road. Better than slave cabins, Byrd thought, but not much.

Ben turned the wagon onto a dirt road, and they left the fields for a thicket. The road was dirt that had frozen and thawed, and the air smelled like mud and the leaves and bugs that had died in it. The trees grew so close together that they blocked the sun. At noon, it was twilight.

Byrd had never seen land like this, with tall trees that grew to three times a man's height, their lower branches bearded with gray moss. Cane grew here too, the stalks as thick as a man's arm. Interspersed with it were silvery trees, their roots gnarled, their trunks twisted, vines snaking from their branches. "What are them twisted-looking trees?"

Ben answered, "Cypress. Grow all over. Good for building because the boards don't rot. If I could mill them I could sell them for good money."

Joe said, "I thought you grew cotton."

"I have a piece of land. But now I run the general store, and I rent the land out."

Byrd had never heard of a town where a black man ran the general store. He asked, "How did you come to have a store?"

"Mr. Levy, over in town, helped me out. Got me supplies, and lent me a little money, too."

They emerged from the thicket into the thin winter sunlight, and Byrd breathed a sigh of relief to see the cotton fields again. The road widened and the mule slowed. Just ahead, where the road was widest, stood a few buildings. A dog lay in the middle of the road, sprawled out in sleep.

Ben stopped his mule cart outside a low-slung wooden building with a covered porch. Puzzled, Byrd asked, "Where's the town?"

Ben frowned. "This is the town." His voice got louder. "Our town. Willow Bend, Mississippi." He gestured towards the sign over the building's door, freshly painted. "That's my store."

Byrd clambered from the wagon, thinking, *Just got here, and I've already made a fool of myself.*

A woman in a gingham apron waved from the porch. She was a little barrel of a woman, with a face as brown as an acorn. She rushed to Joe and hugged him, crying out, "We ain't seen you for years! Can't believe you here!" Byrd stood to the side, surprised that he felt bad that no one was making a fuss over him. He stepped into the street to gaze down at the dog.

Its ribs showed, but it had the deep chest and the blunt nose of a dog used to hunting. Its coat was a dusty yellow, and its muzzle was grizzled white with age.

Byrd asked Ben, "Is this your dog?"

Ben said, "No. Strayed into town a few weeks ago. I feed him and let him sleep outside the store." At the sound of a voice the dog stirred in his sleep and opened his eyes a little. Ben added, "I believe he's a hunting dog who got turned out. He don't move much, but when he do, he walk like my granddad after he got rheumatism."

The dog struggled to his feet. Byrd held out his hand, intending to stroke the dog's head, but the dog snuffled into his fingers and began to lick them. Byrd asked, "What's his name?"

"Don't have one."

Byrd felt a rush of sympathy for the nameless, homeless dog. "Should have a name. Dog needs a name, just like a person." The dog was still licking his hand. "Ain't that right, buster?"

The dog made a soft yelping sound, too gentle to be a bark, and wagged his tail, despite the effort it cost him. Ben laughed. "He agree with you. Answer to Buster. I guess he have a name now."

Ben's wife said, "Ben, are you fussing with that dog?"

"Janie, say how do to Sergeant Byrd."

"Glad to meet you." Janie put her hand on his arm, like a

mother touching her boy. Byrd, whose mother had been dead for ten years, didn't care for it. "How do, Miss Janie."

The store was dark. Oilpaper, not glass, served for windows here. The place smelled of sawdust, paint, flour, and coffee. Behind the counter, a young man set bolts of cloth on the shelves, which were only half full, despite Mr. Levy's help.

Ben said, "This is my nephew, Davey, who stays with us."

Davey was young, but his face was prematurely lined with grief, like a young soldier after a bad battle. Byrd wondered what had made this boy's heart so heavy.

Miss Janie said, "Come on back, the food's ready, it'll get cold." Despite the chill outside, the back room was pleasantly warmed by the stove, where a big iron pot steamed. Miss Janie directed them to sit, and Ben Thornton bent his head. "Thank you, Lord, for this food," he said. Byrd felt ashamed. He hadn't said grace over a meal in decades.

Miss Janie brought the pot to the table and the earthy, smoky smell of cowpeas and greens cooked with side meat filled the room. Joe Thornton sighed. "Smells like home," he said.

Byrd, who was still queasy from last night's beefsteak and crème brulee, fought off nausea at the smell. As a slave, Byrd had eaten cowpeas and greens nearly every day of his life, and he had disliked them ever since.

Smiling, Miss Janie handed him a plate. He swallowed hard and nodded his thanks. He picked up his fork and yearned for a glass of whiskey.

Miss Janie asked, "More for you, Mr. Byrd?"

"No, ma'am, I'm all right."

She shook her head. "You're a spindly man," she said. "You need it." She looked them both over, him and Joe, and offered to wash their clothes. "Since you dusty from the road." As Byrd pushed his food around his plate, she asked, "What is you planning to do? Will you settle here?"

"I haven't decided yet."

Miss Janie said, "Ben would be glad to rent you a piece of land, if you decide to farm."

He'd been a slave, then he'd been a soldier. All his life, he'd had someone tell him what to do. He didn't know what he wanted to do—he was as rootless as a man could be—but he wanted the freedom to consider it. He struggled to be polite to her. "Miss Janie, I'm grateful to hear that."

"Janie, leave him be, he just got here," Ben said.

After dinner, Ben said, "I keep whiskey in the store. Janie don't mind, as long as I don't drink at the table. Would you men like a drop?"

Ben poured whiskey into tin cups and they stood at the store's counter as though it were a bar. Byrd drained his cup and set it on the counter, hoping Ben would pour him another. But Ben did not.

The door opened, bringing a gust of chill air and a man's laughter. "Drinking and it ain't a Saturday afternoon." He was wiry and his clothes were flecked with sawdust. He looked at Byrd with curious eyes. Taking his measure.

Ben said, "My brother Joe came home and he brought a friend with him. Mr. Ambrose Byrd. They soldiered together out West."

"I'm Dan Willis." There were handshakes all around. Willis said, "We soldiered together during the war. We was in the 1st Mississippi."

The 1st Mississippi was legendary among black Union soldiers, and even the Buffalo soldiers of the 25th told tales about them. The men were freed slaves who fought like demons. Byrd said, "That was a fine regiment."

Ben poured Willis some whiskey, and refilled Joe's and Byrd's cups. Willis raised his cup. "Welcome to Willow Bend," he said, and they all drank to that.

An easy voice said from the doorway, "Did you all start without me?"

Ben said, "Jim, come on in and meet my brother and his friend Mr. Byrd."

He wasn't tall, but he was solid, and he had an ease to his

gait as well as his voice. Ben said, "Jim's our mayor. Mayor Truehart."

Truehart had an air of command. He wouldn't have to raise his voice. He'd just have to look at you, and ask you to do what he wanted, and you'd want to do it. Byrd was reminded of his commanding officer in the 43rd Pennsylvania. Sergeant Shaw, a free black man from Chester County, Pennsylvania, had a similar air of easy command. In the worst of the battles for Fredericksburg in 1864, Shaw had walked through the smoke and minie balls with as much calm as a man strolling to a Sunday picnic.

Byrd asked, "Did you serve in the 1st Mississippi, too?"

Truehart nodded. Ben said, "Sergeant. That's what we called him, until we made him our mayor."

A black man ran the general store. A black man was mayor here. Byrd realized he hadn't seen a single white face in Willow Bend. "Do white folks live in Willow Bend?"

Truehart grinned. It was an infectious grin. "We're all black folks here. Willow Bend is a town for black folks."

On Sunday morning, Miss Janie made a generous breakfast of ham and eggs and grits, the first meal Byrd had enjoyed in Willow Bend. She said, "We're going to meeting this morning, and you're welcome to come along with us."

I ain't welcome to refuse, he thought.

The sun came out for the Sabbath day, casting a pale light and warming the damp air. Like the store, Willow Bend's church was newly built, with bright white walls that smelled of fresh paint. Light streamed in through the glass windows. Ben said, "We pooled our money to buy proper windows for the meeting house. And for the schoolhouse, too."

Ben introduced him to the Reverend Baldwin, a well-fleshed man in a well-cut suit. At his side was his wife, Miss Octavia, whose hair was smoothed into curls, and whose soft hand was scented with lavender water. "Welcome, Mr. Byrd," she said.

"You're a Yankee!" he blurted out.

She laughed. "I'm from Ohio. I met the reverend there, and now I teach school in Willow Bend."

Byrd had met more than a few schoolmarms as the war ended, when they came South to teach the freed slaves to read and write. He'd learned his own letters from a serious-minded free black woman from Syracuse, New York. She was pretty too, he recalled.

Willis waved him over. "This is my wife, Miss Maggie." A child nested in her arms and two others, a boy and a girl, pulled on her unadorned gray skirt. "Are these all your young 'uns?" Byrd asked.

"These just the youngest. The oldest married now and have some of his own." She was lean, pared down, and her expression was severe. She took his measure, like her carpenter husband.

Two boys ran past him, shouting and pummeling each other. Just behind them, too stout and too starched into her dress to run, panted their mother, who yelled, "You imps of Satan! You hush and quit that! We going into church!"

Maggie smothered a smile. "Miss Bessie!" she called out. "Come meet Mr. Ambrose Byrd."

At the elbow of the imposing Miss Bessie was her husband, Pete Glover, a man half her size, who spoke to Byrd in a voice so soft it was hard to hear him.

Truehart greeted Byrd and introduced his wife, Miss Niecy, whose calico dress crackled with starch and whose natural hair had been wrestled into a tight braid around her head. Beside her was a willowy girl with a coppery glow under her brown complexion. She wore her starched dress as though it bothered her, and she tugged at the locks of hair that had escaped from the braid over her shoulder. "This is my daughter, Miss Bernie," Truehart announced. "Just turned eighteen!"

So she was older than she looked. Can't decide if she's grown or not, Byrd thought, and won't let anyone else decide for her, either. As a sergeant, he had known many a boy like that, but never a girl.

Miss Janie elbowed past Byrd to grasp Bernie's arm.

"Bernie, honey, our Davey ask after you. Like to see you. We at home after dinner today. Come visit."

Bernie laughed. "If he want to keep me company, he should come hunting with me."

"Niecy, how do you allow such a thing? A grown girl running off to that island with a rifle. Should be at home helping you."

Niecy sighed. "Don't know how she come by it. Sometimes we think the catbird brought her."

"No harm in it, Niecy," Truehart said. "It put meat on the table." He hugged Bernie and beamed. "Bernie the best shot in Willow Bend. Drill a rabbit through the eye at fifty feet!"

Janie said, "Set down that rifle and come see Davey!" As Janie turned her back, Bernie stuck out her tongue, and Byrd smothered a laugh at the girl who dared to sauce Miss Janie.

Truehart said, "Mr. Byrd, have you met Miss Jerusha Smith?"

On the night before he came to Willow Bend, Byrd wandered the streets of New Orleans for a long time, savoring the beauty of the women, who came in every hue from African black to palest ivory. He was loath to find a bawdy house, where he'd have to make a choice. Once inside, he gave the nod to a woman who was slight and fair, like himself, and she smiled at him with a sweetness that unmanned him.

Miss Jerusha was so light-complected that she had a sprinkle of freckles over her nose. Her eyes were green. Byrd recalled the woman in New Orleans with such feeling that he was stricken again.

"How do," she said coolly.

Byrd said the first thing that came into his head. "Miss Jerusha, where do you hail from?"

"Why would you ask?"

"You don't talk like someone born in Mississippi."

Her eyebrows rose a little in surprise. "You hear right. I was born in Virginia."

None of his memories of Virginia were pleasant, but he smiled. "So was I. Where?"

Like him, she looked unhappy to remember. "On a place near Alexandria," she said.

"I grew up on a place near Fairfax." He added, "So we is strangers here, both of us."

She shook her head. "I been here for a long time," she said, and turned away.

Stung, he thought, she's haughty, and she doesn't have a thing to be haughty about.

It was a relief to sit on the hard pine bench with the Thorntons for the service. But he was surprised as soon as Jim Truehart rose to welcome them, both him and Joe. "Welcome to our newest brethren," he said, and Byrd felt a flush spread over his face at being singled out.

After the service, Miss Niecy invited him to take Sunday supper with them, to which Ben said, "Janie won't mind. You go on and eat with them."

The Trueharts, like all the folks in Willow Bend, were house-proud. The front yard was full of flowers, wild roses and black-eyed susans and morning glories, and the steps were carefully swept. The Truehart house was a little bigger than the other houses in Willow Bend, but no grander. Truehart said, "Don't really need more than oilpaper, not in this weather, but Niecy says that someday we'll have glass in our windows, like in the meeting house."

"Someday," Niecy agreed, smiling.

Inside, a pretty rag rug sat before the hearth. A white cloth lay the table, to honor the Sabbath, and it was set with the Sabbath china. Like Ben Thornton, Truehart blessed the meal. It was the food of the frolics of Byrd's youth, the days of rest after the harvest was done: fricasseed chicken, sweet potatoes with butter, and an apple pie. No whiskey, not at the Sabbath table.

They asked after his people. "Don't have none. My mama died ten year ago."

Niecy said, "We sorry to hear it."

"What about your people?" he asked.

Truehart said, "We have two children grown, a son and a

daughter, and their families. They all went to Kansas a few years ago to farm there. It's just Bernie with us now."

Saddened, Niecy said, "They write, but it ain't the same as seeing them. I have grandbabies I've never held in my arms."

Truehart put his hand over his wife's and asked Byrd, "What was it like out West?"

It was hard to talk about the West without talking about soldiering. He said, "Spent most of my time in Texas, soldiering." He glanced at Bernie, who listened with interest. "Soldiering ain't proper talk at the dinner table."

Niecy threw her daughter a warning glance. "I agree, Sergeant Byrd."

Byrd had been restless in the Army, where he was always occupied. In Willow Bend, where he had nothing to do, his skin itched with disquiet. He decided to make the trip into town, if only to touch the goods in the general store and to lose himself in a crowd of strangers. He thought longingly of the saloon, where a man could take a drink in the middle of the day, and no one would make a disparaging remark or stare at him as he raised the cup to his lips.

Byrd wrapped himself in his greatcoat, but the sky was overcast and the air colder for being so damp. He strode down the dirt path, past the dormant cotton fields, and soon, too soon, he was in the thicket, where night fell in the middle of the day. He felt a shiver of dislike at the dead vines on the cypress trees, which looked so much like snakes in the gloom. He thought he heard the sound of slithering in the canebrake, and halted to listen.

Silence, broken by the shrill cry of a bird.

He'd been through worse countryside than this—the Western desert, where Comanches and Kiowas lurked behind the rocks, and the despoiled South, where everything had been burned to the ground and the earth smelled of blood and ash. The thicket, with its stink of decaying mud, bothered him more than any battleground. The swamp was a perfect blind, as soldiers said, and anything could be hidden within it.

When he reached the paved road and emerged into the thin gray daylight, he was so relieved that he thanked God.

In town, he stopped outside the general store, where a group of white men, as idle as Buster, lounged on the porch. Next door, a group of black people, men and women, huddled at the side of Levy's. The men wore the rough clothes of farmers, streaked with dirt, and the women wore stained aprons over worn calico dresses and bound their hair with kerchiefs. They stared at him, but no one spoke to him.

He shook his head and wandered toward the saloon.

The saloon reeked of corn whiskey, as though someone had spilled a jug on the floor. Three unspeaking men leaned against the bar. The saloonkeeper, a thin, weedy man, glared at Byrd. His eyes were an unnaturally pale blue. "We don't serve niggers in here."

All three customers at the bar turned to stare at Byrd. Byrd said, "Sorry to trouble you, sir," and with a soldier's instinct, backed from the saloon until he was in the relative safety of the street.

The next day, just after midday dinner, Byrd leaned against Thornton's counter, listening to the pleasant patter of rain on the oilpaper windows. Since he returned from his visit to town, he spent most of the day in the store, waiting for the company of anyone who strayed in. Truehart opened the door, taking off his coat and shaking off the water.

Thornton, who stood behind the counter, said, "No plowing today."

"Dan just behind me. No carpentering, either."

The light was so dim that Thornton had lit a kerosene lamp against it. Willis opened the door, and with him was Buster, wet and whimpering. Thornton said, "Janie won't like it."

"The weather ain't fit even for a dog," Willis said.

Buster's smell overpowered the usual odors of paint and coffee. He wagged his wet tail and lay down at Byrd's feet.

Truehart laughed. "He stink, but he like you."

"Took to me," Byrd said, oddly pleased.

Thornton asked, "Did you folks need anything?"

"Just came to visit." Willis leaned against the counter, next to Byrd. "How are you settling in?"

"I'm all right."

"What do you think? Will you stay with us?" Truehart asked.

"I might."

"It's a good place," Willis said.

"A town for black folks, that ain't usual," Byrd remarked. "Tell me, how did Willow Bend come to be?"

"Jim, you tell it," Thornton said.

Truehart laughed. "It's a long story. Ask Davey to bring in some chairs from the back."

They settled into the chairs. Truehart rested his hands on his knees in the storyteller's stance and leaned forward. "It were three year ago," he said. "This time of year, between picking and plowing. I'd been cropping for Marse Little and I had money saved up. He'd been my massa before the war, and I'd worked for him since I came back, but I always wanted my own place. So I went to see him."

"Tell him about that house, Jim," said Thornton.

"Just getting to it. I always went over there, every year, to sign the paper to rent from him. The Littles was always rich, even before the war, but afterwards they got richer, and they built a grand new house."

Willis said, "Hired me to build it."

"Never went in the front door—we folks always come round the back—but Dan built them big pillars in front. Two stories high."

Willis shook his head.

"It were even grander inside. All that dark wood, too fancy for Dan to carve. And the ceilings painted gold. When I told Niecy—she used to work in that house, in slavery days—she said the Littles could paint the insides of their chamberpots gold, if they wanted to." He snorted. "Went into Marse Little's study, and he let me set down in a chair. Surprised at that. Asked me why I was there. Told him I wanted to buy land. He told me he couldn't sell me any land to grow cotton on."

Thornton interrupted. "So you went roundabout."

"Told him I wanted the bottom land right by the river. Swampland. Then he asked me what I'd do with it. Roundabout again. Said I'd try to raise some corn and hogs on it. He laughed and said I'd get swamp fever just by walking through it. Asked me how much I wanted. A hundred acres, I said, held my breath. He thought about it—not too long—and told me he'd sell it for a dollar an acre. And he'd give me the island, too, since it was all swampland like the river bottom." He grinned. "When I left I laughed into my sleeve. Dollar an acre. The island for free. Swampland!" He laughed.

"Went there just after he bought it," Thornton said. "We was standing in a thicket, our feet sinking into the muck, and Jim stood still, taking it in. Nothing to see but trees and canebrake. Couldn't figure what he was looking at."

"Where to plant corn, and where to plant cotton," Truehart recalled.

"Couldn't see the field for the trees, couldn't stand on it for the mud, but he could see a cotton field."

Truehart said, "Weren't a cotton field yet. Had to be cleared."

"Put on his driver's voice," Willis said, "his old coaxing voice, that could get you to do anything he wanted you to do. Told us both that if we helped him clear the land he'd give us each twenty acres."

"That were a painful task," Truehart said. "Cut down the trees, clear the brake, pull out the stumps. Then Ben had a good notion."

Thornton said, "We could take the cypresses to the sawmill and get good money for them. Got easier after that. Every cypress we cut down, we profited by."

"Still weren't easy. We worked after we plowed and chopped

to grow cotton for Marse Little. Worked in the evenings, when we was already tired, and on Sundays, when we wished we was resting. Once picking started, we was all too tired for anything else. Even the mules was too weary to work."

Outside, the rain slowed to a drizzle, and the sky turned a lighter gray. Byrd shifted in his chair and Buster thumped his tail on the floor as he dreamed. Thornton said, "Folks came to see it. Weren't much to see. But they were proud that Jim had bought it and that we'd reclaimed it."

Truehart nodded. "Next growing season we each went to Marse Little to tell him we didn't want to sign an agreement for another year. He weren't too pleased, but he said he'd furnish us. Wanted to get us into debt, so we'd owe him once the crop came in. Didn't know we'd been putting by our cypress money and we had enough for our own seed and fertilizer."

Willis said, "Folks began to come to us, saying they'd like to join us, that they'd like to rent from us. We decided to buy more land."

"Not from Marse Little," Truehart said. "Didn't want him to know how well we was doing. Mr. Levy told me that Marse Taillefer had some swampland, river land, he might be willing to sell. Said that Marse Taillefer didn't care much for Marse Little and I should keep that in mind. So I paid Marse Taillefer a visit. He were always a big planter too, but nowhere near as grand as the Littles, and he were glad to stick his thumb in Marse Little's eye. Sold me his land for fifty cents an acre." Truehart chortled. "Just to spite Marse Little."

Willis said, "We cleared that land, and sold the cypresses, and rented it out. A dozen families living here. All growing cotton."

"My gal Bernie told me that she learned in school about them Egyptians, who grow the best cotton in the world in a river bottom. I told her she didn't need to be schooled know that. We grew a fine crop."

Thornton said, "I reckon it's more than a bale an acre."

"Don't know yet. Haven't ginned it." Truehart frowned and

addressed Byrd, as though Byrd understood. "Don't want to take it to Marse Little, because he'll know down to the pound how well we did. Don't know where else to take it. Wish we could buy our own gin."

"Why don't you?" asked Byrd.

"Don't have the cash."

Byrd surveyed the store, furnished with Mr. Levy's help. "Wouldn't Mr. Levy help you out? Lend you money?"

Truehart's voice rose. "Won't buy anything on credit or a note. Don't want to be in debt, not ever again."

Thornton and Willis both nodded. "Why did you call it Willow Bend?"

Truehart said, "Named the day we first surveyed it. Bernie did. Called it after the weeping willows that still grow on the riverbank."

"All ours," Thornton said proudly. "A black town, with a black man as mayor. Tell him about that, Jim."

"Once we had a dozen families here, a hundred people, folks felt like it was a real town. That it needed a mayor. Wanted to appoint me, but I said no. We had an election, like we used to, and we voted, like we used to. So I got to be mayor fair and square."

The rain had stopped and the sky had brightened. Thornton extinguished the lamp. Truehart stretched and said, "Still have a crop to worry about. Want to see if them fields are draining right in this weather. Come with me, Dan?" He rose from his chair.

Willis rose too. Byrd followed them out the door, Buster at his heels. The sun had come out and the air held the promise of spring and a new season for planting cotton. Byrd scanned the road in both directions, seeing the store, the meeting house and the school with fresh eyes. The town of Willow Bend had risen from the mucky dirt, built with the strength and sweat of black folks. Willow Bend belonged to them, and no one could take it away.

Chapter 2

Fort Pillow

After two weeks in Willow Bend, Joe Thornton told Byrd that he was leaving. "Can't stand it. Ben pestering me all the time, and Miss Janie fussing."

"They won't like it."

"Don't care. What about you? You coming with me?"

"Thought I'd stay here for a while."

Joe gaped at him. "In God's name, why?"

"I don't know," said Byrd.

After Joe left, Byrd felt more restless than ever. He wandered down the dirt road to the edge of town, where the cotton fields gave way to thicket. He wanted to find his way to the river shore. He plunged into the swamp.

The air was damp and smelled of dead things, and the mud sucked at his boots. But the river glimmered through the trees. He pushed aside the marsh grass and squeezed through the cypresses. Before him, down a gentle incline at the water's edge, grew the weeping willows that liked water so much. The river ran slowly here, brown with silt, and the river curved in the bend it was named for. Across the water was the island, where another stand of willows grew. Where Bernie took her rifle to hunt.

It was about twenty feet away, close enough to swim. He took off his muddy boots and left them on the bank. He'd have to be careful of his step once he was on the island.

The water swirled with mud and silt. He hadn't reckoned on getting dirty in water. It didn't feel deep, but rivers were tricky. If the bottom dropped suddenly, the eddy might pull a man down. This water seemed peaceful. He wondered if there were alligators in the river. He hoped not.

As he neared the island's shore, he swam past flocks of ducks, mamas with half-grown ducklings, which quacked furiously as he swam by. The geese, protecting their goslings, honked at him, and a mama goose tried to nip him when he swam too close. "Easy," he said, as though she could understand him.

At the edge of the island was a shallow sandbar, where the water only came up to his knees. The shore itself was wet sand, marked with the tracks of birds, the webs of ducks and geese and the forklike feet of herons. A canoe had left a scrape here. Bernie's boat. The beach was wide but not very deep, only about ten feet into the island.

Beyond the beach grew a thicket like the one on the river shore, where willows gave way to cypresses. He found his way through the trees. The ground was damp beneath his feet, but it was sandy and held his weight. The ground had been tamped here. Someone had made a path. Was it Bernie, or someone before her? He didn't try to sight it through the trees. He felt for it with the soles of his bare feet.

The trees grew dense here, as on the shore, and filtered the sun. At midday, the light was cool and green, as though he were still in the water. About ten feet into the thicket, the land began to rise. He moved quietly through the trees, listening. He heard the calls of the birds, the ducks who liked the river, and the waders, the herons, who lived on land and nested in the trees. Since there was marsh here, and standing water, there were likely frogs, too. But frogs were quiet during the day.

The path rose sharply up the hill. Even though it wasn't far above the level of the shore—when he looked back, he guessed about forty feet—it was a climb rather than a walk. The herons nested here, and when he disturbed them, they made a raucous cry. He was sweating and thirsty, but he kept going. He wanted to crest the hill.

At the top of the hill was a glade, ringed with cypresses, where the trees parted like a doorway. He slipped inside. The ground was covered with moss. He bent to touch it and was pleased to find that it was dry. The trees twisted together overhead, filtering the sunlight, making it feel cooler than on the beach. It was like a room outdoors. He sat, the moss forgiving under his backside. He wondered what it would be like to sleep here, with moss for a mattress and cypress branches for a roof that would let in a view of the stars.

Curious about the other side of the island, he left the glade to peer through the thicket. On the other side of the hill, the land flattened. Covered with scrub and vine, it was level, and larger than the beach where he'd landed. He edged through the scrub and his feet found another path that didn't go down to the shore, but curved, and led him to the sound of water. Running water. At the stream, he cupped the water in his hand and drank. Sweet water.

He thought, A man could stay here, if he wanted to.

In the thicket again, he moved slowly though the dense growth of cypress, the roots and branches twisted and tangled around each other. He stepped slowly toward the shore until the dirt turned to mud beneath his feet. The mud stopped him.

At the shore were inlets that gave way to muddy, soupy swamp. He didn't want to risk walking there. A man could sink into the mud and not be able to progress a single step.

His clothes were wet and he had sand in his underdrawers. He didn't care. He wanted to return to rest on the hill and repose in the glade. For the first time since he arrived in Willow Bend, it pleased him.

Byrd watched as Davey rearranged the bolts on the shelf. "Do you need any help with that, young man?"

Davey shook his head. "You still a guest, and my uncle say that we don't put a guest to work."

Byrd left the store to sit heavily on the stairs. Buster, who slept the porch, woke and came to nose Byrd's hand. Byrd scratched the dog's head and Buster wagged his tail with pleasure. "You mighty happy doing nothing," Byrd said.

Truehart walked down the street. He waved at Byrd. "I'm going to town this morning," he said. "Mr. Levy has some goods for Ben. You're welcome to come with me."

Byrd straightened up and took his time. No reason to let Truehart see how eager he was to go somewhere. "I might."

"The wagon's in back. Jump in."

The sun was bright enough to penetrate the thicket, and the smell of something new and green overpowered last year's rot. Birds called and trilled as they gathered Spanish moss for their nests. Byrd felt warm enough to take off his jacket.

In town, Truehart pulled the wagon up to Levy's and waved to the crowd of ragged men and women who waited at the side door. They waved back, calling out, "Jim! How are you, Jim!"

Byrd asked, "Who are those folks?"

"Knew them when I cropped for Marse Little. They still do." Truehart frowned. "Don't have much to show for it."

Levy's wasn't much bigger than Thornton's, but the light streamed in through big glass windows. The wooden counter stretched the length of the store, and behind it, the shelves were crammed with dry goods on one side and hardware on the other. The place smelled of starched cloth and machine oil.

Mr. Levy was broad and burly, with a deeply lined face that put Byrd in mind of the late President Lincoln. He said, "How can I help you, Jim Truehart?" Didn't call him Mister, but didn't call him boy, either.

"I've come for Ben's stuff."

"Who is this with you?"

Truehart introduced Byrd. "How do you find Willow Bend?" Levy asked.

He talked like the peddlers who came to the little towns of the West, Jewish men from Russia who carried their livelihoods on their backs. Byrd was glad to meet another stranger. "It's a good place," he said, also speaking to Truehart.

Levy said, "Did your wife like that calico I sold you?"

"Yes, sir, she did. Said it suited her."

"Anything else today?"

Truehart said, "Don't need it right away, but I'm thinking about a new rifle. A Winchester."

Levy said, "Hope there ain't trouble where you are."

"No, sir. Just for hunting. We hunt deer and rabbit. Eat what we hunt."

Levy took down a rifle from its spot on the wall behind his head. He laid it on the counter. "The newest Winchester," he said. "A fine gun."

Truehart asked, "May I touch it?"

"How else would you judge it?"

"When I bought from Marse Little's shopkeeper, he didn't let us touch the goods."

Levy said, "I hear he gives short weight."

Truehart didn't reply. He bent over the rifle, looking at the gleaming stock and the bright barrel. He said, "It's a fine thing. I ain't quite ready to buy. I need to save up some money first."

"I can put it on account. You can pay me when you sell your crop."

Truehart put his money on the counter. "No, sir, don't care to be in debt. Wait until I have enough cash for it."

"Anything today?"

"Just a little flour."

Levy filled up the sack and set it on the counter. Truehart dropped his voice. "Mr. Levy, I'd value your advice."

"About what?"

"About the crop I made last year."

Levy's eyebrows rose. "I don't know how I can help you."

"I have some bales of cotton I need ginned."

"Mr. Little has a gin. You don't take it to him?"

"I don't work for him anymore. Take it elsewhere, if I please."

Levy didn't reply. Truehart dropped his voice so low Byrd had to strain to hear. "Thought you might know where."

Levy hesitated, and the lines on his face seemed to deepen. Truehart waited, pressing his hands hard into the counter. "It may be trouble," Levy said.

Truehart said, "You helped Ben."

Levy stared at Truehart's hands, straining against the counter. Lowering his voice to match Truehart's, he said, "I might buy some cotton from you."

"Mr. Chatham need to gin it."

"Why shouldn't I take him cotton to gin?" Levy said defiantly. "I'm free to buy and sell, as I like."

Truehart gripped the edge of the counter even tighter. "I'd be obliged, Mr. Levy."

Josiah Hood, Willow Bend's blacksmith, was at work when Byrd came to see him. Byrd waited for him to lay down his hammer. All of the farmers of Willow Bend had powerful shoulders, but Hood had even more powerful arms. He was very dark of skin, an African black, and he had the broad cheekbones and full lips of Africa as well. He was in shirtsleeves, and he had sweated his shirt through.

Nearby, his wife Lizzie had set her washtub, and she was up to her elbows in soapy water. Lizzie's lips were curved upward, smiling even when her face was at rest.

Byrd asked Hood, "Wondered about that shack you have next to your house."

"Built it when we moved here, just to have a roof over our heads." He gestured toward the shop. "Live a better house now."

"Might a man rent it from you?"

"It's awful tumbledown."

"Be glad to pay rent. Pay you for meals, too."

Puzzled, Hood said, "Thought you were staying with the Thorntons."

"It's time for me to find my own place."

"Peculiar for a man to want to live alone." Hood glanced at his wife.

Lizzie looked up from her washtub to grin. "If I had to stay with Miss Janie, I'd want to be alone, too."

The next day, Byrd opened the door to his new place. It was only a little bigger than the cabin he'd grown up in. The oilpaper over the windows dimmed the daylight. The Hoods had given him a narrow bedstead, a rough little table, and a chair once painted white, now weathered and peeling. The cornhusk mattress crackled when he sat on the bed. Under his hand the coverlet felt rough, and its edges were worn ragged. The pillow was flat with use.

No one in Willow Bend had much. He knew the Hoods had done their best for him. Surrounded by Willow Bend's castoffs, Byrd felt lower than he'd felt in a long time. He wanted whiskey—not the single cup taken in Thornton's, where everyone else had a farm and a family to tend to tomorrow morning, but the bottle of a man who had nothing else to do and nowhere else to go.

As Byrd leaned against Thornton's counter, wondering more than ever why he'd stayed in Willow Bend, Truehart stepped into the store and said to Byrd, "I need some help around my place, if you'd like to earn a dollar."

Byrd straightened up. "What is it?" Byrd worried that Truehart might ask him to plow or to hand him a hoe. He'd refuse that.

"Need my henhouse fixed up."

Behind the counter, Davey smothered a smile. Byrd said, "Don't fool me, man."

"It ain't fooling. Willis busy, and who else help me? Wouldn't ask my daughter to lift a hammer."

"If you need it."

Truehart nodded and held out his hand. Byrd still had his doubts, but he shook it.

For makework, it was hard and dirty. He cleaned out the henhouse first, then hammered and nailed as Truehart directed him to. Drove him to. Whenever he flagged, Truehart stopped by to stay, "Looks good, Mr. Byrd, just needs a little more over here." Byrd had been driven by men who hated slaves, then by sergeants who acted like they hated soldiers. Truehart praised him, and Byrd was chagrined that it pleased him so much.

At the end of the day Truehart gave him a dollar in silver dimes. "Won't let it carry as a debt," he told Byrd, and the dimes were a satisfying weight in Byrd's pocket as he tramped back to his shack.

Not long after, early one morning, someone knocked on the door of the shack. "Who is it?" he croaked.

"Dan Willis." The door creaked open.

Byrd sat up. His head ached. "What do you want?"

"Wondered if you'd like a job of work today."

Byrd coughed and spat. "Haven't even had breakfast yet."

"We can eat in the wagon on the way."

Byrd sat up, blinking against the light, and scratched his chest through the underclothes he wore to sleep in. "What's the hurry, man?"

"Marse Little wants me today."

"Ain't your boys willing?"

"Too busy plowing."

"Why ask me?"

Willis grinned. "Jim said you were handy with a hammer."

"Don't anyone ever say no to this man Little?"

"Wouldn't want to try it. Come on, man. Breakfast, and money at the end of the day."

Grumbling, Byrd dressed and went outside to splash water on his unshaven face. On the way, between bites of pone, Willis said, "Marse Little is the richest planter in the county." Byrd didn't reply. "He own ten thousand acres. Grow cotton, corn, vegetables, fruit. Mostly cotton."

Byrd chewed and swallowed. "That's a big place."

"He was always the biggest planter in the county, even in slavery days. Got bigger in the last ten years, since cotton went so high. Can't complain, since he builds all the time and asks me to work whenever he does."

It was hot for late winter, more like full spring. The sun burned through Byrd's coat. They turned into a driveway, planted with magnolia. The Little place was a mansion bigger and grander than any antebellum place. It was three stories tall, with a piazza on the first story and a balcony that spread the length of the house on the third, painted dazzling white, with full-length windows flanked by dark shutters. It had eight columns in front, which reached the full height of the house, the ones that Willis had constructed. The great white door was twice a man's height, but they wouldn't use it. Willis knew where he belonged. He didn't stop in the driveway. His business was in back.

Byrd asked, "What are we working on?"

"Marse Little wants me to help his gang build a new stable."

Byrd looked at the stable, which was long and low-slung, big enough for a dozen horses. "Don't see anything wrong with the old one."

"Ain't grand enough," Willis replied.

Behind the old stable, two men, dressed in rough, patched clothes, not much better than slave clothes, stood next to a pile of fresh lumber. They waved and greeted Willis. "Who's the new man?" Willis introduced him.

Willis set Byrd to sawing boards that the other men had measured. Unlike pine, which was silky and fresh, this wood smelled earthy and sour, and felt greasy to the touch. "What is it?" Byrd asked Willis.

"Cypress. Like from our swamp. Better than pine. Don't rot."

As Byrd worked, the plantation bustled around him. A tall

woman passed him, a bundle of clothes balanced on her head, the place's washwoman. A woman in a calico dress and a fresh apron, a house servant, stopped to watch them work, her arms crossed, her face lined with weariness.

"Who is that?" Byrd asked Willis.

"Miss Delia. Keeps house for Marse Little. Cousin to Miss Niecy in Willow Bend."

Byrd sweated in the sun. He took off his jacket and his hat, and wiped his forehead with his shirt sleeve. He said, "I need to set a moment."

One of the men on the place laughed. "Don't let Marse Little see you lingering."

Byrd shook his head and poured himself a cup of water from the pitcher that one of the men had brought. Like in slavery days, he thought. Pitcher and dipper at the side of the field. Cup in hand, he walked into the shade, and sat to drink it.

At noon the men broke for midday dinner. The two men on the place returned to their cabins to eat, while Willis and Byrd rested in the shade. Willis said, "My wife always packs enough food for a gang. Would you like some?" When Byrd saw the second tin plate and cup and spoon, he knew that Maggie Willis had done it on purpose. He wondered why, since she disapproved of him so.

As they ate, Willis said, "Jim told me you did good work for him."

Byrd frowned. "Didn't need his henhouse fixed."

"He likes to look after people."

"I can look after myself."

Willis laughed. "Jim's a good man. I've known him since we was slaves together on the Little place. He's a little jumped up these days, being mayor. Don't mind it."

Byrd saw the flash of the gold-tipped cane before he saw the man. As Little came close, Willis set aside his plate and swiftly rose to his feet. Little stopped before the two men and said, "Dan, boy, how's the stable coming along?"

Willis dropped his head and said meekly, "It coming along fine, Marse Little."

Little waved his cane at Byrd. "Who's this? Tell him to stand up and show respect."

Byrd didn't move. His voice pitched low, Willis said, "Stand up, man."

Taking his time, Byrd carefully set down his plate and stood. He held himself straight and tall as a soldier at attention.

Little said, "Now I remember you. You're the nigger who thinks he's a sergeant!"

"When I mustered out of the U.S. Army, I was a sergeant. Had the chevrons to prove it," Byrd replied.

Smiling, Little said, "Are you naysaying me?"

"No, sir. Just stating a fact. Like it's a fact the sun is shining today."

"Didn't I tell you to school him?" Little asked Willis.

Willis tried to make light of it. "Marse Little, we don't hold much with what he says. He like a hornet, flying and buzzing. We brush him away."

"You can shoo a hornet, or kill a hornet, but you don't leave him in the house to sting you," Little said.

"Yes, Marse Little."

Little laughed. Byrd remembered that laugh, full of malice. Little grinned as he stroce away, gold-tipped cane flashing in the sun.

"I ain't a hornet. I'm a Buffalo soldier," Byrd said angrily.

Willis let out the anger he'd held close while Little was there to hear. "Man, if you don't act right around Marse Little, you won't be a hornet or a buffalo. You'll be a dead nigger."

That evening, Byrd stopped at Thornton's, where Truehart was already there, a cup of whiskey before him. As Thornton poured some for Byrd, Willis flung open the door.

Truehart asked mildly, "Something bothering you, Dan?"

Willis glared at Byrd. "I'm just fine, if Mr. Sergeant Buffalo Soldier don't get me in trouble."

"What kind of trouble?"

Willis smacked his hand against the counter. "Ask him how he acted around Marse Little today."

"I ain't a slave, and I won't act like one," Byrd said.

Truehart said, "We ain't slaves, none of us. But we ain't fools, either. We don't make trouble for ourselves, making Marse Little mad at us."

"Won't call him Marse."

"Call him sir. But don't disrespect him."

Thornton nodded, like he was listening to the Reverend in church. Byrd felt the day's anger surge through him. He set his cup on the counter with a thud. "Look at you, all of you," he said. "Free men, and you act like niggers around this man Little. Like you never got free at all."

Willis grabbed Byrd by the shirtfront. "Are you calling me a nigger and a slave?"

Byrd gripped Willis' arm and pulled his hand away. "You heard me," he said.

Willis made a fist and threw a punch that would have landed on Byrd's jaw, if he hadn't moved fast enough. Byrd recovered, but before he could lunge at Willis to land a blow, Truehart pinned his arms behind him and said, "Easy, man." He looked at Willis, who was panting with anger and effort, and he said, "You, too."

Truehart tightened his grip on Byrd. "If you plan to stay here, you act peaceable."

Byrd growled, "Let me go."

Truehart released him and pushed him towards the door.

"Won't stay where I ain't welcome," Byrd muttered, slamming the door behind him.

The sound woke Buster, who slept outside the door at Thornton's. He whined a little as he opened his eyes. Byrd knelt down to rub the dog's hard head. Buster licked his hand. "Poor old boy," Byrd said softly, his anger dissolving. "Broke up your sleep." Buster sighed and put his head on his paws. Byrd stroked the dog's flank until he was sure that Buster was asleep again. Then he straightened and walked the few steps home.

In the dark, his place was even meaner than in daylight. The room smelled of sweat and unwashed laundry, like a slave cabin during harvest, when everyone was too work-weary to wash. He lay awake on the lumpy mattress and the thin pillow and thought about everything that bothered him. His father, whom he never knew. His mother, dead these past ten years. That he had no wife to warm him and no children to cheer him.

The scars on his back itched and burned, no matter how he shifted, reminding him of the whipping that had put them there. He thought of himself at eighteen, a runaway for the third time. He hid in a thicket of pine trees, so afraid of recapture he could scarcely breathe, and started at every rustle, thinking it was the slave-catcher with his dogs. He waited until the only sound he heard was the call of an owl. Then he ran until his legs ached and his lungs burned.

In daylight, he stumbled toward the Union encampment, sighting on the blue uniforms as he'd once sighted on the Drinking Gourd. The contrabands saw him first. One of them, a very black man in a jaunty blue cap, called out to him: "You're all right! You're free now!"

The Army put him to work with the other contrabands, hauling wood, digging ditches, and washing dishes. Just about anything but fighting, all the way through Virginia and into Pennsylvania. He was at the battle of Gettysburg, but he worked for the quartermasters, cooking for the officers. As the battle raged, he asked the man in the blue cap—Cato, his name was— why black men couldn't sign up to fight.

"Black man with a gun? They afraid of us."

As a contraband, he learned to read in the Sunday School run by the pretty free black woman from Syracuse, who led them in prayer before they began. He was surrounded by grown men and women like himself, their brows furrowed, their hands clenched around the slate pencils as they labored over their letters. "A is for apple" were the first words he ever deciphered. A childish thing, but to this day his heart filled with pride to remember it.

He began to pick up the newspapers the officers discarded, sounding out the words until they made sense to him. His reading improved, and he eagerly read the news of the war, which he had a stake in, and the latest words of President Lincoln, whom he revered. He liked *The Liberator* best, because it was so hot against slavery.

On a bright day in early spring, in a leisured moment after the breakfast dishes were done, he sprang up, paper in hand, to shout at his friend Cato: "They're mustering in black men! They're raising a regiment in Philadelphia!"

Cato whooped with joy as he tore off his apron and threw it on the ground. That day they both boarded the train for Philadelphia.

Byrd and Cato, who now called himself Charles Highgate, lingered over the coffee served with midday dinner at Camp William Penn.

The camp, which housed all the black regiments in Pennsylvania, had been quickly built, but it was as solid an Army post as any for the white men. Thousands could stand on the parade ground, and the sight of so many black soldiers swelled Byrd's chest with pride. A few weeks after he arrived, Frederick Douglass, *The Liberator*'s greatest voice against slavery, came to address them. Oblivious to the heat of the spring sun, Byrd stood at rapt attention as Douglass exhorted them to fight for freedom.

Today, Byrd lifted the cup to his lips and drank deep of it. It was still a luxury to drink coffee every day, just as it was to carry a rifle and to be called "Private Byrd." In the heat, Byrd wore his heavy blue coat buttoned to the neck, as befit a soldier.

Their commander, Sergeant William Shaw, came loping past, and they rose and snapped themselves to attention. "At ease, Private Byrd, Private Highgate," he said. "Sit down and take your ease."

Shaw was a black man, but he was a soldier with a sergeant's chevrons. Byrd had never before taken an order from a man he respected. If Sergeant Shaw ordered him to sit, he'd sit. "Thank you, sir," he said.

"Save your strength," said Sergeant Shaw. His voice was firm—even on the parade ground, it carried so well he never had to shout—but he was smiling. "We drill in half an hour."

Byrd was fascinated by Sergeant Shaw. He said to Cato-turned-Charles, "He talk just like a Yankee!"

"Educated. I hear he go to college for a year."

Byrd marveled, "Born a free man, and his daddy born a free man, too. Own a farm in Chester County in Pennsylvania. A hundred acres, all theirs. Think of it!"

"Did he show you that little card he carry around? Picture of his wife?"

"No, I ain't seen it."

"She's white!"

Byrd shook his head. "Must be awful light-complected."

"No, he told me she was white. Just like that! As though it were the most usual thing for a black man to marry a white woman!"

"Were she pretty?"

Charles snorted. "Never looked at a white woman close enough to know. But he tell me he believe so."

The day had been warm and the evening, only a little less so. The camp smelled of the sweat of men and horses, of manure and latrines, of oil and spent gunpowder, and of fried meat, boiled coffee, and tobacco. Outside, someone who was not quite sober was singing, as beautifully as a lullaby, the refrain to "John Brown's Body."

In their barracks, the man to Byrd's right, who had just learned to read, struggled through the Bible that a pretty colored woman from the Methodist Church had given him. In the corner, a group of four men played at cards, gambling with pebbles, since their pay money had run out.

Byrd shucked off his coat, since it was warm enough for shirtsleeves. He unfolded *The Liberator*, which he now bought for himself out of his pay, and laid it on his lap to read it.

Byrd read and re-read the paper. He let it slide to the floor and asked Charles, "Did you hear what happen to our men at Fort Pillow in Tennessee?"

"Did we lose a battle?"

"Worse than that."

"Ain't nothing worse than losing a battle," said the man who had been reading the Bible.

"Man, you look ashy. What happen?" asked Charles.

Byrd was too agitated to sit. "The Rebs stormed the fort. We surrendered. Put up the white flag for them to know it." The card players began to listen. Byrd said, "They came up the hill waving a black flag. Yelling out 'No quarter! No quarter!' And then they began to shoot at us."

"After we surrender?" The men began to mutter in disbelief.

"Shot at men who put down their arms, waved their handkerchiefs, called out that they surrendered."

The men rose from their cots and drifted to stand so they could hear Byrd speak. He expelled a breath. "Shot everyone they could. Shot them point blank. Shot men who were wounded. Shot men who were crawling away, half dead."

One man said, "Can't be," and another echoed him, "Ain't right." Like in meeting, when Byrd went to meeting as a boy.

"Do you know that half of the soldiers at Fort Pillow were colored? The Rebs singled them out. Said they wouldn't take a nigger prisoner, that they would kill us all. Put their eyes out with carbines. Stabbed and beat black men before they shot them."

The murmur grew louder. "Can't be, Lord. Can't be."

"They shot the contraband boys who worked on the breastworks." A shiver of shock ran through the group, men who had been contraband. "Shot the little ones who waited on the officers. One of them grabbed a little 'un, ten year old, and said, 'Stand still so I can shoot you good.'"

"Ain't right." Louder, angrier. "Ain't right."

"They robbed the dead, black and white. Buried them rough. Not everyone they buried was dead."

"Buried alive!"

"Put a black man into a barn and nailed it shut. Then they set it afire. Left him to burn to death."

A man sobbed out, "Great God Almighty!"

Byrd's heart went hard. "The man who commanded it was called Forrest, General Forrest. He rode over the body of a colored man and laughed about it. When a Reb said, 'We'll kill them all,' he said, 'No, keep them alive, and we'll carry them back to their masters in slavery.'"

The Bible reader wailed, "Help us!" Charles shouted, "Damn them all to hell!" The men erupted in a howl of rage and pummeled each other in their haste to shove outside to shout out their fury.

Sergeant Shaw, who billeted next door, came running. Breathless, he demanded, "What's the trouble here?"

The hubbub stopped, and they stood at attention.

"Sir?" Byrd said.

"Yes, Private Byrd?"

Byrd raised his voice to his commanding officer. "Did you hear what the Rebs did to our men at Fort Pillow?"

Shaw's mouth went taut. "Yes."

"Shot us like hogs!" "Buried and burned alive!" "Murdered in cold blood!" "Damn Rebs, kill them all!" "No quarter! No quarter!"

Shaw raised his hand and his men fell silent. Lines of pain creased his face, and he spoke with effort. "We aren't brutes. We're men, and we're soldiers. We fight like soldiers, with honor." He studied his men, whose bodies and souls bore the scars of slavery, and he said, "We'll fight like the devil, but we'll fight as soldiers. That's how we'll remember Fort Pillow."

The cry went up: "Remember Fort Pillow!" It became a chant. "Remember Fort Pillow!"

They took it into battle, when they were first tested in the operations against Petersburg. The Rebs gave out their yell and the men of the 43rd answered it: "Remember Fort Pillow!"

The din swallowed Byrd's voice. Sergeant Shaw would never hear him. He cried out: "Avenge Fort Pillow!"

Byrd carried his rage over Fort Pillow, and the cry, into every battle he fought.

As Byrd lay sleepless in his bed in Willow Bend, the scar on his face ached and burned. As much as he tried to push the memory away, he recalled it.

Two of his fellow slaves, men twice his size, dragged him from the plantation's makeshift prison into the yard, where all of the slaves were gathered. They stood in silence, their heads bowed, around a fire in a shallow pit, which burned low and hot. The overseer held the iron in the flame. The brand glowed, a terrible ember. He said regretfully, "First time you ran away we beat you. Didn't stop you."

Byrd thrashed in the grip of the men who held him. In the same regretful tone, the overseer said, "Stay still, Ambrose, or we'll do worse."

The iron sizzled as the brand pressed against his cheek and seared his flesh. He smelled himself cooking like a pig in a barbecue pit. He howled against the pain until the overseer hit him in the head with the cold end of the iron and he passed into darkness.

After he mustered out, Byrd wasn't done fighting yet. He went back to Virginia to find the man who had scarred his back and branded his face.

After the war, Byrd's old place was in ruins. It had been the site of battle more than once, and the soil was ruined for tobacco or corn, soaked in blood, full of human and horse remains, polluted with char and bullet and minie ball. The air still smelled like blood and rot and sulphur. The plantation house was so badly damaged that no one could live there. Even the slave cabins had suffered. Byrd stood before the mean little houses, looking at the one he once lived in, and his heart rejoiced that no one would ever live there again.

The overseer had a four-room house, better than a cabin but not as fine as a planter's house, and it had been ruined too. The overseer was gone, just as the planter and the former slaves were gone. Disappointed, Byrd took to the road, intending to walk back to Fairfax. The landscape oppressed him. It was though he were still at war, still in battle.

He passed a cabin that survived the war. Outside it, a man and a woman, former slaves, were breaking the earth with a hoe. No plow, and no mule, either. They waved in greeting. "Ambrose!" the woman called.

"Salley!"

When he knew her before the war, she was young, round in her face and plump in her body. Now she was gaunt, and her hair was threaded with gray. He didn't know her husband, who looked older than she did. His pants were worn ragged at the hems and he went barefoot.

She said, "Never thought we'd see you again." She invited him in and insisted on giving him something to eat. She served him all they had, rough bread like the soldiers ate, cornmeal and water mixed together and baked in the ashes.

He asked after his old place and the people who used to be on it.

Salley said, "All the black folks left. Ran to the Union lines during the war and just ran after."

"The white folks left too. Your old Marse, he went to Washington," the man said.

Byrd's eyes glittered. "What about his overseer?"

"That man who was too mean to live? He still here. Found a place to hole up," Salley said.

"Where?"

"In the countryside." The man looked at him with curiosity. "You ain't intending to say how do, are you?"

Byrd rested his hand on his pistol. "Your wife said it. He too mean to live."

Husband and wife regarded Byrd, dressed in his Union tunic, carrying his Union sidearm, and a look passed between them. Bottom rail on top now, the former slaves said, as they saw their former masters brought low. The man pointed the way through the trees. "You follow that road, you find him."

Byrd said, "I won't keep you." He got up to go. He knew how badly despoiled the countryside had been. He gave them good Northern coin to thank them for the trouble they had taken to feed him.

On the road, Byrd was a soldier again, listening for the step of a picket, tensed for the sound of a shot. He stopped at a little house where the steps had collapsed, the walls had been scorched, and all the windows had been destroyed. Nothing grew in the yard. No chicken pecked, no hog rooted, no dog lazed. Did anyone live here?

He approached quietly, pistol in his hand. At the base of the ruined steps he called out the man's name.

Someone poked a rifle through the opening that had been a window. A familiar voice, roughened by war and drink, called out, "Who the hell are you?"

Byrd said, "Come out and see for yourself."

The door creaked open. He was dressed in the tattered remains of a Confederate uniform, and he carried an ancient musket. He held the gun with difficulty, since he was missing a leg, and he supported himself on a crutch. "Damn free issue nigger!" he said, pointing the weapon at Byrd as best he could. Then he recognized the man in the Union tunic. He said, "Ambrose?"

Byrd raised his pistol. He saw red, like waves of blood, before his eyes. He aimed as sure as he'd ever aimed. The man cried out, "Ambrose!" and fell to his knees, too stricken to keep his grasp on the musket. Byrd walked close. He pressed his pistol to the man's temple. The man pleaded, "Ambrose! Don't shoot me!"

Byrd held the pistol steady and said, "This is for whupping me when I ran away. This is for branding my face. This is for calling me boy, and black bastard, and nigger. This is for treating me worse than a hog."

The man bent his head, as in prayer. He began to cry. "Ambrose! Show mercy!"

Byrd said, "No quarter," and shot him in the head. He fell to the ground and Byrd kicked the body in the side to make sure he was dead. Satisfied, Byrd put his sidearm back into its holster and walked away.

We're better than that, Sergeant Shaw had said, but Byrd knew he was not.

Byrd didn't want to see the men at Thornton's the next day, but he longed for a drink of whiskey. He asked them, "May I join you?" Polite and formal.

Truehart said, "If you act peaceable."

He wouldn't humble himself before a man, but he'd humble himself for a drink. "Do my best."

Willis arrived, looking sideways at Byrd. He nodded to Thornton, who poured him a cup of whiskey.

Byrd drank, set his cup down, and said nothing.

Willis said, "Didn't think you wanted to be here."

Byrd swallowed hard. "Don't mind it."

"Glad to hear that," Willis said stiffly.

"Shouldn't have raised my hand to you."

Willis nodded.

"Wasn't right."

Willis turned to Byrd and held out his hand. Byrd shook it. Willis said, "I need some help on the Little place tomorrow, if you're willing."

"I am."

The others drank a cup, and when the other men left Thornton's store, Byrd remained. He said, "I'd like another cup."

"Don't you have a job lined up with Dan tomorrow morning?"

"That's my lookout, not yours."

"Hate to see a man drunk," Thornton said mildly.

Byrd began to feel angry. "Do you keep a saloon or a meeting house?"

"Easy, man. Easy."

Byrd was shaking. "I can't sleep. Can't bear to dream. Can't stand to remember."

Thornton looked at him with saddened eyes. He poured another cup of whiskey. As Byrd fumbled in his pocket for money, Thornton said, "No, keep your money. We all have things we can't bear to remember."

Byrd began to look like a man who didn't have a woman to look after him. His shirt wasn't clean, and his hair and beard grew ragged.

A little girl—a Glover, he thought—asked him on the street, "Why don't you comb your hair?"

He said, "When I fought the Indians, they called us black men Buffalo soldiers. Because our hair looked like a buffalo's coat. Do a buffalo comb its hide?"

"Don't know," said the little girl. "Do a buffalo look raggedy?"

That night, Byrd asked Thornton for a third cup of whiskey, then a fourth, and later, still not drunk enough, he begged for the bottle. Thornton shook his head and let him have it. "As long as you set quiet," he said. Byrd sat quietly on the porch in the dark and drank until he had finished the bottle. When he stood, he was unsteady on his feet. He staggered into the road where Buster slept in the dirt. He bent to pet the sleeping dog's head. Buster woke, licked Byrd's hand, and went back to sleep. Byrd fell, too drunk to rise. He put his head on Buster's warm, obliging flank.

Someone tapped his shoulder. "Mr. Byrd?" he said. Truehart shook him, just a little, the way he'd shake his own boy to get him out of bed.

Byrd groaned and forced his eyes open. Still half-asleep, he said, "I'm so sorry, Sergeant Shaw."

The next day, as Byrd bought nails for Willis in Thornton's, a woman's voice drifted through the door. "Mr. Truehart, it's a disgrace, the way that Mr. Byrd drinks too much and falls down in the street."

"Miss Maggie," Truehart said. Willis' wife, who fed him when he worked with Willis. "He's been a soldier. He's lived rough for a long time. He's seen death. I don't blame him for feeling troubled in his mind and his heart."

"I don't like my children to see it."

Truehart laughed. "Miss Maggie, if the worst thing your children ever see is a man passed out from too much corn whiskey, they should feel lucky. Much uglier things in this world than a man drunk."

Byrd was surprised. It wasn't exactly respect, but it was understanding. Truehart knew his heart. It bothered him. Sergeant Shaw saw into him, too, and he hadn't always liked Shaw's scrutiny. He hadn't lived in a way to make Shaw proud, either.

Chapter 3

Willow Island

Byrd found himself longing to return to Willow Island, but he was reluctant to swim there again. Everyone in Willow Bend had a boat, a skiff or a flatboat. He asked Willis if he built boats, too. "I do," Willis said, "but if you want to fish you can borrow my boat when I ain't using it. My fishing rig, too."

"Thank you," Byrd said, surprised that Willis would be so generous.

Willis added, "Whatever you do, don't take Miss Bernie's boat."

"Why not?" asked Byrd, suddenly itching to do what he shouldn't.

"I made it special for her birthday. Jim wanted a little pirogue like they use in them swamps down the river from us. No one touches it but her." Willis grinned and said, "Prettiest boat I ever built."

Hearing about Miss Bernie rankled with Byrd. He was polite to her at Sunday meeting, which he attended, even though he wasn't much of a believer, and he usually had a sore head after Saturday night. Last week, Miss Janie badgered Miss Bernie about getting married, as she had every week since Byrd had come to Willow Bend. Bernie grinned. If Miss Janie's back was turned, she would have stuck out her tongue again. She sauced, "When I meet a man who's a better shot than I am, I'll marry him."

Miss Janie puffed herself up. "You know that Mr. Ambrose Byrd, lately of the U.S. Army, was a sharpshooter for most of his soldiering life."

Bernie laughed, a sweet sound like a rivulet of water. She replied, "He may be a sharpshooter when he's sober, but he usually ain't!"

It stung him to be so harshly judged by a girl whom he barely knew, and he didn't forget it. His drinking was none of her business, as her unmarried state was none of his. A few days later he told Willis how much it irked him. Willis said to him good-naturedly, "Miss Bernie is mighty tender about wild creatures when she hunts, and mighty rough on any man who might go hunting after her."

A few days later, when the moon was out, Byrd slipped down to the riverbank. He carried a bedroll and a piece of pone he'd saved from midday dinner. He was sober, an unfamiliar sensation, and not a bad one. He didn't want to try to maneuver Willis' boat unless he was sober. The boat was a little skiff, trim and well-built. He pushed it from its mooring on the shore and eased himself into it. The fireflies were out, a lovely flash of bright green that sparkled on the water of the river. The moon lit his path to the island. The water was calmer than during the day. Quieter, too, since the gauntlet of geese and ducks was asleep.

The frogs were wide awake, and their sound rent the night. He heard the chirping of the cricket frogs, and the trilling of the chorus frogs, and the deep sonorous call of the bullfrogs. He'd once held a cricket frog in his hand, feeling its light feet and slimy skin, and he was astonished that such a little thing could make such a noise.

It wasn't easy to find his way in the dark. He blundered

before he found the path and got mud on his boots and trouser legs. He remembered to look for the path with his feet, not his eyes, and he could step where someone else had trod and make his way up the hill to the glade.

Inside, the trees filtered the light, as they did during the day. The moonlight was faint and slightly green, and it put him in mind of the fireflies on the water. He sat. The moss was drier than it had been a week ago, and softer. He didn't need a blanket to cover him. He stretched out and let the night air flow over him. He listened to all the creatures that called and peeped and chirped and cried at night. It wasn't quiet, but it was peaceful. The stars glimmered through the openings in the canopy that the live oaks and cypresses made overhead. He was alone, but for the first time since he'd come to Willow Bend, he wasn't lonely. Every bone and sinew in him eased and he fell asleep.

When Truehart asked Byrd and Willis to help him load a wagon, Byrd was puzzled, but he agreed. As soon as Truehart unlocked the shed behind his barn, Byrd understood. The shed was bigger than Truehart's house and it was filled with cotton. A little cloud of loose fluff floated through the door and settled gracefully at Byrd's feet.

Truehart said, "Mr. Levy agree to buy some cotton. Today we take it into town to sell."

"All of it?" Byrd asked.

"One load to start. If it go well we take the rest later."

As Byrd shoveled the cotton into the wagon, the fluff went up his nose and into his mouth, where it tasted linty and dry. Truehart laughed as Byrd put down his shovel. "Now you a proper country nigger," he said. "You got cotton fluff in your hair."

Willis shared the front seat of the wagon with Truehart, but Byrd had to scramble into the wagon. He thought that cotton would pillow him, but it was full of seeds and leaves and sticks that stuck into his backside like his old cornhusk mattress. It was a relief to arrive at the gin, where Mr. Levy waited for them, and to clamber from the wagon.

Mr. Chatham, who ran the general store, also owned the town's gin, which sat directly behind his store. Chatham stood in the back door and watched as Truehart descended from the wagon to greet Levy.

Chatham was a big, ruddy man, whose belly strained against the cloth of his waistcoat. His watch fob glinted bright gold in the sun, and he took out his watch, also bright gold, so big it filled his substantial palm. Don't need to know the time, Byrd thought. He just like to fondle that watch. Chatham closed his fist over the watch and returned it to his pocket.

Ignoring Levy, Chatham strolled up to Truehart and said, "Jim, what's this? Don't you crop for Mr. Little?"

Mayor Truehart, Sergeant Truehart, removed his hat. Rounded his shoulders. Dropped his eyes. He said meekly, "Mr. Chatham, sir, grew this for myself." Not the crisp yes, sir! of a soldier. The soft, slurred "suh" of a former slave.

"Do Mr. Little know you're bringing it here?" Chatham asked.

Still looking down, Truehart said mildly, "No suh, didn't want to bother him about it."

"He could gin it for you. Buy it from you, too. Save you the trouble of bringing it into town."

"Mr. Little isn't buying it. I am," Levy interrupted.

"Didn't think you were in the cotton business." Chatham took a step toward Levy.

Levy didn't step back. "I buy and I sell. Just like you."

Chatham stepped closer. "I've been in this county for thirty years," he said. "I know every planter and every nigger and most of them are in debt to me." His hand went to the bright gold of the watch fob. "I knew the man who ran your store before you come here. Didn't last more than a year. Folded up and left."

He addressed Truehart, who was still standing with his hat in his hands and his eyes on his shoes. "Jim, boy, pull the wagon onto the scale and we'll weigh it."

Truehart hesitated. Chatham said, "Four dollars for every hundred pounds."

"Begging your pardon, Mr. Chatham, suh. That's seed weight, and I ain't selling seed today."

"Four dollars is a lot of money."

"Suh, want to sell the cotton. Ginned and baled so we can weigh just the cotton."

"Why go to all that trouble?" Chatham said. In his mind, Byrd heard it different: "I can cause you trouble."

"Suh, last I heard, cotton's going for ten cents a pound. More, if it's graded high." Soft-voiced. Round-shouldered. Looking half his usual size.

"How do a nigger know so much about the price of cotton?" Chatham sneered.

"Suh, I been growing cotton all my life, I reckon I know something about it."

"I ain't sure I can oblige you, Jim."

Levy was so agitated that he bounced from foot to foot. He burst out, "I'm buying! You'll oblige me!"

Chatham took out his watch again. The gold dazzled Byrd's eyes and he had to look away.

"Mr. Chatham, suh."

"What is it, Jim?"

"Folks know you for a good business man. For a fair man, too." Chatham didn't speak, and Truehart went on, wheedling. "It ain't on my account, suh. It's on Mr. Levy's account. I know you'll treat him right, suh."

Chatham hesitated. Byrd thought, Truehart's put him in a spot. If he says no he's admitting that he ain't willing to treat a white man right.

Reluctantly, Chatham said, "All right. I'll gin it for you." He motioned toward Willis and Byrd. "Hey, you! You can help Jim load it into the gin."

More shoveling, and more fluff to breathe in. Byrd began to hate the taste of cotton. He yearned for a shot of whiskey to take that taste away.

They waited as the cotton ran through the gin and the presser. Compressed and tied, it emerged as two bales.

Chatham said impatiently, "You niggers need to set it on the scale to weigh it."

Truehart, Willis and Byrd lifted the bales, grunting with the effort, and heaved them onto the scale.

Levy crowded Chatham, craning his neck to read the number on the scale. Chatham didn't like it. "A thousand pound," he said sourly. "Bright white. You'll get your ten cents a pound."

Truehart said, "Suh, don't bright white go for more? Eleven, twelve?" He let his eyes slide toward Levy. "Give Mr. Levy his due."

Chatham threw a venomous look at Truehart. "Take your ten cents a pound and get the hell out of here."

On a warm afternoon, Byrd wound through the trees and found now-familiar path up the hill to the glade. Inside it, he stretched out on the soft carpet of moss and closed his eyes. He heard the calls of the birds, the domestic sounds of ducks and geese, and the wilder whistles of the herons and the keening cries of the hawks.

The sound of footsteps, noisy on purpose, surprised him from his drowse, and his heart pounded as he sprang to sit up. Her voice came to him from the opening in the glade that was like a doorway. "Didn't mean to startle you, Mr. Byrd," Bernie said.

From his vantage point on the ground she seemed even taller than usual. She wore a plain dress of faded calico, hiked up to save the hem from mud, and a straw hat against the sun. She carried her rifle slung over her shoulder, and around her waist she had tied a leather game bag, which sat heavy on her hip.

He asked, "Any luck yet?"

"No. Not yet."

"I heard your daddy boast about you. Can you really shoot a rabbit through the eye at fifty feet?"

A small smile. "Try to. It don't spoil the meat."

"Ain't easy to hit such a small target. I was a sharpshooter. I know."

At the shrill cry from above, she raised her head and pointed toward the sky. "Look between the trees," she whispered.

The bird spread its great barred wings and soared upward, until it looked as small as a sparrow. It circled, scouting the brush on the hill, and suddenly folded its wings to dive at a terrifying speed for the ground, so swiftly that the rabbit didn't cry out. The hawk climbed back into the sky, its bloodied prey in its beak.

"Red-tailed hawk," she said, her eyes shining. "Best hunter on the island."

"Better than you, Miss Bernie?"

She laughed. "Eagles here too. Fine hunters. Wings like this—" she extended her arms outward—"and them beautiful feathers glinting in the sun."

"You don't mind if I come here? To be quiet? Sit, and watch and listen?"

She flashed him a smile. "Course not, Mr. Byrd." She ran down the hill, her long loose hair flying.

Byrd landed his skiff on the island next to Bernie's canoe. He slipped across the beach, shading his eyes against the sun, and eased into the thicket.

New marsh grass grew in the damp earth, and where he trod on it, it released a floral fragrance that twined around the odor of mold and decay. The new growth of the cane was only knee-high and supple enough to bend as he passed. Above, the live oaks had put out a lacy cap of foliage, and the tender feathery leaves on the cypresses smelled of fresh sap. The sun filtered through the young leaves and suffused the thicket with a soft green light.

Birds trilled and called, chirped and peeped from their nests high in the live oaks. Little animal feet scurried through the marsh grass. A skeeter whined softly by his ear and he brushed it gently away.

She was so quiet that only the color of her skirt gave her

away. She stood like a young tree, the sweet green light streaking her face and her dress. He didn't move. Didn't even dare to take a deep breath, afraid that the slightest motion would alert her and that she'd start like the rabbits she hunted.

She raised the rifle to her shoulder. Set her feet in a stance to handle the kick, if she fired. But she did not. Watched. Listened. Waited.

Something bolted to safety through the marsh grass. She lowered the rifle. Good girl, he thought. Don't waste a shot. Don't alarm the rest of them. Only shoot what you can hit.

She listened again, and at a sound so small that Byrd missed it, she swung the rifle to her shoulder, in the easy motion of long practice, and in a moment, sighted, aimed, and fired. The rabbit's lifeless body slid to the ground as softly as a sigh.

But she didn't retrieve it. She waited.

With a scout's instinct, he edged toward her, not wanting to spoil another shot for her. But her ears were sharper than a scout's. When she turned, she wasn't startled. "Mr. Byrd," she said, in a low voice.

"Miss Bernie."

She smiled. She was herself again, no longer a wild creature but a girl with a rifle. "I'll walk with you to the glade, if that's where you're going."

She retrieved the rabbit and he followed her as she sprinted up the steep incline. In the glade she unslung her rifle and sat cross-legged, revealing her ankles, which were slender and scratched like a child's. She saw him looking and yanked her skirt down. She pulled a piece of pone from her pocket. "Would you like some, Mr. Byrd?"

Their fingers touched as she handed him a share and she pulled back her hand. Startled now. Took too big a bite of her pone and nearly choked on it.

He said, "You put me in mind of an Indian when I saw you in the woods."

She chewed and swallowed. "My mama tells me that her granddaddy was an Indian. A Choctaw."

"Never met a Choctaw where I was. Mostly Kiowas and Comanches."

"Are they good hunters?"

"They are, Miss Bernie. They hunt buffalo."

"Must not be hard to hunt a buffalo, it so big a target," she teased.

"No, Miss Bernie, it is. Buffalo dangerous. Run like the wind, and if them horns don't maul a man, a buffalo can knock him down and break his bones."

"Why did they call the colored soldiers after the buffalo?"

He rubbed his hand over his untrimmed hair. "Not just this It were praise for the way we fought. They thought we was as fierce as the buffalo."

She nodded. "When you were out West, did you ever see that Wild West Show? Mr. Buffalo Bill's show?"

"As a matter of fact, I did, Miss Bernie."

"I read all about it in the *Greenwood Messenger*. Is Miss Annie Oakley really as good a shot as the newspaper say?"

He wanted to laugh. Her mama and daddy didn't want him to talk about soldiering in the West, but she wanted to hear about Buffalo Bill. "She's a fine shot. Never missed one of them clay pigeons, not once."

"Mr. Byrd, do you think a colored girl could join a Wild West show?"

It came out of his mouth without his having to think about it. "That's no life for a gal."

"Not you, too!"

He didn't know what she meant, and he waited to hear from her.

"You sound just like my mama. Whenever I pick up my rifle to go hunting she sigh and shake her head and say, 'It ain't natural for a gal to be so handy with a rifle.'"

"She worry. She want what's best for you."

"I know what she want for me. She want me to go that school in Holly Springs to learn how to be a teacher, like Miss Octavia." She rested her hand on her rifle. "Wear a starched dress, and stay indoors, and teach the little 'uns their ABCs." She curled her hand around the rifle barrel. "If I had to act like Miss Octavia I'd be bored to death."

He knew a rebellious nature when he saw one. He thought of her in the forest, as untamed as the creatures she hunted. He said, "Don't blame you, not a bit!"

She started to laugh, and he joined her, even though he knew he shouldn't.

"Would you come hunting with me, Mr. Byrd?" she asked, her face alight with their shared amusement.

"Yes, Miss Bernie, I would."

Truehart enlisted every man and every wagon in Willow Bend to load the rest of his cotton to take it into town. By the time they were done, Byrd's skin itched with cotton lint, as though he were wearing an extra layer under his shirt. He rode with Willis and he took shallow breaths, hating to let any more cotton up his nose.

They made a convoy, ten wagons, each so heavy with cotton that a pair of mules strained to pull it. The mules trod carefully on the dirt path through the thicket, and Byrd felt his skin itch with impatience as much as with lint.

He recalled escorting a convoy out West, a group of settlers bent on breaking ground in country that the Comanches still called home. That was dry country, where the dust went in his nose and mouth and coated his skin. No trees grew there, only clumps of tall grass that could cut a man's face if he rode by too fast. Beyond the grass were the hills, rough tumbles of rock, where the Comanches might be hiding. Byrd recalled scanning the horizon as he preceded the wagon train, his breath shallow and his eyes stinging with the dust, every sinew braced for the sound of pounding hooves and the cry of war.

Today, in the Delta thicket, he shifted on the seat of Willis' wagon and listened for the sounds beneath the call of birds, the snuffle of mules, and the creaking of the wagon wheels. He stared into the thicket's dimmed light, scouting for the trouble beyond the now-familiar landscape.

He didn't feel less wary on the paved road. As the wagons creaked and the mules trudged toward the town, he wished he'd brought his sidearm.

In town, their ten wagons filled the ginyard. Truehart descended from his wagon first, and as the rest of the men halted their mules, they slid from the wagon seats to bunch behind Truehart.

Levy, who had seen them arrive, came running into the ginyard, waving and calling out, "You're all right?"

As though they might not be, Byrd thought.

The back door of the general store creaked open. Chatham leaned against the doorway, surveying the wagons and the phalanx behind Truehart.

Truehart stepped forward, making himself small, and spoke softly. "Mr. Chatham, suh, I come to sell the rest of my cotton to Mr. Levy today. Be obliged if you'd gin it, suh."

Chatham didn't move from his position in the doorway. "Can't oblige you, Jim."

"Ain't for me, suh. For Mr. Levy."

"Can't oblige him, either."

Levy demanded, "Why not?"

"Don't want any trouble," Chatham said, as indolent as if he was talking about the weather.

Levy started forward, but Truehart touched his sleeve, nothing more, to restrain him. "Mr. Levy, suh." Levy halted. Truehart said, "No trouble, Mr. Levy."

Levy shook Truehart off. He strode towards Chatham and growled, "Get out of my way. Let me do business."

Chatham straightened up. His bulk filled the doorframe. He reached into his pocket.

Without realizing it, Byrd pulled himself tall, his shoulders back, his feet apart, his belly flat. He focused his gaze straight ahead. Next to him, Willis unbent himself to look ahead, and the rest of the men of Willow Bend raised their heads and straightened their spines. As Chatham searched in his pocket, all of them stood behind Truehart, in the stance drilled into them when they first became soldiers.

Chatham drew his hand from his pocket and Truehart's company observed without a word.

Chatham pried open the cover to consult the big white dial. He snapped the watch shut. "Go on home, Jim," he said. "Take your boys and your cotton on home." He turned and stepped over the threshold into his store.

Byrd had expected trouble, and he had been right about it. Not shooting trouble, but something else. Levy touched Truehart's shoulder and said quietly, "I know a man in Greenwood. A *landsman*, a Jew. He buys cotton. Let me talk to him."

Truehart let Levy's hand rest there. He nodded, unable to say, "Thank you," or "Mr. Levy," or "suh."

When they returned to Willow Bend an hour later, Byrd was sticky with cotton lint and heartsick at the thought of unloading ten wagons full of loose cotton. Truehart stopped outside Thornton's and said, "I'd like a drink, and anyone else who wants one is free to join me."

All of them crowded into Thornton's. Truehart pushed his way to the counter, gulped down a full cup of whiskey, and banged the cup on the counter instead of asking politely for another. He turned to address every man in the room. "It were Marse Little," he snarled. "He talk to Mr. Chatham, warn him off. I bet he summon me tomorrow to chide me. 'Why didn't you bring it to me, Jim? I'd gin it for you.'" He clenched his hand into a fist. "Gin it for me, and give me short weight, and pay me in furnish instead of cash, and reckon so that I'm in debt." He growled with rage. "My cotton, that I grew. Bright white, worth twelve cents a pound." He turned back to the counter so he could pound his fist on it. "Damn him! Never do business with him again. Never be in debt again!"

It rattled Byrd to see Truehart in a fury. It seemed wrong,

like thinking of the reverend in the privy. The reverend went to the privy, like everyone did, and Truehart could get mad and drink too much, if something drove him to it. But Byrd didn't like it. He excused himself after one drink and left with Willis.

Willis looked as worn as a man who'd been picking cotton all day instead of carrying it in a wagon to sell it. Byrd followed Willis as he took the dirt path that cut through Truehart's fields, past the neatly plowed rows where the seeds would uncurl in the sweet warm air to produce another year's worth of bright white cotton. Byrd asked, "Why do he hate so much to be in debt?"

Willis said wearily, "It go back ten year."

"What happen?"

Willis said, "We set in the shade." He gestured toward an ancient tree with a great crest of foliage. Willis sat heavily on the ground and Byrd joined him.

Willis said, "After the war we was all loyal Republicans. Stood up for the county conventions, organized speeches and rallies, helped everyone go to vote. We was proud to do it. Went to the polling place, all the men from the 1st Mississippi, in our Union coats. The Democrats didn't like it, but as long as the government kept their men here, to watch over things and defend us, we was all right. No one bothered us. But in 1876 the Federal men went home. Them Democrats saw their chance, and they made it rough during the election." Willis' face was ashy.

"How bad were it?" Byrd asked.

"It were just before the election. Two men come to see me. A man named Dixon, a friend of Marse Little's, and Chatham, before he got so big in the county. I know they in the Klan, but they so bold they don't even cover their faces. Come in broad daylight, for my wife and children to see. Dixon put a gun to my head and he tell me that if I ever vote again, he kill me."

Byrd remembered the shock of the news from Fort Pillow, a man's voice sobbing out, "Can't be, can't be…"

"They go to see Jim and tell him the same thing. Then they do worse to him."

Byrd thought again of Fort Pillow. There were things worse than death.

"They burn his crop in the field to put him in debt to Marse Little. And he were in debt, for three long year. He work in the sawmill when he weren't in the field, and Miss Niecy go back to the Little place to work as a servant. It were a bitter time, and it still burn in him."

Byrd sprinted up the hill to the glade, where Bernie waited. Now that the trees had fully leafed, the glade was even more private than before, and he was acutely aware of being alone with her. He stood at a respectful distance, as though they were talking after meeting, and teased her. "Miss Bernie, I thought you were going to bring me a rifle."

"But I did, Mr. Byrd."

"Don't see it. Are you going to lend me your Winchester?"

"Not the Winchester!" She laughed and picked up the rifle that was hidden in the flowers at her feet. "My old rifle. It ain't a repeater."

He took it from her hands and hefted it. "A good gun. A Springfield, like I used in the war." He raised it to his shoulder, feeling the places where her hands had worn it.

"Have you hunted rabbit, Mr. Byrd?"

"Never hunted anything so small, Miss Bernie."

"They're hard to hit. Hide in the grass, startle easy, never bound towards you, only away." She moved so close that he could feel her heat. She smelled fresh and unripe, like a green apple. "I can show you."

He moved the rifle from his shoulder to point the barrel down. "Miss Bernie, you know it ain't safe to stand so close to this gun."

"Safety's on."

"You know better." As he'd speak to a young recruit.

She drew back, her hand on her rifle strap. "We go into the thicket," she said, her voice smaller than before.

He followed her as she slid through the trees, the dirt damp under his feet, the grass dense around his knees. He startled an early mayfly into flight, and he brushed away a cloud of gnats and some skeeters, too.

He matched her uneven pace, glide, stop, glide, stop. A scout's pace, silent and watchful. It was strange to be so alert in a place that held no danger. Straining for the sound of little hopping feet and the flash of a white tail.

He edged towards her, not wanting to flush any rabbits, until he was alongside her. She bent close, like a child confiding in her daddy. She whispered, the puff of her breath warm on his ear. "We go quiet. Follow me."

Slide through the trees. Stop to study the grass. Wait. Sight. She didn't shoot. Couldn't get a clear shot.

Around them, the thicket teemed with movement, the grass and the vines in a fever of growth, the gnats and skeeters boiling up from the ground, the birds shrilling and shrieking in their determination to mate and nest. But he and Bernie were silent in it.

It ain't the shooting she cares for, Byrd thought, marveling that he held a gun in his hands and felt a perfect sense of ease. This wild place is a refuge.

She disturbed the quiet with a shot, and the animal fell to the ground. She grinned. She retrieved it, holding it by the ears.

"Shoot it through the eye?" he asked, remembering to talk low.

"Quiet," she whispered back.

He trailed her as they found another spot to watch and listen and wait. He said, "Let me give it a try."

He raised the rifle to his shoulder. He knew he was a fine shot—he could kill a man at fifty feet—but as a bunny hunter, he found himself hesitant. He wanted to best her. He wanted to get his own rabbit clean through the eye.

Look for movement in the grass. Stand still, don't startle when it does. Take your time. Look for the gleam in that little eye, and aim for it.

He saw the grass move and heard the faint rustle. He waited. The rabbit froze. He sighted on the ears, which quivered ever so slowly. Waited again. The rabbit bolted just as he fired, but he heard it fall.

She said, "Let me find it," and in a moment she returned with the dead rabbit in her hands. "Hit it in the side," she said. "Tore it up."

"No good, then."

"We leave it for them big birds to eat." She laid it on the ground to offer it to them. She came close and laid her hand on his arm, a warm, firm touch. "Mr. Byrd, don't look so crestfallen. We try again."

He met her eyes. He had never looked into them before. They were a deep velvety brown, flecked with a copper color like the undertone to her skin. He said, "Yes. We do."

They kept going. Slide through the thicket. Stop. Wait.

And he saw it, its head showing through a parting place in the grass, and he sighted and shot and knew, even before it fell, how well he had hit his target. He said to her, "No, I go for it," and grabbed it by the ears to hold it high to show her. "As good as you did. Through the neck."

She put the rabbit into her game bag. "We'll make a hunter of you yet, Mr. Ambrose Byrd," she said. It was unseemly that she called him by his Christian name, but the sound of it was sweet on her lips.

Unaccustomed feeling surged through him. He laid his hand on her back, the way he'd encourage a young soldier. And she smiled at him with a radiance that he had never seen on a young soldier's face.

After she left, Byrd was loath to leave the island. He sat on the hill until the sun began to set and the frogs began to call. He rowed slowly across the river, and he lingered on the way to his shack. He opened the door and shut it gently. He lay quietly on the bed and closed his eyes. The smell of green apple seemed to fill the room and to overpower everything that was soiled and sour. He thought, If I'd married after the war I'd have a gal her age. Might have been a hunter and a sure shot, like her. Full of regret, he let himself admit the thought he couldn't drink away.

He loved Bernie the way a father loved a daughter.

Truehart strode into Thornton's, and at the look on his face, Thornton got out the whiskey jug without being asked. Truehart shook his head. Thornton asked, "Why not? All right to get mad here, with us."

Truehart glanced at Byrd. "Now I understand why you say it. Don't want to call that man Marse."

"What happen?" Thornton asked. Truehart gestured toward the jug and Thornton poured him a cup.

Truehart glared at him. "Tell you when I tell everyone at meeting this Sunday."

That Sunday, Byrd shifted uncomfortably on the hard pine bench. He was still surprised to find himself in church every Sunday. But all of Willow Bend went to church, and he was now part of Willow Bend. Bernie sat with her mother in the front row, her braid untidy, and Byrd wished with all his heart he could tell her to comb her hair proper before church, and that she would mind him.

Before the reverend began the service, Truehart strode to the pulpit. "Excuse me, Reverend, need to be mayor for a moment, have some town business to discuss with everyone."

The Reverend stepped aside. "Go ahead, Mayor Truehart."

Truehart stood with his shoulders back and his hands curled at his sides. He surveyed the room, his gaze settling on each face. "Most of you know that I go to see Marse Little this week. He summon me, just like I thought he would, after we try to sell my cotton. But he surprise me." His eyes rested on Byrd, and Byrd wondered if Bernie had said anything to her father. "It weren't about the cotton or the ginning."

"What were it?" Thornton called out.

Truehart's eyes swept the room again. He had the commander's ability to look at everyone and to make the crowd feel that the words for him or her alone. "He want to buy the land back from us."

"Don't fool us!" The words escaped Willis.

"Why would I fool about such a thing? He offer ten dollars an acre for it."

"What did you tell him, Daddy?" Bernie sang out.

Truehart nodded at his daughter and softened for a moment. Then he addressed the crowd again. "I tell him I ain't inclined to sell. That we have to talk it over, all of us, since I ain't the only one to decide. We all decide."

"Don't even have to ask," Thornton said grimly. "Ain't inclined! He could shoot me, and my widow wouldn't sell it to him, either."

Willis cried out, "What do he think? After we clear it, and plow it, and plant it, and reap what we sow, we give it back to him?"

Thornton rose to his feet. "No!" he called out. Willis rose too, and called it back to him: "No!" Niecy and Bernie both stood, echoing the cry: "No!" Around them, women rose, their dresses rustling, and men stood, their boots heavy on the floor, and even the children stood, glad of a chance to make a noise in church. "No!" they shouted. "No! No! No!" until the roar was like a battle cry.

After Truehart's announcement in Thornton's, Byrd felt uneasy in Willow Bend. He craved the quiet of Willow Island as much as he craved a drink of whiskey. He rowed to the island, not knowing whether he wanted to be alone or alone with Bernie.

The air was thick and wet, holding the promise of rain. The gnats had multiplied since his last visit, and he brushed them away from his eyes and spat them out of his mouth. He climbed the hill and had to halt a moment, because his heart pounded in his chest at the memory of the smile on Bernie's face.

No wife to warm him. No child to cheer him. But at the top of the hill was Bernie, who made him regret that he'd never married and that he'd never raised up his own flesh and blood to be a rebellious spirit and a good shot.

He hadn't bothered to be quiet and when he entered the glade, she was on her feet. With that bright smile on her face. "Mr. Byrd."

"Yes, Miss Bernie?"

She came close enough for him to smell her green apple scent and raised her eyes to his. "Mr. Ambrose Byrd." Ambrose. the name that his dead mother had called him. That only a wife would call him, if he had one.

"What is it, Miss Bernie?"

Before he could stop her, she flung her arms around his neck and pressed her lips to his ear, her breath warm with a confidence that was not a daughter's for a father.

"I love you."

Byrd was speechless. He never knew that a good churchgoing girl might sniff out love the way a rabbit sniffed out a hunter.

Oh, Lord. How she had misunderstood him. How he had misunderstood her. He put his hands on her arms and gently tried to pull them from his neck. "Miss Bernie, no."

She didn't move her arms and he'd be damned if he'd force her. "You're the only man I've ever loved."

That shocked him into speech. He struggled to find the right way to say it. "I love you like your daddy's brother would love you. Proud of you. Pleased with how you turned out. Glad for you if you find a man to marry who will cherish you."

"I'd marry you, if you asked me."

"Miss Bernie, you don't want to marry me."

"But I do."

He tugged on her arms until she let him go. He retreated far enough so that she couldn't reach for him again. "Listen to me."

Unease crept onto her face.

"I'm too old for you. I've lived too rough. I ain't kind. If you married me, it would be a misery for both of us."

The bright smile disappeared, like a fire snuffed out. He

said, "You find a young man to be sweet to you. That's who you should marry."

She put her hand to her eyes. The thought of her tears knifed him. "Don't want one. They all fools. You ain't a fool, Mr. Byrd."

He had wanted to be fatherly with her, but all he had was the voice of the man in the bawdy house, telling the bought woman that he could never stay. "I've been a fool, and if I let you talk sweet to me, and kiss me again, I'd be a bigger fool. I ain't marrying anyone right now, least of all you."

The tears overflowed and rolled down her cheeks, silvery streaks on the coppery skin. She pulled away. He hadn't prayed for a long time, but he would ask the Lord's forgiveness for making Bernie Truehart cry.

In a ragged voice, she said, "I'll go."

He stood stiffly, his hands balled into fists at his sides. He didn't dare to touch her. The words came from him like blood from a wound. "Miss Bernie, I'm sorrier than I've ever been in my life."

She turned away, sniffling hard against the tears. "Don't care," she said, and she fled down the hill. She was gone.

Byrd sat on the hill, his heart so heavy in his chest he could barely breathe. He didn't move, save to brush the skeeters off his face. No matter what he thought, he wasn't her daddy or her daddy's brother. He couldn't be a suitor to her, even if he wanted to. If she was old enough to know her own mind—which she wasn't—Truehart would never allow him to keep company with her. He wasn't fit to court her. He was a stranger to Willow Bend, he was a drunk, and he was a fool.

Chapter 4

Jerusha

Byrd woke and winced at the dim light that filtered through his oilpaper windows. When he sat up he was assaulted by the pain in each temple. He was sweating, and his sweat stank of whiskey. His gut recoiled at the smell.

He staggered outside and vomited behind the shack. Quivering, his head hanging low, his headache worse than ever, he wiped his mouth on his sleeve.

"Mr. Byrd?" It was Miss Lizzie.

He shook his head. The nausea returned, made worse by embarrassment.

She handed him a cup of water. He took a sip, unable to take more, and gave it back to her.

"Miss Jerusha have a root for that," she said.

He bent over to retch again, and when he stood up, he lurched into the road. Jerusha's house wasn't far—she lived just next to the Truehart place—but every step sent further pain into his head and misery into his stomach.

He stumbled up her front steps and leaned against the doorjamb. He called out hoarsely, "Miss Jerusha?"

She came unhurriedly to the door, wiping her hands on her apron. "What is it, Mr. Byrd?"

"I have a powerful bad headache. Do you have a remedy?"

She wrinkled her nose. "Did you drink up all your money, too?"

Anger made his belly roil again and he'd be damned to hell if he'd vomit on her doorstep. "I ain't asking for charity."

"Come in."

She led him to a chair and he fell into it. The small sounds she made as she opened her cupboard, set a jar on the counter, and knocked a spoon against a tin cup aggravated the pain in his head. But the cup she brought to the table smelled strong and pleasant, like wintergreen.

"What is it?" he asked.

"Birchbark tea. Good for headache. Go on, drink it."

He drank. The wintergreen immediately soothed his throat and quieted his stomach. He sat up a little straighter.

She asked, "Can you tolerate some breakfast?"

The headache began to ease like a fist unclenching. "Think so."

As she cut pone and poured coffee he was able to lift his head enough to stare at the glass jar she kept on the table, filled with a bunch of cut black-eyed susans. Odd thing to do, when they grew wild everywhere. On her table they glowed, like brown eyes in a bright coppery face.

Hadn't drunk enough to forget.

She watched as he ate, an appraising gaze, as though she wanted to examine his innards to find what ailed him. He began to regret that he'd come to see her. He should have slept off his whiskey. He'd promised her he'd repay her, and he didn't like the idea of being in debt.

"Better?" she asked.

"Yes."

She laughed. "I haven't put you to work yet. We go to the barn."

They walked through the pasture, where her cow stopped grazing to raise its head. The cow was smaller than a horse, but considerably wider, with a Guernsey's black and white splotched coat.

Jerusha said proudly, "Her name Honeysuckle but I call her Honey. Do you want to meet her?" Not waiting for his reply, she hurried across the grass, and he trailed after her. When he got close enough, the cow nosed him with a soft black muzzle and licked his hand with a big soft lolling tongue.

Jerusha laughed. "She like you!" She put her arm around the cow's neck and crooned, "How's my Honey? How's my girl?"

Byrd thought, She don't talk sweet to anybody and she hug that cow like it her sister.

Jerusha led him into the barn, where the straw was ankle-deep and clotted with manure and the stink of manure was overpowering. She said, "Haven't had time to muck it out today."

"One cow make all this mess?"

She laughed. "Ain't you ever tended to a cow?"

"I was a soldier. Had a horse to tend to."

"Shovel's over there." She was still laughing.

He shoveled out the shittened straw onto the manure pile behind the barn and wished he hadn't left the Army. He sweated as he worked, the last of the whiskey coming out of his pores. When he finished he leaned against the shovel and wiped his forehead with his sleeve. She approached with a light step. "How are you coming along?"

He bit his tongue against what he'd like to say to her. What he'd said to the Army man who had commanded him to clean out a latrine.

"I just churned butter and there's fresh buttermilk. Glad to pour you some."

He followed her back into the house and sat again at the little pine table. The buttermilk was cold and sweet-sour. He drained the cup and sighed as he set it down.

She had oilpaper windows, like everyone in Willow Bend, but she had hung curtains, bright white, and between them the oilpaper gleamed like sunlight.

"How's your head now?" she asked.

Surprised, he said, "Headache's gone."

"Anything else troubling you?"

"Why would you ask that?"

"A man who drink usually have trouble."

Byrd was used to flattery—bought women traded in it—but Jerusha's sympathy caught him off guard. He admitted, "Don't sleep well. Wish I had something to help me sleep."

"Drink makes it worse."

He rose and turned to go. "Asked for a root. Don't need a sermon."

She grasped his wrist and pulled him back. "Wait," she said. "I have something for you."

She came back with a twist of brown paper that stank of rotten grass, worse than the muck in her barn. He made a face. "What is it?"

"Valerian root, ground up. Take it with some honey."

He said, "If I can stand it."

"Don't want anyone to lean on valerian. Ain't good for you. And don't take it if you been drinking."

"Why not?"

"Ain't usual, but you might stop breathing in your sleep, never wake up."

He held the twist of paper in his hand, not sure if he wanted to take it with him. "What do I owe you?"

"You can stop by to muck out my barn again."

He held the paper between two fingers, unwilling to put it into his pocket. "If this stuff don't kill me."

She said, "When you get riled you flush. Light-complected enough to show." She put her hands to her own face. "As bad as I do." She was smiling.

Riled and flushed, he said, "Would I see that, if I riled you?"

"You might, if you came to supper this Saturday night."

"Miss Jerusha, don't make a fool of me." He clenched the twist of paper in his hand, and the smell leaked through his fingers.

She closed her hand over his fist, her veins prominent under the fair skin. "This Saturday night."

Buster heard the hooves on the dirt road first, and barked a warning and a welcome that sent Byrd and Thornton into the street. Byrd strained his eyes to spy who it might be. "He's white," Byrd told Thornton.

Thornton said worriedly, "Never had a white man visit Willow Bend before."

The stranger hopped from the horse. He was a slight man, jauntily dressed in a checked suit and shiny new shoes. His eyes darted in restless motion and his arms were restless at his sides. Even his hair was impatient. When he took off his hat it sprang upward to curl in the heat, despite the pomade he'd put on it. He surveyed the wary faces that greeted him. "Where's the cotton you want to sell?" he demanded.

Thornton edged away and the man held out his hands, surprised and unarmed. "Didn't Joe Levy tell you I was coming?"

Thornton stammered, "No, sir."

"Where can I find Jim Truehart?"

"We bring him," said Thornton, and before he could ask Byrd to fetch Truehart, Byrd was off to find him, running like a man pursued by Comanches. He waved his arms and yelled at Truehart, "There's a man come to buy your cotton!"

Truehart didn't run, any more than Sergeant Shaw would have, but he moved more briskly than usual. The stranger's face broke into a grin. "I'm Jake Rosenbloom, from Greenwood. Cotton broker. Joe Levy said you had a fine crop of cotton you needed ginned." When Truehart didn't reply, Rosenbloom added, "Joe told me about the trouble you had at the gin with Chatham. I didn't come to make trouble for you. I came to buy cotton. Can I see it?"

Truehart said, "Mr. Rosenbloom, you talk so fast I can hardly make out what you say."

Rosenbloom grinned again and opened his arms wide. "I'm from New York," he exclaimed. "That's how we talk!"

Truehart led the way and Rosenbloom hurried behind him. Byrd and Thornton followed, their eyes never leaving the excitable stranger. Truehart unlocked the shed and Rosenbloom grasped a loose boll. He examined it in the sunlight, pulled on it to check the fibers, rolled the strands with his fingers, and brushed it against his cheek to feel how soft it was. "Good clean cotton," he said. "Bright white."

"Twelve cents a pound?"

Rosenbloom nodded. "Take it down to Greenwood and I'll gin it and weigh it for you."

"Ten wagons full, sir," Truehart said. "Worried about trouble on the road."

"Don't worry. I'll go with you."

Truehart stared at the short, dapper, jaunty man before him. "Will we be all right, sir? With them wagons on the road to Greenwood?"

Rosenbloom reached into his left pocket and brought out a fistful of silver dollars that shimmered in the sun. "These should to help us along, and if that don't work, I have this." From his right pocket, Rosenbloom removed a pistol with a flourish.

Byrd laughed. He thought, Little banty rooster of a man, no taller than I am, with a pistol in one pocket and a fistful of bribe money in the other. He called out, "I have a Colt just like yours. A peacemaker!"

Truehart warned, "You leave your sidearm at home, Mr. Byrd."

They loaded up the wagons and by midday, they were on the road to Greenwood. Rosenbloom and Byrd rode together up front, and Truehart brought up the rear. Ten wagons, moving as slowly as a tired mule, and only one man with a firearm to defend them. Despite Rosenbloom's jaunty demeanor, Byrd was thinking like a scout, and he didn't like their chances.

"Someone's down the road," Byrd told Rosenbloom. "Man on a horse."

He was a stranger, a young man with sandy hair. He challenged Rosenbloom. "Who are you?"

Rosenbloom shot back, "Who are you?"

"Don't matter," the young man said. "What's your business here?"

Rosenbloom's hand stole toward the pocket where he kept his bribe money. "Bought a load of cotton up near Itta Bena."

"Who are all these niggers?"

"They cropped it and they're taking it to Greenwood for me." Rosenbloom held out two silver coins.

The sandy-haired man ignored the money. "Is one of those niggers named Jim?"

Byrd started. Rosenbloom yanked his hand back and replied in irritation, "I don't know. Didn't get introduced."

"You're lying. You bought Jim Truehart's cotton and you're going to gin it down in Greenwood."

Rosenbloom rose from his wagon seat in his agitation. "That's none of your damn business," he said.

"Mr. Little thinks it is."

Rosenbloom danced with ire. "I don't know Mr. Little, and I don't know you. Get out of my way."

The man didn't pick up the reins or nudge his horse to move.

Rosenbloom pushed his hand into his right pocket and pulled out the gun. The stranger regarded him without alarm. Gripping the gun, Rosenbloom said, "There's a man in Greenwood who got in my way. Kept me from doing my business. He's still limping."

The man guffawed. "Didn't come to shoot," he said. "Just came to chat." He kicked the horse in the ribs and they galloped away.

Byrd stood before his cloudy little mirror and stared at his reflection. The little Glover girl had been right. He looked raggedy. He needed a pair of scissors to trim his beard. He'd buy it at Thornton's, and when he came back he'd use his sliver of soap and his washrag to clean himself up for Miss Jerusha.

At Thornton's, he asked Davey, "Do you have a pair of scissors? The kind a man can use to trim his beard?"

Davey said, "My uncle can barber, if you want a trim before you see Miss Jerusha."

Irritated, Byrd said, "Just need a pair of scissors."

Outside, in the street, he scratched Buster around the ears. "Everyone about to bother me to death. Do anyone care if you go to visit a gal dog?" He rubbed Buster on the head and Buster raised himself up to bark.

Back in his shack, he found that his good shirt had lost a button, and he accosted Miss Lizzie at the pump. "Miss Lizzie, would you sew on a button for me?"

A smile on that pleasant face. What would it be like to be married to a pleasant woman? "Glad to help you look fine for Miss Jerusha."

He sat in her kitchen as she sewed, her fingers brown and capable against the fabric. He said, "Do everyone know she ask me to have supper with her?"

"Everyone talk to everyone else around here. That's how we watch out for each other."

"Don't think it's a danger for a man to set at a woman's table for supper."

"Were you ever married, Mr. Byrd?"

"No, I wasn't."

Miss Lizzie snipped the thread and let the shirt lie in her lap. "I've known Jerusha since she was a girl on the Little place, just sold away from her mama. She got married and her husband was sold away, too. She never saw him again." She snipped the thread and handed him the shirt.

He carried the mended shirt back to his shack and thought, Don't ask a woman who used to be a slave anything about what's done. Who was your daddy? Can't tell, even though everyone can see it, your skin so fair. Where's your mama? Gone. What happen to your husband? Sold away.

That evening, he strolled to Jerusha's house in the sweet evening of spring, as the sun slanted low over the cotton fields and the nightbirds began to call softly to lull their nestlings and their prey. Tonight, unburdened by headache, he took pleasure in the sight of the flowers in her front yard, columbines and Virginia bluebells like the ones he'd grown up with, painted daisies that reminded him of the West. Her steps were swept so clean he was sorry to tread on them. As he lingered at the door, he savored the smells of apple pie and greens cooked with bacon.

She wore a pretty dress, newly ironed, and her hair fell in curls around her face. Her cheeks were pink. She smelled of soap and starch and the roots she handled, a smell that was sweetly floral and bitter just beneath.

She had set the table with china dishes and put flowers in a glass vase. They were bachelor buttons, blue and spiky. She had put out candlesticks and lit the candles, the smell of clover honey mingling with the smell of beeswax. Against the far wall— how could he have missed seeing it last time, in a one-roomed house?—was her bed, the pillows plumped with goose feathers, the coverlet brightly quilted in a pattern of red and blue.

He was uneasy to be in the company of a woman he hadn't paid for. He wondered what he could talk to her about. She laid the table with the food, catfish and hushpuppies. He waited for her to say grace, but she did not.

He asked, "You don't bless first?"

"Talk to God as I need to. Don't bother Him all the time."

"I ain't much of a believer," he admitted.

"Didn't think so, the way you fidget when the Reverend give a sermon."

Just when he felt at ease with her, she had to jab at him like a skeeter. But she smiled. "You flushing. Did I rile you?"

He carefully finished chewing a bite of hushpuppy and set down his fork, as polite as a man in a restaurant in New Orleans. "Yes, ma'am, you did."

"Do you like it here? In Willow Bend?"

That fair face. Those cheeks light enough to turn pink. Those green eyes. He didn't lie to her. "Don't know yet, Miss Jerusha."

"You ain't easy, living here."

He admitted, "Don't think I'd be easy anywhere."

She said, "I thought so." Glimmer of a smile. "You was a soldier, and soldiers don't stay in one place."

Outside a mourning dove called in soft lament. Did doves recall what was lost? Did their hearts ache for it? He knew what that felt like. The candlelight flickered over her face, making it darker and paler at once, shadowed and eerie and so beautiful that his heart ached. His manhood, too.

After dinner she surprised him. She offered him whiskey. "Didn't think you approved of whiskey, Miss Jerusha."

"A little whiskey is all right. It's good as a medicine, too. I don't approve of too much whiskey, that's all."

Under her gaze, he slowly drank from the half-filled cup she gave him, and didn't want more. Pleased, warmed, he set the cup down and asked, "Miss Jerusha, how did you come to settle in Willow Bend?"

"Knew the Trueharts from back in slavery days. I worked under Miss Niecy in the kitchen, after slavery was over. She was always kind to me, and when she learned that I knew roots, she told her friends about me. Surprised me that people would pay me for it. Pleased me to set something aside. When Mr. Truehart had a notion to start a town, where black folks might live and make a living, I thought it was a good idea to join them."

"How did you come by your cow?"

"Got her from some folks who decided to move to Kansas."

"From here up to Kansas? Why would folks do such a thing?"

"You never heard of them Exodusters?"

"No, did not. Who were they?"

"That's what the folks who went to Kansas called themselves. After the book of Exodus, because they were leaving a place that oppressed them, and after them dry, dusty plains up in Kansas, where they don't get rain like we do."

"Oppressed them? What happen here, to send them away?"

"After the massacre."

Byrd sat at the table, his whiskey untouched. He said slowly "Massacre?"

"No one told you?"

"Not about a massacre. Was it here?"

"Not here. The next county over."

"What happen?"

The mourning doves called again, and the owls answered. Her face clouded. "We was all Republicans, to remember President Lincoln who freed us. Even us ladies who never could vote. Always had a parade on Independence Day, and when the men went to the courthouse to cast a ballot, we went along and cheered for them. Ever since the end of the war, always sent a Republican to the legislature in Jackson, and sent some Republicans to Washington, too."

Her face was pale and haunted in the candlelight. "The next county over, all the black folks were Republicans, just like us. There were a white man, a Union Army man, who run for the legislature in Jackson, who said that black folks should own their farms and sell their cotton for their own benefit. The Democrats hated him, and it were no secret that they belonged to the Klan."

She said, "Were a big rally out in the countryside. People come from all over to hear the candidate. When they was all gathered together, a horde of Klansmen come riding up. The Klansmen shoot him dead, and then they shoot folks in the crowd. Not just men, but women and children. Fifty people, innocent folks, come to hear a man give a speech. Shoot them all dead, and bury them in a mass grave."

"And then the ruffians go into the countryside and seek out all the black folks they could find. Dragged them from their houses. Shot the men dead. Left the women and girls alive to outrage them."

She shuddered. "To this day no one go near the place where the massacre happen. People say the dead linger there, too restless to go to heaven or to hell."

Byrd thought of the trouble on the road to Greenwood. "Was it Mr. Little's doing? The massacre?"

"Never knew. Always wondered. We did know about the man who led the band who did it. Tall man with only one eye. Colonel Loveless."

As a soldier, Byrd had been in many places before a battle. He had learned to distrust a peaceable countryside. It could erupt suddenly, full of smoke and blood and death. He had been wrong to feel at ease in this place, which seemed so much at peace. A black man, like a hunter, needed to stay wary.

The next time Willis went to the Little place, he reluctantly took Byrd along. "You keep out of sight, and you keep your head down."

And as they worked—Byrd keeping his head down, trying to stay out of trouble—two men visited Little, one stocky and short, the other younger, taller, sandy-haired. The man who'd stopped them on the road to Greenwood. Willis' face tightened and he bent his head lower than ever, trying to keep out of sight himself. Byrd asked, "What's the matter?"

Willis whispered, "That short man, that's Mr. Dixon."

"What business do he have here?"

"We both stay low," Willis said.

As Byrd sawed boards behind the stable, he heard Little ask Willis, "Where's that jumped up nigger you had with you last time? Little fair-complected nigger?"

Willis' voice changed. Softened. Went back to slavery. "Don't know, Marse Little."

"I believe you do, Dan. Where is he?"

"Don't want any trouble, Marse Little. Just to do this job for you."

"If you see him, tell me."

"Yassuh."

What did Little want with him? Byrd was fully a scout

again, scenting danger, and until he and Willis finished the day's work he was alert and uneasy.

By the time Willis and Byrd left the Little place, their money in their pockets, the sun was just beginning to set. The March air was warm when the sun was high, but began to chill as night came on. The birds that called and chattered so loud during the day were settling for the night, their songs soft and drowsy. The swallows, who came out at dusk to feed, swooped through the sky as the light failed, with the sideways flight that made Byrd think of bats.

At the edge of Little's land, the cotton fields gave way to uncleared brush, where uncut canebrake, as tall as a man, grew between the twisted cypresses. They couldn't see the animals who lived in the undergrowth, but they could hear a soft rustling as they moved: swamp rabbits, birds that hopped on the ground, snakes as they slithered. Getting ready for the night, some to rest, some to look for food.

Willis was uneasy. "Don't like being out at dusk," he said. He slapped the reins over the mule's neck. Betsey was even-tempered, but like all mules, she was steady rather than swift. He said, "You go on, girl. Go on home," but the mule didn't quicken her pace. He frowned. He said, "Do you hear that?"

Byrd's ears as well as his eyes were sharpened by apprehension. "Something rustling in the trees." Something bigger than a bunny rabbit.

The rustling got louder. Uneasy, Willis said, "Noisy for a hunter."

It wasn't a hunter. Byrd knew, as he always knew. "Get down!" he cried out, pushing Willis down and shielding him. The shot whistled over their heads and landed in the bark of a cypress on the other side of the road. "Don't sit up!" he said roughly to Willis. "He ain't done yet."

Another shot, another whistle, another bullet lodged in the trunk of the cypress. Byrd, who felt his heart pound and his blood rise, turned his head—not sitting up—to look at the trajectory.

The shots were aimed clear. He said to Willis, "Don't think he intend to hit us."

Willis was shaking. His voice low, he said, "Don't matter."

This time, there was a low laugh. Then the shot, aimed over their heads, into the cypress again. As the bullet lodged in the trunk of the cypress, a mocking voice said, "Are you afraid now, sergeant nigger?"

It was the voice of the young man who had been on the road to Greenwood. Byrd's mind was fully alert. And then footsteps, loud on purpose, away from the road, the sound of someone crashing through the canebrake.

Jerusha asked him to visit again, and Byrd couldn't bear to come empty-handed. He asked Davey Thornton about a proper gift for a lady. "For Miss Jerusha?"

Byrd couldn't be sharp with Davey. "Yes, you young busybody, it is."

"She might like a ribbon. Green ribbon to go with them pretty green eyes."

"No. Want something a little better. What else might suit?"

"A handkerchief." Davey drew a tray of neatly folded handkerchiefs from the case. Byrd bent over them, afraid to touch the dainty cloth. What might please her among these scraps of lawn and lace? "This one," he said. "The lace have a pattern of flowers in it."

It cost him as much as whiskey money for a week, but he didn't mind.

Davey wrapped it neatly in brown paper and cut a length of the green ribbon to tie it shut. He said to Byrd, "I think she like the ribbon, too." He smiled. "A gift from all of us."

Byrd shook his head as he left the store. In the street, he stopped to pet Buster, who woke up with the attention. Aggravated, he bent down and spoke to the dog. "Did you see that gal dog? Was she sweet to you? Do everyone gossip about it?" Buster, responding to his voice, snuffled a little and licked his

hand. He scratched the dog's ears and went back to his shack to put on his clean shirt.

He lingered on the way to Jerusha's place, smelling the last of the season's honeysuckle and the first of the roses. He was more than a visitor today, with this gift in hand, and the blood rushed to his face and elsewhere, which the women in the bawdy houses had always appreciated.

When Jerusha opened the little package tied with ribbon, she blushed deep and hard. She said, "Don't know what to say."

It gave him pleasure to tease her about minding her manners. "Just say thank you."

"I do thank you."

"Davey Thornton knows I bought it for you."

She laughed. "I reckon all of Willow Bend knows."

He laughed too. "Can't sneeze in Willow Bend without everyone knowing."

Still holding the gift in her hand, she moved close. Her voice low, she said, "I know another way to say thank you."

"Do you." He warmed from his face to his chest down to his belly.

She looked into his eyes. "Are you teasing me, Ambrose?"

His given name, that Bernie had called him by. That his wife would call him by, when he found her. "No, I ain't."

She twined her arms around his neck and touched his nape. He'd rarely felt a touch so gentle. He leaned forward, wanting to kiss her.

She let her hands slip down to rest softly on his back. The spot that he told the women in the bawdy houses to leave alone.

He started from her as though he'd been scalded. "Don't touch me there."

She said, "Does it hurt?" The healer's question, and the healer's gaze.

"No."

"War wound bothering you?"

"No."

"What's the matter, Ambrose?" she asked.

He sat heavily in the nearest chair and stared at the floor. Finally he said, "I was whupped, back in slavery days."

She waited. He said, "I ran away twice. They whupped me raw both times. Put salt in the wounds to make them hurt and keep them from healing right. The second time they branded me. R for runaway. That's why I keep the whiskers. You can't see the mark underneath."

She was silent. She waited.

He wiped his face, shamed by the tears. "The third time I ran away to the Union Army as contraband. Never came back. Been free ever since."

She gently touched his shoulder and asked, "Is that all right? To touch you there?"

He nodded.

She tightened her grip on his unscarred flesh. She said, "Who of us ain't damaged? All of us who came up in slavery?"

Byrd lounged on the porch of Thornton's, sweating in the heat, and Buster lay at his side. Buster's ears pricked up through his indolent drowse. Byrd heard it too: the whir of buggy wheels and the trot of a horse, long before the visitor appeared. Byrd was the first to see the smart little buggy drive up, drawn by a very pretty chestnut horse. The man who held the reins was huge and fierce and very black. Beside him sat the small, smiling, cane-wielding figure of Hiram Little.

Little jumped from the buggy. He surveyed the dusty street, the plain wooden church, and the modest store. His gaze strayed beyond the road to the cotton fields. Not addressing Byrd, but sure that Byrd could hear, he said, "So this is Willow Bend? Ain't much of a place." Little glanced at Byrd without seeing him. "Where's Jim, boy?"

Byrd rose. Little chortled. "Oh, it's you! Sergeant nigger! Don't just stand there, boy. Go get Jim for me."

Byrd ran toward the Truehart place. He ran past the neatly plowed fields, where the new crop was just putting its shoots through the soil. He ran to find Truehart in one of those fields, hoe in hand, bent to chop the weeds that choked the tender young cotton plants.

Gasping, Byrd called out, "Mr. Little is here. In Thornton's."

Truehart brought down the hoe with enough force to sever a clump of cotton plants along with the weeds. "Damn," he said, and flung the hoe to the ground. He stared at the ruined plants and shook his head. "Won't ever be ready," he said, and straightened and set his shoulders back, reminding himself to be a soldier. They trooped to Thornton's in the cadence that was as familiar to Byrd as taking a breath. Byrd found himself singing softly, the marching song of the colored troops, calling for glory and recalling John Brown's body. Truehart said sharply, "Watch yourself."

When they arrived at Thornton's, the coachman, who was as massive as a live oak and as unblinking as a blacksnake, stood three feet behind his master. Little smiled. "I have some business with you, Jim. Inside."

Little sauntered into Thornton's, the coachman a few steps behind him. Truehart followed, keeping a respectful distance. Byrd bounded up the steps, and the coachman fixed him with a hard stare, warning him.

Thornton, who stood behind the counter, spoke politely, as though he entertained Little's custom every week. "Marse Little, how do."

Little surveyed the store, as he had gauged the town, and said, "It's a sorry little place, Ben."

Thornton didn't reply.

Little smiled again, the mirth with so much malice in it. "Didn't bring your cotton to me, Jim," he said. "Had to take it into town. When Chatham told you no, had to take it down to Greenwood."

Truehart didn't reply, either.

"I went down to the county courthouse and I found out how much land you have around this place you call your town."

The silence was like a breath held in.

His voice rose. "Three hundred acres."

The silence made him louder. Little brandished the cane in Truehart's direction. "Three hundred acres!"

So quiet that they could hear the skeeters whining outside.

"What does a nigger need with three hundred acres!" Little slammed his cane against the counter, hard enough to leave a mark on the wood.

Byrd started. It was too much like the sound of a cane on a man's flesh.

Flushed with rage, Little shouted, "Didn't we warn you? Don't you recall?"

In the silence, Byrd thought of the gun to the head, and the cotton burned to the ground, and the grave, the next county over, where the dead would never lay to rest.

Chapter 5

Stand and Fight

After the shooting, Willis was cool with Byrd, and Byrd was surprised when Willis asked him if he'd like work again.

"Thought you didn't want me on the Little place."

"Ain't for Marse Little. It's for Jim. Wants me to build him a new barn, and I need help."

Byrd hadn't been on the Truehart place for weeks, and as he hesitated, Willis said, "Don't have to say yes. I know you don't care much for Jim."

"Don't mind him so much." He still didn't feel right around Bernie, and he knew she felt the same way about him. But that wasn't his secret to tell anyone. "Be glad of the money, if you'll have me."

"I'm asking, ain't I? Don't think you'll get into too much trouble building Jim Truehart a barn."

Byrd and Willis joined Truehart at one corner of the Truehart table, listening to his plans for the new barn. Outside, Niecy's chickens fluttered and pecked and cackled in the run behind the house. At the other end of the table, Niecy kneaded dough for bread, the slap of the sponge against the kneading board rhythmic and reassuring. She hummed as she pressed her palms into the dough, a hymn that Byrd recalled his mother singing: "O Happy Day."

They heard the brush of feet on the steps, and a voice called through the open door. "Niecy?" She slipped inside without waiting to be invited. She had high cheekbones like Niecy's, but there were deep lines around her mouth. She wore the starched dress and stout shoes of a house servant. Byrd hadn't met her, but he had seen her on the Little place.

She was out of breath. "I can't linger," she said. "I stole away. If Marse Little asks where I am, someone will lie for me."

Like in slavery days, Byrd thought.

"Tell us, Delia," Truehart said.

Delia cast a look at Byrd. "Haven't met him," she said.

Byrd thought, She has trouble to tell and she don't trust me. Niecy said, "This is Mr. Byrd, who stays with us in Willow Bend."

Instead of "How do," she said to Byrd, "I know of you. Marse Little's man shot at you."

All three men met her gaze. Byrd said, "That's true, ma'am."

"Marse Little had a visitor today who scared me to death." Delia took a deep breath. "I never thought I'd see that one-eyed man with the eye patch again, not as long as I lived."

Byrd sat up straight. He wasn't wearing a sidearm, but his hand went to the spot on his belt where the holster would sit.

Both Trueharts gazed at Delia, and Truehart asked, "Colonel Loveless?" Delia nodded.

"Why in God's name would he be back here to talk to Marse Little?" Niecy asked.

Delia said, "Marse Little wants his land back and he don't care how he gets it. Asked Colonel Loveless to do what he can."

Everyone was silent. Finally Niecy asked, "What do you think he'll do?"

Delia raised panicked eyes to her cousin's. "What do you think, Niecy? Don't you remember?"

Niecy wiped her hand across her face, leaving a trail of flour on the coppery skin. "Can't forget," she said.

Delia said, "No one knows I came here, or that I told you." Niecy nodded, and Delia was gone.

Niecy's pleasant face was hard and set. She said to her husband, "Told you we'd pay for naysaying Marse Little."

Truehart sat heavily at the table, his shoulders burdened. He clasped his hands together and rested his chin on them. His gaze was far away. Byrd had seen that look, the soldier's look, seeing and hearing the battle, years after it was over.

"This one-eyed man, Colonel Loveless. Is he a soldier? Or do he just call himself one?" Byrd asked Truehart.

Truehart roused himself and said, "Confederate officer. Fought under General Forrest in the war."

Byrd's voice rose. "Forrest? The one who murdered our men at Fort Pillow?"

"The very one."

"Was he at Fort Pillow?"

"Believe so."

Now Byrd fell silent. Byrd stared past Truehart, lost in his own memories. The burden of Fort Pillow had gone with him to Texas, and now it had come back with him, more than twenty years after the fact, to Mississippi. The ghosts of the massacre wreathed around the ghosts of Fort Pillow and filled the room like smoke.

That evening, Byrd's unease compelled him down the street to Thornton's. The day had been pleasant, but the evening air had turned dense and wet. There was a thunderstorm brewing a few miles away. As the sun set, sheet lightning flashed, brighter than a swarm of fireflies. He could hear the noise in Thornton's before he set foot on the porch. The door was open and the room was lit with kerosene lanterns. The smell of kerosene fought with the smell of sweat and the smell of whiskey.

The store was so crowded that there was no room to walk

to the counter. Just inside the door, to his surprise, Byrd found himself pressed against the rotund body of Reverend Baldwin, who never came into Thornton's because he disapproved of drink. "How do, Reverend," Byrd said.

"How do, Mr. Byrd." Reverend Baldwin wiped his face with a clean handkerchief. "Dreadful news today." With him was William Rice, the oldest and frailest man in Willow Bend. Byrd had never seen him at Thornton's, only in church, where he sang in a quavering voice. He echoed the reverend's words: "Terrible news!"

Byrd wanted a drink. He tapped the shoulder of the man nearest him. The man didn't budge. Byrd said, "May a man get past you?"

He turned. It was Willis' son-in-law, who never came to Thornton's either, since he preferred to spend his evenings with his wife and family. He said sharply, "Don't push me, man!"

Byrd said, "Didn't push you. Just walking through."

Around him, men talked in voices loosened by drink, so loud that all that came to Byrd was the occasional word. "Loveless. Massacre. Terrible. God help! God damn!"

It was not like companiable Thornton's. It was like a saloon, where Byrd had spent too much of his time out West.

Byrd elbowed his way to the counter and called out, "May a man get a drink?"

A hot and harried Davey picked up the jug and said, "This one almost empty." Thornton snapped at him, "Pour him some and get another. You know where we keep it."

Willis leaned against the counter, elbows planted there. Truehart surveyed the room from the far wall. Keeping an eye on it, Byrd thought.

"Move over, man," Byrd said to Willis.

Willis turned to him, his eyes glittering. He smelled of whiskey. He said, "Never had any trouble before you come here. Never got shot at before you come here." He raised the cup to his lips. "Now we all in trouble. Because of you."

"That ain't true and you know it."

Willis shoved him against the counter, hard enough to bruise. Byrd said, "Damn you, it were bad enough for you to be angry with me. But I won't be blamed! Not for something that happen ten year ago!"

"What do you know about what happen ten year ago?"

Byrd lost his temper and shoved him back. "What do it matter?" he shouted. "What do you care?"

Willis grabbed Byrd by the shirtfront and raised his fist. Truehart put a rough hand on Willis' shoulder. He didn't need to raise his voice. "It ain't him and you know it."

Panting, Willis let Byrd go. Truehart gripped his shoulder, the way he'd grip a growling dog. Truehart said, "It's Marse Little. It's always been Marse Little, from the day we decided to build up Willow Bend."

Willis faced Truehart but he spoke to everyone, calling it out. He shouted, "Thought I'd be safe in Willow Bend! Thought my wife and my children would be safe! And now we ain't!"

There was a shocked silence, and then every voice was raised in such a hubbub that it had no words, only the roar of men in fear.

Truehart raised his voice as though he were on the battlefield. "Stop!" he shouted. "Listen!" But they continued to shout, and they began to shove. In the street, Buster howled in alarm.

Byrd had been a commander too. He found the voice that had carried over the war cries of Kiowas and Comanches. "Hey!" he bellowed, and he whistled loud enough to hurt a man's ears. The roar diminished. "Shut up and let the man talk." They muttered and complained, but he reckoned Truehart could talk above it.

Truehart strode into the middle of the crowded room and called out again, "Stop! Quiet!" He waited as they lowered their voices, quieting like a dog that had howled itself out. He said, "Mr. Byrd ain't the danger to us."

A murmur of protest. "No, listen. It's Marse Little and his man, that one-eyed man, Colonel Loveless. They're the danger to us."

Willis turned his anger on Truehart. He said, "Could have

gone to Kansas when I had the chance. Safe in Kansas, instead of waiting here for that one-eyed man to come back and finish what he started."

Byrd said, "Ain't no one stopping you. The train go north to Kansas every day. Get on it, if you want to."

"Are you calling me a coward?" Willis demanded.

"You have a fight on your hands. Are you going to stay here, or run to Kansas? Up to you."

"You don't know," Willis cried out. "You weren't here."

The soldier and the temper rose together in Byrd. He crowded Willis. "I know what happen, ten year ago."

Willis swayed on his feet. "It ain't your wife in danger. It ain't your child. It ain't your house. It ain't your place. It ain't your fight!"

The men in Thornton's began to mutter, then to raise their voices. "He don't know! He weren't here! It ain't his fight!"

"I was a soldier," Byrd said. "Thought you were, too. Soldiers stand and fight."

Willis raised his fist and so did Byrd. Truehart lunged between them and pushed Willis roughly out of the way. He grabbed Byrd by the collar. He growled, "I'm ashamed of you. All of you. Drinking like cowards. Fighting like dogs." He released Byrd, who glared at him, rubbing his nape and straightening his shirt. "Won't stay in this room with you."

He let the door slam as he left.

A shamed silence swept Thornton's, like the headache after too much to drink. One after another, the men set their cups on the counter, mumbling goodnight to Thornton as they slipped away.

Buster whined as Byrd approached him, but Byrd ignored him, and hastened towards his shack.

Someone followed him, with the easy lope of the soldier. Truehart came abreast of him. "Mr. Byrd." Byrd halted. Truehart said, "From now on we be careful, all of us. Don't go anywhere alone, not even in broad daylight."

For the second time that day, Byrd rested his hand on his hip, where he was used to feeling the grip on his sidearm. Truehart saw him do it. He said, "And don't give anyone reason to start a shooting match."

After Truehart's warning, the soldier in Byrd was fully awake. A soldier needed ammunition. Thornton's sold cartridges, but he didn't want to buy them from Thornton and to listen to another lecture about being careful. He decided to visit Levy's in town.

Truehart's words still nettled him. Jim Truehart wasn't his sergeant or his daddy, to tell him to take a companion when he left Willow Bend. Byrd had been a soldier and a scout for twenty years in dangerous places and he figured he could walk down the road by himself in broad daylight. But he wasn't going without improving his chances.

It gave him satisfaction to load and holster his sidearm and to buckle on his gunbelt for the Colt revolver that was just like Jake Rosenbloom's peacemaker. It pleased him to feel the weight of the pistol on his hip and the pressure of the holster against his thigh. He put on his long Western coat, and buttoned it closed. He was armed, but the world didn't need to know it.

As soon as he arrived in town, he saw the young sandy-haired man who had stopped them on the road to Greenwood and who had accompanied Dixon on the Little place. He lounged on the sidewalk outside Levy's, in the company of another man who was a stranger. The sandy-haired man wore a good city suit, not a farmer's nankeens, but he was dusty and unkempt, and today his face was red as though he were sunburned or drunk. His companion, a head taller, had the powerful shoulders and the tanned neck and hands of a farmer and his nose looked as though it had been flattened in a fight.

When Byrd stepped onto the sidewalk, the sandy-haired man blocked his way. "Where are you going, nigger?"

"Came to do my business at Mr. Levy's, sir." He said it sharply, like a soldier.

The sandy-haired man said, "You're the nigger who thinks

he's a sergeant. Sergeant nigger!" His friend, so much bigger, barred the door. Byrd didn't move. Still polite, he said, "Let me by, sir."

Mr. Levy opened the door. "Mr. Dixon, Mr. Painter, let the man come in." He cajoled, "How can I make a living if my customers stand in the street?"

So the sandy-haired man was a Dixon, too.

"He's a nigger who needs to learn some manners," Dixon said.

Friendly, joking, Levy said, "His money is as good as anyone's. Let him come in."

"Learn you some manners, too, storekeeper," Dixon replied, and the two men swaggered down the street to the saloon.

Inside the store, Byrd expected that Levy might say, "Be careful," or "Mind your manners," but all he said was, "I recall you. Came in here with Jim Truehart. How can I help you today?"

"Need some cartridges for my sidearm." Byrd rested his hand on his hip, where the gun hung on his belt under the coat. "A few boxes."

Levy shook his head, but he retrieved the boxes and set them on the counter. "Do you want to put it on account?"

"Don't want to run a debt," Byrd said. He unbuttoned his coat to pull the money from his pocket.

Levy saw the pistol. "Is everything all right in Willow Bend?" he asked. "There's no trouble?"

"No, sir," Byrd said pleasantly, and put his money on the counter.

Levy said, "I hear things. Can't always say how. Take care. Can't say more."

Byrd thought, A white man, a stranger to me, and he warn me, too.

When Byrd left Levy's, he saw Dixon and his friend Painter leaning against the wall of the saloon, watching him go. They didn't speak, but he felt their eyes on him.

His skin began to prickle, as it always did when there might be trouble.

The road away from town took him close to the river, where the land was muddy and the trees grew close together, the pines and cypresses lashed with vines. A thicket on either side of the road. A good hiding place. Wary, careful, he was a scout again, listening for voices or footsteps. He stopped. He waited, listening, trying to get his bearings.

He unbuttoned his coat and rested his hand on the grip of the pistol. In the West, he could use it and no one would be the least bothered that he had defended himself. But here, if Byrd shot Dixon—if he killed Dixon—Dixon's family and his friends would kill Byrd. And then they would massacre the people of Willow Bend, without waiting for Loveless to plan for it.

He cursed himself for a fool. Truehart had been right.

He couldn't use the sidearm, but he still could fight. A man without a gun had his fists and his feet and his teeth. They'd come from behind, he thought. Thinking they'd surprise him. Thinking he couldn't fight them both at once. He wouldn't run into the thicket, where he might not have an advantage. He would meet them on the road. He stood still, listening and waiting.

They were drunk and careless, and he heard them well before they came close to him. Singing. "Dixie Land." Byrd hated that song as much as he hated the Rebel yell. He felt the sap of battle rise in him. How drunk were they? He might be able to topple them and run.

As soon as they saw him they broke into a run. "Hey, nigger!" Dixon called out. "Sergeant nigger!" He was laughing. Drunk and laughing and winded. Dixon came towards him, his arms outstretched, like a man celebrating instead of planning to grab someone to pin him. Byrd waited. When Dixon was close enough Byrd bent low and ran right into him, knocking him off balance, and as he staggered, Byrd hit him hard in the gut. He fell, gasping in pain and surprise, and Byrd turned to grapple with Painter.

But Painter was steadier on his feet than Dixon. He rushed Byrd, trying to get a grip on him, but Byrd twisted away. "Damn you," Painter said. Byrd dodged as Painter tried to grab him. Painter yelled, "Dixon, damn you, get up!"

Dixon rose to his knees. He groaned. Painter hesitated and Byrd rushed in to hit him in the belly. Painter grabbed his hand and twisted it. Byrd roared with anger and kicked Painter hard in the knee. Painter cried out and let go Byrd's hand, bending over with pain. Byrd rushed him, hoping to topple him, but Painter grabbed him by the shoulders instead. They wrestled like that, and Painter, bigger and heavier than Byrd, had the advantage. They fell together, but Painter rose to his knees and pressed Byrd's face into the dirt.

Byrd struggled, but Painter tightened his grip. Dixon was still groaning, but he managed to stand upright. Painter yelled, "Come here and help me subdue the bastard!"

Painter yanked hard on Byrd's collar to drag him upright. Byrd coughed and gasped for breath. Dixon hobbled close enough to spit in Byrd's face. As Byrd twisted away, Dixon said, "Came to teach you some manners."

Byrd thrashed in Painter's grip, but Painter held him fast. Dixon charged him, flailing, and drunk as he was, he landed blows on Byrd's face. Byrd felt his eye puff up and his lip split. He felt blood leak from his nose.

Dixon, his hand wet with Byrd's blood, grabbed a fistful of Byrd's coat and used it like a towel to wipe his hand. He saw the gun, and Dixon pulled up Byrd's coat, the way a man would pull up a woman's dress, to reveal the sidearm. Panting, Dixon said, "That's too good a gun for a nigger."

With difficulty, Byrd said, "Army issue sidearm. It's mine."

Dixon said, "Told you to learn some manners," and straightening up, he punched Byrd in the gut. It knocked the breath out of him. Dixon punched Byrd again. And again, until he sagged in Painter's arms. Dixon reached for the gun and held it so that Byrd could see it. "Better than mine," he said, and he put it in his pocket. "Are you mannerly yet, nigger?"

Byrd said nothing, but there was no fight left in him. Painter let him go and he fell to the ground, doubled up, spitting blood.

Dixon kicked him hard in the ribs. "Are you mannerly now?"

Byrd groaned.

Dixon bent down, Byrd's sidearm in his hand. He pressed it to Byrd's temple.

Painter said uneasily, "We weren't supposed to kill him. Just scare him."

"He ain't scared enough." Dixon cocked the gun. "Are you scared now, nigger?"

Byrd lay with his knees drawn up. He was silent.

Painter grabbed Dixon's arm. "Leave him be," he said.

Dixon rose. He kicked Byrd again in the ribs and Byrd rolled over and groaned again. Dixon said, "That was for the rest of the niggers in Willow Bend."

When they were gone, Byrd lay in the road, feeling the blood drip down his face. With difficulty, he sat up, then stood. Those damn cowards stole my sidearm. My sidearm, he thought. Anger surged through him. Fueled by fury, he straightened up as best he could to limp back to Willow Bend.

By the time he arrived in town he was barely able to stand. He staggered into Thornton's and slumped against the counter. "Give me a drink, Ben."

In alarm, Thornton called in back to Davey. "Get Miss Jerusha. Hurry!"

Byrd lay his head on the counter. "Don't feel so good," he muttered, and slid to the floor. Thornton eased him on his back and slipped something under his head. "Rest quiet."

Byrd closed his eyes. He heard the rustle of a skirt and the quick footstep. He forced his eyes open. He wanted to say, "Don't fuss over me," but only a groan came out.

Jerusha dropped her basket and fell to her knees beside him. She cradled his bloodied face between her hands and cried out. "Ambrose! Oh, Ambrose!"

Then he fainted away.

Byrd was only half-aware in the days after his beating. Through a haze, he heard voices, low and worried, but he was too weary to understand what they were saying. He heard the sound of a dog whining and thought he must be dreaming. God knows what Jerusha had given him.

When he woke he didn't recognize where he was. The coverlet was clean and whole. The room had been aired and tidied. He was in his own room, he realized, but someone had improved it a great deal. He smelled broth. Jerusha, her face tired and worried, sat at his bedside, holding a bowl.

He heard the sound of snuffling and a low whine. Felt a warm weight on his feet. He said, "Buster!"

Jerusha said, "He pined for you. Cried and whined and wouldn't stop. So we brought him in to stay with you. Jumped right up on your bed."

The dog pushed his nose into Byrd's hand and snuffled a little. Despite the pain, Byrd sat up and held out his hand for the dog to lick.

It all came back to him—the beating, the theft, and his shame at lying on the floor of Thornton's while Jerusha wept over him like a wife.

"Can you set up?" she asked. She held out the spoon. "Let me help you."

"I ain't a baby," he said. "I'm a grown man bruised up. Can feed myself."

"Worse than bruised up." She shook her head. "Hurt bad."

"What did you give me?"

"Poppy juice. Deadens pain, helps you sleep."

"Who was talking while I was asleep?"

She said, "While you were abed, everyone in Willow Bend came to see you. Worried and upset and sorry you were hurt."

"Mr. Willis? Mr. Thornton?"

"Everyone. Miss Bernie came to set by your bedside. Watched you and Buster sleep."

He sat up, despite the pain. He rubbed the dog's head and ran his hand over the prominent ribs. "Pined for me," he said, smiling. Suddenly he felt weak and dizzy. He lay back on the pillow, plumped by Jerusha's hand.

Jerusha said, "You lie down and rest."

"Don't need to be ordered about like a baby."

She laughed a little. "You feeling better," she said. "Got your temper back."

She watched him eat. When he handed back the empty bowl, she asked, "Why is you always mad, Ambrose?"

"Don't know. Born mad. My mama used to tease me and tell me I was like an angry little bird, always diving and pecking at something."

Jerusha said, "Not all birds are little pecking things. Some birds are big and fierce and proud. Like eagles."

"Or buzzards!" he said, laughing. He put his hand to his side. "Lord, it do hurt when I laugh."

The Trueharts came to see him, Niecy carrying a pie in a basket, Truehart beside her. Niecy set the pie on the table and said, "No, don't get up, you don't look like a man well enough to get up." She said to Jerusha, "We leave them men to visit," and Jerusha left with her to give them privacy.

After the women left, Truehart sat in the rickety chair by the bed. "How do you feel?"

Byrd sat up as straight in bed as he could. "Feel better than I look." He knew how bad he looked. Jerusha had handed him the little mirror this morning and he saw the puffed eye, the bruised nose, and the split lip.

"We all worried about you."

"I'll be all right."

"We all sorry you got hurt."

Byrd sat up straighter. "Why? Didn't I bring it on myself?"

Truehart winced. "Don't no one say that," he said. "Weren't meant for you. Meant for all of us."

"You'll need to be ready," Byrd said, but he was suddenly worn out, and he lay back against the pillow.

"Can't use the help of a wounded man." He rose. Awkwardly, he said, "You rest quiet and heal up."

Finally alone, Byrd dressed, intending to see who might be at Thornton's, but Truehart had been right. He wasn't well enough to go anywhere, not yet. He slumped into the rickety chair and thought of the men who had attacked him, and the one-eyed man who commanded them.

If this man Loveless had followed Forrest after the surrender, he'd been a Klansman, still fighting his side of the war as Byrd had continued to fight for the Union. Klansmen played at being soldiers, but they weren't soldiers. They were ungovernable. They fought folks who were unarmed. They murdered people who were innocent.

Just like the Comanches, who struck terror into the heart of every white settler in Texas. Byrd knew how to fight a band of Comanches. You didn't need a battle line and a cannon on each side. You needed a band of men who were crack shots. You needed to surprise them.

Byrd stood up. His side ached every time he drew breath, but he'd been hurt worse. He needed to go out. He needed to look at Willow Bend with the eyes of a scout.

Buster jumped from the bed, even though it cost him, and wagged his tail as he waited for Byrd. Byrd laughed. "Can't bend down to pet you, old boy," he said. "Hurt worse than you today." Buster nuzzled his hand and Byrd bent down, even though it cost him, to fondle the dog's soft ears.

Byrd turned to go. And heard the soft yelp. Wherever Byrd was going, Buster wanted to follow. Byrd said, "You stay put." Buster lay down on the floor, whining a little, and rested his head on his paws.

Byrd limped around Willow Bend and thought about how to surprise a band of raiding men. The town was defenseless, flat and open. The fields and cabins weren't safe, either. Anyone could ride over those level, cleared fields, shooting as he went, hitting

anyone he aimed at. The woods on the edge of town wouldn't admit a battle. But anyone who ran into the thicket would become prey to be stalked and hunted and captured, then killed one at a time. There was no chance for a battle in the town, in the fields, or in the uncleared thicket.

The island, he thought. He'd go back to the island—he'd even risk meeting Miss Bernie—and he'd look at it with his mind on a fight. He'd look at it afresh—not as his own peaceful refuge, but as a bastion for a battle.

That afternoon, ignoring the ache in his side, he carefully rowed over to the island. The ducklings and goslings were half grown, but their mamas were still upset to see him. He landed on the beach and waded to the shore. He lingered at the base of the hill to put himself in the frame of mind of someone who had never set foot on this place.

He crested the hill, resting after each step. He knew his way, but a stranger wouldn't. He thought of the trouble the Rebs had scaling the hill at Little Round Top. This was a taller, steeper, and much muckier hill. Harder to climb, easier to defend. If you put sharpshooters in the right spots, behind the trees, an attacker wouldn't see them until he'd become an easy shot. He thought about using sharpshooters and crept between the trees, trying to see vantage points. You could string them all along the narrow path that Miss Bernie had made.

He thought about the swamp side of the island, the mucky side, and realized that no one could land there. It would suck a man under and trap a horse's leg before breaking it. Anyone who came to attack would launch from the other side. If you were positioned right, you'd see them coming. You'd have plenty of warning. You could be set to shoot as they straggled onto the shore.

He felt the old excitement. The old heat, before a battle. He saw the advantage of the island in a fight. He felt like a soldier again. He sat in the glade, turning the idea over in his head.

He heard the light step on the path. She hesitated on the threshold of the glade, fidgeting with her rifle strap, as uncomfortable as he'd ever seen her. "You don't look well, Mr. Byrd."

He rose, panting with the effort. "I feel better than I look."

Her face creased with concern. "Don't get up."

"No, I won't stay to trouble you."

She spoke in a rush. "Mr. Byrd, I can't tell you how sorry I am for acting the fool with you, the last time we was here."

So that was her worry. "I should have been wiser. I'm grown. I'm sorry too." It hurt to stand upright, but it hurt more to speak to her.

"You didn't say anything to my daddy?"

"Of course not. It wasn't my secret to tell anyone."

"It's so peaceful here," she said. She raised troubled eyes to his. "Will we have to fight?"

"What do your daddy say?"

"Won't say. Just keeps saying he has to figure it."

"What about you?"

Her hand went to her gun. She touched it to reassure herself, as he'd done the day his sidearm was stolen. She said, "I'd fight, if I had to."

The father's feeling came back to him and surged through him so hard that it hurt his bruised side. "Miss Bernie, with all my heart, I hope not."

"Haven't you heard what happened to the gals in the massacre?"

He thought of Jerusha's face in the candlelight as she told him. "Had a thought about this man Loveless and his men. How to fight a battle we can win." He gestured around the glade. "This is the place for the battle."

"The island?"

"Best place to stand and fight."

"Tell my daddy."

He wanted to clasp her hand, but he didn't dare. "Let me figure it, and I will."

"He's intending to call folks together after Sunday meeting."

Her eyes were unwavering on his face. "Tell him then. Tell everyone in Willow Bend then."

He hadn't drunk whiskey since he was hurt, but that evening he limped to Thornton's in the humid dusk and Buster followed him. Neither of them moved very fast. Byrd said, "We're a sorry pair, ain't we?"

He let Buster in first and Truehart called out, "Come in, Mr. Byrd, and join us."

Willis leaned against the counter, his gaze intent on the cup before him. He and Willis hadn't spoken since their altercation. Buster ambled to the counter and nosed Willis' leg. Willis ignored the dog and said stiffly to Byrd, "How are you?"

Truehart scolded, "Can't you see? Still bruised up. Get him a chair to set in."

Willis hauled a chair from the porch. Truehart asked Byrd, "Do you want a cushion? Or a blanket?" even though it was so hot a man wanted to unbutton the collar of his shirt. Byrd said, "All of you as bad as Jerusha," but he had to lower himself carefully into the chair, and he gasped as he settled into it.

Truehart handed him a cup of whiskey as though he were too weak to get it for himself and they waited for him to drink. "Don't stare so," he said.

Willis said, "Miss Jerusha said you were beaten near to death."

"She were upset. I'm better. I'll be healed up soon."

"Glad to hear it. Wouldn't want my last words to you to be hateful."

Byrd took a long draught of the whiskey to hide his satisfaction at Willis' apology.

Willis let his gaze linger on Byrd, but he addressed Truehart. "Do you recall, before the massacre, when we used to vote? How we used to put on our Union coats, and buckle on our sidearms, and go together to the voting place? Them buttons shining in the sun. Together, like we was marching."

"Of course we recall," Truehart said.

"Remember, the ballots with the Union flag on one side, and the eagle on the other, so no one could mistake them, even if he couldn't read? How we held our ballots high, flying that flag, so everyone could see how we voted?"

Thornton said, "So we'd know if anyone tried to steal the ballots."

Willis drained his cup. "How we'd walk out proud. Done our rightful duty. Like soldiers." He sighed. "Fighting for freedom."

The old comrades of the 1st Mississippi were silent.

"Why don't you put this business to a vote? Ask folks to vote on it?" Byrd asked.

Truehart looked at Byrd, the man none of them expected to throw in his lot with theirs. "Ain't a bad idea."

Willis said, "It's a good idea, Jim. Let everyone have a say and a vote."

"Can't say until I figure it."

Willis looked at his former commanding officer. "Have to figure it quick."

"I know," Truehart said. "Have to figure it smart, too."

They were silent again.

Thornton asked, "Mr. Byrd? Another cup?"

Byrd felt weary, the exertion of the day catching up with him. "I've had enough."

Willis said, "Can't believe what I just saw. Go home and tell Miss Maggie about it. Ambrose Byrd saying no to a cup of whiskey." He began to laugh.

Byrd made a show of leaving his empty cup on the counter. "Have to keep a clear head."

Thornton joined in, and even Truehart grinned. Byrd and Buster limped down the steps of Thornton's to the sound of friendly laughter.

That Sunday, after the sermon and after the service, Truehart stood before the people of Willow Bend in the tunic he had worn as a Union soldier, decorated with the chevrons of a sergeant. He held his cap in his hands as he surveyed his friends and neighbors. Then he spoke.

"All of you know that Marse Little asked us to sell back the land we bought from him. But it wasn't enough to ask us to sell it, and to allow us to say no. Marse Little wants our land, and he wants us gone. Most of you know by now that Marse Little has hired Colonel Loveless to run us off our land. And do to violence by it."

They knew. But there was still a shocked silence. Then a babble of voices.

"Just like the massacre."

"We got to run away and hide."

"Won't run anywhere! Not after I worked so hard!"

"Outraged and then dead."

"Not that one-eyed man! He got the devil in the only eye in his head!"

"Hide on the island."

Truehart raised his hand in the gesture that meant "halt." He said, "One at a time, so we can all have a say."

Thornton rose. The storekeeper who seemed so placid and soft behind the counter stood as tall and powerful as a bear. "I know that all of us remember that massacre. My nephew Davey lost his mother and father, and I know many of you lost kin and friends. We know what they did there. We know that Loveless led them and commanded them to do it. I can't sit by. I can't run away. Don't know how we do it, but we fight them. That's my piece to say." He sat.

Niecy sprang to her feet, her fists curled tight against her skirt. Tears glistened in her eyes. "They didn't know, when the massacre happened. They like lambs at the slaughter, standing there innocent while those Klansmen came by with rifles and pistols. Outnumbered them, and used deadly force on folks who didn't have anything to defend themselves but a hoe or a stick. But we know. We can lock up, and go away, and be safe somewhere. Marse Little won't try for this land forever. He give up, and we come back. But we safe somewhere until it's over."

Charlie Robinson, whom Byrd didn't know well, stood up to speak. He said, "How we be safe? You know Marse Little won't give this up. If we run, we already lost the fight. He take it back and we crawl back to him to crop shares again. The Union Army freed me, and I've been a free man ever since. I'm staying right here. I got a sidearm, and a rifle, and I can defend myself and my family. And I will."

His wife, Miss Louisa, said fearfully, "What about our babies? What about our gal? Don't you recall what they did to the gals before they shot them dead?"

The room erupted in a melee of voices, all loud and fearful and angry. "We protect you." "You can't!" "Anyone touch my wife, my sister, my daughter, I kill him." "They kill you for it afterwards."

Byrd stood, tall and still. He let the roar subside. He let them stare at him, at the blackened eye, the split lip, and the way he held his hand to his side, since it still hurt every time he drew breath. They gazed at the stranger who had taken the beating meant for all of them, and waited to hear what he had to say.

"The island," he began. His voice was sober, and it carried well. "If we want to fight, we gather on the island, and we defend ourselves from the island. Can't send a troop there, because the canebrake's too dense, and the land's too mucky. Can't climb the hill through them trees and vines. Can't get to the crest without being seen. That's our bastion, and we go there, and fight there." He looked around the room. "Stand and fight on the island."

Thornton said, "What about our families? Our stock? Our crop?"

"Take everyone along. Put gals and little'uns behind the front lines. Take the stock, too. Don't know about the crop. You'll have to figure it."

Someone said fearfully, "What if they burn it? Burn our houses, too?"

Byrd said, "Replant the crop. Rebuild the house. You can, if you're alive."

The room was quiet. Finally Truehart said, "Mr. Byrd, what you say makes sense. But around here, we ponder everything together, and decide everything together." Truehart sounded as though he didn't know if he should be exasperated or pleased.

Byrd surveyed the room, as though he were about to take a vote at that moment. He let his gaze settle on Truehart, one commander to another.

Truehart said, "We need to frame this up so we can debate it, like we used to do at our Republican conventions. Then we can vote on it, like we voted for mayor."

Out of turn, Bernie called out, "Can I vote?"

Truehart said, "Everyone over twenty-one can vote, like for mayor. Men and women both. First we got to figure out what we're voting about."

At the door of the meeting house, Byrd spoke to Bernie in a low voice. He said, "He slid right over it. The island."

Equally low, she replied, "Didn't naysay it."

As though Bernie were much younger than eighteen, Truehart said, "Bernie, honey, you go on home and help your mother get Sunday supper."

"Yes, daddy," she said obediently, but before she turned to go, she grinned at Byrd. Forgiving him, reminding him.

Truehart asked, "What was that about?"

Byrd was out of practice lying. He tried to sound easy as he said, "Miss Bernie invited me to come hunting with her on the island not long ago."

"Show her what a good shot you are?"

He'd gladly make a fool of himself to spare Bernie trouble with her father. "Did my best. A bunny rabbit's a mighty small target."

"Thought you were a sharpshooter."

Byrd laughed, but he had to put his hand to his side against the pain it caused him. "Never fought a bunny rabbit for the Army."

In the days before the vote, the town of Willow Bend buzzed with worried and angry talk, a sound Byrd could hear as plain as the rasp of the crickets that lived in the swamp. People huddled together in the street, arguing the point one way and the other. They didn't invite Byrd to join, but they didn't lower their voices either.

Byrd lay on his bed in the shack, Buster asleep at his feet. He didn't like to admit that he still hurt so much and that he still tired so easily. Tonight, for the vote, he wanted to be able to stand up straight.

The light in the room was soft and blue—he had learned to gauge sunset by the color of the oilpaper—and he sat up. His side still hurt every time he moved too fast. Buster woke. When Byrd swung his feet onto the floor, Buster jumped down, nosing Byrd's hand, begging to go with him. Byrd sighed as he stroked the dog's head. "You stay here," he said. "You get to rest them old bones of yours."

The day had been near-summer, bright and hot, but now the air cooled, making his skin prickle in a pleasant way. Byrd knew the path down the street—he had walked it and staggered it at every time of night—but tonight the familiar dark was silvery with moonlight.

She slipped beside him. "Full moon," she whispered. "Ain't it glorious?" In the moonlight, Bernie's plain calico dress was silvery, too. An unseen bird called, a low sound, hooting and cooing at the same time. "Great horned owl," she said. "Hunts at night." And she slipped away, as quietly as the great birds hidden in the live oaks.

At the church a crowd had gathered, talking softly in the darkness, holding kerosene lanterns in the moonlight. They had become familiar to him, but the night cloaked them and made them unfamiliar again. When he got close enough the strangeness melted away.

Charlie Robinson held out his hand. "Good to see you back on your feet, Mr. Byrd." Byrd nodded. Willis' daughter-in-law rocked her fretful baby in her arms. She said to Byrd, "We came to see you but Isabella fussed so we didn't stay. Didn't want to bother you."

"That was kind of you, Miss Carrie."

The Glover boys ran and shouted, running and shouting excited to be awake so late. Their mother admonished them "You quiet down before we go into church!"

A soft hand, scented with lavender water, pressed his. "The Reverend and I prayed for you," said Miss Octavia. "We're glad that you're recovering." Touched, Byrd answered, "Thank you, Miss Octavia, I feel better now."

Miss Janie bustled up, her hand outstretched to lay on his arm. "Mr. Byrd," she said breathily, "We worried so when you got hurt!"

She means well, he thought. "Thank you, Miss Janie."

The little Glover girl who called him raggedy pointed at him and sassed, "Is it true Miss Jerusha witched you when you were sick?"

Jerusha was at his elbow. "Witch him! What kind of foolishness is that? Gave him medicine to quiet him and heal him."

The little girl stared at her bare feet. Bessie Glover swept up. "Don't pester Miss Jerusha," she said sternly. "Mr. Byrd, we is all glad to see that you are better," and she herded all of her badly behaved children into the church.

Byrd and Jerusha walked into the church together.

Inside, the moonlight shimmered through the windows. On the pulpit, in the back, and on the tables under the windows sat kerosene lamps, which cast shadows like a campfire.

The room smelled of the sweat of people who had worked hard all day, the musk of men who chopped cotton and the tang of women, who kneaded bread, weeded gardens, nursed children. Truehart wore his Union Army coat, the polished buttons glinting in the lamplight. Willis wore his uniform, as did Thornton, even though he had become too stout to fit the coat of the private he'd been twenty years before.

When they were all settled—they talked low, humming,

making a sound like skeeters over the swamp—the Reverend asked, "Mayor Truehart, will you stand with me?" Truehart rose to take his spot as sergeant and mayor.

Truehart asked, "People, are we ready?" At the sound of his voice they quieted and turned their faces towards him. "I'm glad to see all of you tonight, even though I ain't at all glad for the reason we're here. We're in danger, and we're going to decide what to do. Reverend Baldwin will lead this meeting, according to the rules of order that he know."

Baldwin said, "We need someone to make a motion to vote on. Who will make a motion?"

"I will," said Bernie. She stood, slender and tall, her voice resounding. "I ain't old enough to vote, but I want to put forth that motion."

"Miss Bernie, I'm sorry, but if you can't vote, you can't make a motion, either," Baldwin said.

Willis said, "I make a motion to vote on whether we stay to fight."

"Do we have a second?" Baldwin asked.

"I second it. That we stay here and fight," said Thornton.

"We have a motion. That the people of Willow Bend will stay to fight." The room was quiet as Baldwin explained, "We will take a call of the roll for everyone old enough to vote. Say 'aye' for yes, and 'nay' for no."

Truehart faced them, the sergeant observing the troops. "Everyone here free to vote as they see fit. Ain't no shame in saying 'nay.' Ain't no shame in deciding to go. You'll be welcome back, God willing, once it's over." Another sweep of the room, turning to survey them with his whole body. "But whoever says 'aye' needs to stand together." He stepped back. "Call the roll, Reverend Baldwin."

Baldwin called out the first name, the full and legal name, to add to the dignity of the occasion. "Sergeant James Truehart, how do you vote?"

"Aye."

"Mrs. Berniece Truehart."

"Aye."

Baldwin went around the room, calling out the names. The men's voices low and sonorous, the women's voices higher and sweeter. "Aye. Aye. Aye." When Baldwin came to the oldest people in the room, William and Amy Rice, who sat side by side hand in hand, they both responded in quavering tones, "Aye."

Baldwin called out, "Mr. Ambrose Byrd. How do you vote?"

Byrd hadn't expected to be called. Hadn't expected his vote to count as a citizen of Willow Bend. Jerusha squeezed his hand. He struggled to his feet, and he felt the worry and sympathy cover him like a blanket. He stammered as he answered. "Aye."

Baldwin referred to the paper where he had tallied the votes. "Fifty-nine aye," he said, "and none nay."

Bernie began to clap. The Glover boys, who needed no encouragement to make a noise, joined her to clap and stamp their feet. "Stand and fight!" Thornton called out, and the crowd responded to the call in a joyful din of celebration. "Stand and fight!"

Byrd sprang to his feet, not minding the pain, and grabbed Jerusha by the hand, pulling her with him. "Stand and fight!" he cried out. "We'll stand and fight!"

Willis began to sing, his barely audible through the noise, the marching song that every black Union soldier knew so well. Byrd thought of his earliest fighting days in Virginia, in the midst of black men who marched with the loose-limbed walk of Africa, even though Sergeant Shaw had drilled them like West Pointers. He recalled the smell of summer in the Virginia countryside mingled with the smell of gunpowder and fire, as the song rose from the throats of free black men of Pennsylvania and just-freed contraband of Virginia, about the soul of John Brown, who marched with them and rallied them to fight for the Union.

Now, in Willow Bend, black men in blue joined the song that all of them recalled so well, their fighting cry against slavery.

Bernie began to sing, the hymn of battle that the pious Northerners had always preferred, and the rest of the women joined her, their voices sweet and rich.

They sang in the flickering light of the kerosene lamps, their faces shadowed but joyful, and Byrd recalled his fighting days again, of campfires in the shadow of battle in Virginia and of gunfire on the Western plains.

They rose and sang as one, men and women, soldiers and farmers, the marching song and the battle hymn, of glory and of the truth that would march on forever.

Afterwards Truehart detained him. "Wait until everyone go home and come on with me. I got something to show you."

Holding a kerosene lamp, Truehart guided Byrd through his fields and into the thicket. The moonlight was dim here, and the lamp shed little light. Overhead the great owl called, and as they edged their way in their darkness, something small and frightened scurried through the brush. Something else slithered. "Where are we going?" he asked Truehart, to make a human sound.

The trees thinned. Truehart held up the lamp to show him the shed, surrounded by swamp. The smell of decay and mold was powerful here. Truehart unlocked the door and beckoned to Byrd to come inside.

It was damnably hot in the shed. "That's it," Truehart said, shining the lamp.

Byrd stared at the gun. He had seen its like more than once. It was a 12-pounder, the cannon that Civil War artillery regiments liked best to use, since it was one of the lightest made, and the most portable. "How in hell did you get ahold of a Napoleon?" he asked Truehart.

Truehart grinned. "Came upon it."

"No one leaves a Napoleon for someone to come upon."

"When the Federal marshals left in '76 they went in a hurry. Didn't take all their gear along. We're all Union men. We figured it was rightly ours. So we took it and hid it away."

Byrd was still staring. "Ammunition, too? Did you come upon that?"

"Powder and a box of canisters, too."

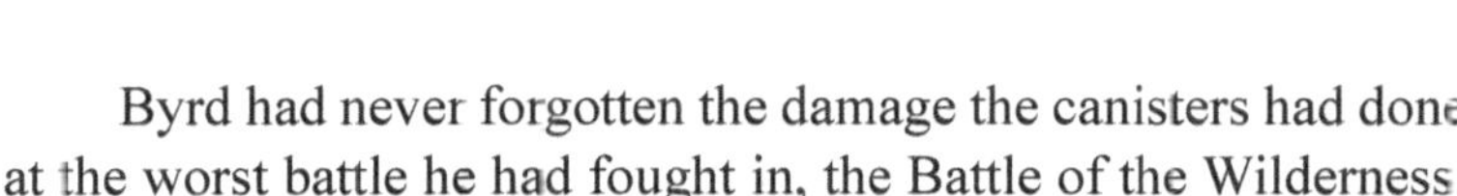

Byrd had never forgotten the damage the canisters had done at the worst battle he had fought in, the Battle of the Wilderness. "Good God, man. A Napoleon and canisters!"

"After the massacre, I thought we might need them," Truehart said. "I'm mighty sorry that I was right."

Chapter 6

The Two Sergeants

Byrd hopped from the skiff as soon as Willis beached it, so eager that he didn't mind the unhealed bruises. Behind them, Truehart landed his bigger and more ungainly boat, and both he and Thornton clambered onto the shore.

All four of them stood on the unshaded sand, sweating in the midday sun. The river was sluggish and green in the heat, its surface clouded with gnats. Truehart wiped his face with his sleeve and Willis slapped away a skeeter from his neck.

Truehart said, "It's big enough for a battle. Cannon behind, a row of riflemen around it. If you have enough men."

"Not here," Byrd said. "Follow me."

Truehart frowned, but Willis came with Byrd, and Truehart and Thornton lagged behind them. Byrd led them to the weeping willows that shielded the hill. Truehart said, "Trees and canebrake in the way, everything growing in muck. Can't thread your way through." His frown deepened. "Where do we set the cannon? Can't have a battle here."

"Not here, either," Byrd said. "Follow me." He slipped through the opening in the thicket that Bernie had made.

Truehart squeezed through, and Thornton, an even bigger man, struggled behind him. Willis asked, "Are you fooling with us, Byrd?"

"No, I ain't. Watch where I step and come after me."

Truehart said, "How can we? It's all over muck!"

"Look down."

Truehart said, "What is that? Did them Indians wear a trail here?"

Byrd laughed. "No. Only your gal, who takes after her Choctaw great-granddaddy."

Thornton asked, "Do the trail run up the hill?"

"Follow me."

Byrd, who knew his way, slipped lightly up the hill, but the others blundered and crashed through the trees. From the live oaks, the nesting birds shrilled their distress, and overhead, the great red-tailed hawk shrieked in alarm. The cypresses gave off a stink of skunk, and the mud underfoot smelled of wet green things going to rot in the heat. The skeeters swarmed and sang in the wet air.

Behind him, Willis cursed. "Damn these skeeters, they eat me alive."

Panting, Truehart said, "Man, slow down, can't move fast in this muck."

Byrd waited, and as Truehart caught up, he said, "Did you hear that?"

That odd sound, a gliding rustle, something moving through the trees. "Snake?" Willis asked.

Byrd halted, froze, listened. Nodded. None of them stirred. Byrd strained to see. But a cottonmouth was well-hidden here, its body undistinguishable from the color of mud, doubly sheltered by the low light of the thicket. All of them were silent and still. They waited until the slithering sound grew fainter, so faint that it was swallowed up by the calls of the birds that flew between the branches of the oaks and the cypresses.

Byrd broke the human silence. "Follow me," he said, and he ran lightly through the trees to crest the hill and linger outside the glade.

Sweating and panting, all three of them straggled behind him. Truehart asked, "How do we get a cannon up here? Unless it have wings and can fly?"

"Build a road. Hell of a place for it," Willis said. "Uphill through them trees."

Truehart said, "Damn you, Byrd, if you're fooling with us—"

"Follow me." He slid into the glade, as lithe and easy as a snake. Willis came after him, and Truehart and Thornton strained through. Truehart said, "Ain't enough room in here for a cat to turn around. Where would we put a cannon and a band of men even if we got them up here?"

"We clear it. The thicket's all on flat ground. Enough room for the gun and the men." Willis looked thoughtful. Taking a measure.

Truehart's voice rose. "A cannon and a troop up here? Not enough room, even if you cut down all them trees."

"Can't you see?" Byrd asked. "We put sharpshooters all the way up that hill. Hide them in the thicket. Won't many men get past them. Shouldn't need an army up here to stop whoever does get through."

"Can't win a battle just by sharpshooting," Truehart said.

Byrd, who had proposed the island and voted to defend it, felt free with his opinion. "We ain't defending Vicksburg. Don't need a long line in front, and another behind, and cannon flanking both." Byrd gestured toward the slope of the hill, all the way down to the beach. "We'll be hidden in them trees. We'll see them, but they won't see us. They come up that hill, and we pick them off like we're slapping skeeters at a picnic."

Truehart said, "Ain't no proper battle."

"Don't want a proper battle. Want a battle we can win. We take our advantage as we can," Byrd said.

Truehart's voice rose. "What kind of a war did you fight out in the West? Hiding behind a rock to kill them Indians?"

"Sharpshooting. Sharpshooting surprises 'em. We want to surprise 'em."

Truehart said hotly, "Ain't a proper way to fight. A coward's way."

"After what I done for Willow Bend, you're calling me a coward?"

"Look at you. Can't keep your hair combed. Can't even keep your shirt clean. Can't trust you to do anything I ask, and can't trust you to stay sober."

Byrd glared at Truehart. "Don't have to take any order from you. You ain't my commander. Or my daddy."

"I rose to the rank of sergeant during the war. Earned it. Don't you forget that."

"You was a sergeant twenty years ago. I been a soldier every year since. Mustered out as a sergeant. First sergeant. Top man. What rank was you?"

Truehart rushed Byrd and grabbed him around the neck. Byrd ducked and kicked Truehart in the knee, enough to bring him to the ground. Truehart overpowered Byrd and pinned him to the ground. He rubbed Byrd's face in the dirt. Panting, he said, "Don't you mock me. Disrespect me. Make a fool of me. Do you hear me?"

Thornton rushed to pull Truehart off Byrd. "Great God Almighty, Jim," he shouted. "He's still bruised up from that beating. Get off him!"

Truehart released Byrd, and when he stood he was ashy. Byrd rose slowly, from his knees, brushing the dirt from his face. He wasn't hurt, not any not worse than before. He felt like grinning. Truehart had lost command of himself in full view of Thornton and Willis.

"Byrd, you're a damn fool. Jim, you're another," Willis said.

Thornton said, "You two shake hands and act proper."

Panting, his shirt dirty, his hair disheveled, Truehart growled, "If he agree to act like a soldier, I'll shake his hand."

"I am a soldier. If he agree to call me sergeant I'll shake his hand all day long."

Thornton glared at Byrd and laid a heavy hand on Truehart's shoulder. "Jim. Great God Almighty. Never saw you so hot at a black man."

"Never met a black man who disrespected me like he does."

"You mayor. Not king. Not God. We're all free men. I'm allowed to disagree with you. Disagreeing ain't disrespect," Byrd said.

Willis shook his head. "Look, I can bring that cannon up here or not. I can build a road or not. But I got to know, one way or the other. And it don't reassure me to watch you two fight like roosters in a cockpit."

Byrd brushed the dirt from his sleeves and beat the worst of the mud from the knees of his pants. "You been telling me this ain't my fight. Maybe it ain't. I can go and leave it for you. See how well you do without me." He slipped from the glade. As long as they could see him, he sauntered down the hill. On the beach, spent, he lowered himself to the sand, elbows on his knees, head in his hands, like a boy too proud to cry.

He heard Truehart's tread well before he heard the voice. "May I set?"

"What do you want?"

Truehart sat on the sand. "Joe Thornton said that you were a good soldier, but you had a disorderly nature. Said the army kept you in order."

"Fighting keeps me in order." He met Truehart's gaze. "Like commanding keeps you in order."

Truehart took out his kerchief and wiped his face with it. He put it back in his pocket. "For a raggedy stray man, you mighty canny."

Raggedy and stray, like Buster. "How else do a man surprise an enemy?"

"Shake on it? Both of us sorry?" Truehart held out his hand to Byrd.

"I'll abide by that," Byrd said. "If you will."

"Don't start up with me, Sergeant Buffalo Soldier."

"I won't."

Byrd nodded. He extended his hand and Truehart shook it, then clasped it in a rough brotherly way. Truehart said, "Willis have a good idea. He figure how we use the sharpshooters and we use the Napoleon."

"How?" Byrd asked.

"We hide the Napoleon in the glade. We cut a path uphill. Let the sharpshooters stand on either side so they can hit them ruffians as they come up. The sharpshooters do what they can, and if the ruffians break through, we use the Napoleon. Clear the hill and fire the canisters."

Byrd said, "I think I could manage with a dozen men. I need to go back and study the path and the trees before I know for sure."

Truehart said, "I know I can find you a dozen riflemen. That leaves me enough to man the Napoleon."

As Truehart left, Byrd thought, don't know who won that round. Can't tell, with Truehart.

Truehart's effort to recruit riflemen was no secret, and the day after the fight on Willow Island, Byrd was in Thornton's, passing the time of day with Davey, when two of the Glover boys came into the store together, laughing and jostling each other. The tallest, nearly a man at sixteen, strode up to the counter and announced, "My daddy says were going to fight. He's going to be a sharpshooter and I'm here to buy cartridges for his rifle." His younger brother shoved him aside. "We're all going to fight," he said, grinning. "I'd stand and fight, if I had a rifle."

The elder Glover regarded at him with scorn and laughed. "You couldn't hit the broad side of a barn if you was standing right next to it."

"All kinds of ways to fight," Davey said thoughtfully.

Stung, the younger Glover said to Davey, "You can't even see to fight. You'd have to put on spectacles first!"

Davey tucked in his chin and put the box of cartridges on the counter. "You tell your daddy it's on his account."

The younger Glover reached for the box, but the elder grabbed it from him, laughing, and turned to run out the door.

Byrd said, "Hey!"

Startled, both boys gaped at him.

The tone of command returned to him. "Do you want to be soldiers?"

"Yes, sir," both of them said.

"Then you handle those cartridges careful. They ain't a toy."

The elder boy cradled the box to his chest, and both boys ran off, laughing and jostling each other.

Davey leaned across the counter and dropped his voice. "Mr. Byrd, may I ask you about something?"

"Surely, young Mr. Thornton," Byrd replied, wondering what Davey might possibly ask of him.

"I want to help, since I can't shoot. I thought I might scout."

Byrd felt a cold breath of fear in the hot little store. "How would you do that?"

"Get close to this Loveless and overhear what he plan to do. Then report, like Miss Delia done, to warn us." Davey's eyes glittered.

Byrd, who never prayed, thought, Dear Lord, keep this boy from harm. But he asked calmly, "And how would you do that?"

"Offer to be a servant to Loveless. Follow him, and listen to what he say, and tell everyone here what I find out."

Byrd, seasoned scout and spy, said, "You can't do such a thing."

"Why not?"

"Because if he find out, he kill you."

Davey tucked in his chin, his sign of strong emotion. "When the massacre happen, I was here, visiting my aunt and uncle. My mama and daddy perished at Loveless' hand." The tears came. Davey wiped his eyes with his sleeve. "Why were I spared, when they died?" Byrd said nothing, because there was no comfort to offer. Davey said, "I carry that with me, every day. I never forget it, Mr. Byrd." He raised his tear-stained face. "I do whatever I can. Go into danger, if I have to."

"Not like that." Byrd's voice rose. "A scout don't have to stand in the thick of danger. He need to find someone who can tell him what he need to know."

"Like Miss Delia."

He was quick, Byrd realized. A good quality for a scout. "Yes. Like Miss Delia."

"I could go to the Little place. Go with Mr. Willis, pretend to be his helper. Find a reason to talk to Miss Delia. Fool Marse Little."

"Still need to be careful."

Davey leaned farther forward over the counter. "I was a playactor, when I was in school. Since I had the best memory, and could recall what I needed to say." He hung his head and dropped his eyes, acting the slave as though he'd been born to it.

Byrd was fascinated and chilled. "It ain't like the playhouse, Davey. If you falter they won't catcall you. They'll hurt you." Byrd shuddered, thinking of Davey threatened and beaten. "Or worse."

"I know." Davey's eyes gleamed, deep and wise and so sad for a boy that Byrd's heart ached for him.

"Your uncle has to say yes. And Mr. Truehart, too."

"Would you talk to them? Persuade them?"

Byrd was surprised that Davey would trust him. "We go together, right away."

"Thank you, Mr. Byrd." Davey clasped his hand.

Byrd leaned over the counter to embrace Davey. It was like embracing his younger self. "We all help you, and prepare you, and guard you against danger, as much as we can."

They went together to find Truehart, who stood with Willis by his old barn, talking about how to build the new one. Byrd interrupted them to tell what Davey had proposed.

Truehart shook his head. "I can't let him do such a thing. It's too dangerous."

Byrd said, "He knows he'll have to keep his head down."

Willis said, "Jim, he'd be under me, and I'll help him. And if he play the fool, he should be all right."

"Don't like a bit, that he pretend like he still a slave," said Truehart.

Byrd said, "Ain't about free or not. Can't be free if you're dead."

Truehart's voice rose. "Don't need you to tell me." He checked himself. "Dan, if you watch him, and help him, he can go. But if he's in any danger, bring him right home." He shook his head and addressed himself to Byrd. "Especially after what happen to you."

After Willis left, Truehart said stiffly to Byrd, "We'd welcome you to share supper with us." The smell from the Truehart house was savory. Truehart said, "Niecy cooking one of those rabbits Bernie shot."

Byrd said yes.

As he washed his hands and face at the pump in the yard, Bernie emerged from the house, wearing a dirty apron. Byrd grinned. "You been in the kitchen."

Bernie achieved a look that would have been a blush of embarrassment on a lighter face. She bent close to whisper. "I heard you're looking for sharpshooters to stand on the hill. My daddy's been talking to every man in town who can shoot straight and true. Ain't that what sharpshooters need to do?"

"It is, Miss Bernie."

She straightened. "I'm a good shot."

Before he could stop himself, he said, "Better than a good shot. A fine shot."

"Better than some of my daddy's friends who stood beside him in the war."

He spoke low. "It's one thing to shoot a critter for your dinner. It's another to shoot at a man who wants to kill you."

"I ain't afraid of danger."

Oh, Miss Bernie. Don't ask me to make you a soldier. Don't

ask me to send you into battle, and to harden your heart, to put you in danger, and to scar your young flesh and your sweet soul. Not just because you're a gal. But because I couldn't bear to see you hurt, even to get a splinter in your finger. "Miss Bernie, I can't let you stand with the sharpshooters."

She said, "Gals can vote in this town. Why can't we fight, too?"

"Don't think you're risking your life to vote in Willow Bend. Sharpshooting's a different story."

"If those men found me, and caught me, I'd be in as much danger as if I were sharpshooting." She looked steely.

He said, "If I said yes, I'd never hear the end of it from your daddy."

"He'd have to say yes, too. But he'd hearken to you, if you asked him."

"Don't think he'd say yes."

"Have to ask to know. Would you help me? Ask him together?" She handed him a cloth to wipe his face.

He took it. "Can't promise what his answer will be. Will you abide by it if it's no?"

"Don't know yet what he'll say, and won't guess until I do."

After dinner, Truehart invited Byrd to sit with him on the little porch. Truehart lit a pipe, and the smell of sweet tobacco mingled with the fragrance of Niecy's evening primroses. Bernie came out and sat, perching on the edge of her chair. "Daddy, I know you're raising a regiment to defend us against Loveless and his men." Truehart nodded. "And that you want Mr. Byrd to be charge of the sharpshooters."

"That's right."

"We need all the good shots we have."

"We surely do."

"Daddy, I'm as good a shot as anyone here. Maybe better. Mr. Byrd thinks so, if you ask him."

Truehart was silent, and they all listened to the night sounds of early summer. As the dark came, as the air cooled, the crickets in the grass began their song, muted and melodic. The night birds came out—the swallows with their lopsided, swooping flight, and the owls, who called to each other from the oaks, getting ready to hunt and eat.

Bernie said, "I want to join up. Stand with the sharpshooters. Fight."

Truehart looked at Byrd. "What do you say?"

"She's a fine shot."

"About this. What do you say about her standing with you? Do you think it's a good idea?"

"No, sir, I don't."

"What did you tell her when she asked you?"

"Told her no."

"Then why did you come to me? Knew I'd say no, too."

"Thought she'd take it more serious if it came from you."

He looked at Bernie. "It is no."

She looked beyond the cotton field, down to the shore, across to the island. "If they broke through, if they caught me, I'd be in more danger than I would as a sharpshooter."

Truehart clenched his jaw. "Don't need gals shooting and being shot at. God help us if you need to defend yourself." She was about to open her mouth when he said, "You won't get round me on this. Don't try. I don't have to ponder. No."

"Thought you were going to stand by me, Mr. Byrd." She rose stiffly, her head down and her shoulders sloping like a soldier after a long march.

The fatherly feeling welled up in Byrd, and envy ached behind his eyes and dried up his throat. They both watched her go. In a low voice, Truehart said to Byrd, "You cherish her, don't you?"

Equally low, Byrd said, "Like you do."

He rose, too full of feeling to sit still. As he left, it bothered him more than he liked to have common cause with Jim Truehart.

He didn't think she'd gone to the island at night, but he threaded his way down to the spot where she launched her canoe. She sat on the shore, gazing at the island, her head propped on her hands, watching the fireflies over the water.

He sat beside her. "I won't naysay your daddy."

She raised her head. "If I were a boy, would you have me?"

"In a moment."

"You know how good a shot I am."

"Don't matter. I won't rile your daddy."

"Don't know why I asked," she said, irritated.

"Miss Bernie." He put his hand on her arm and he was pleased that she didn't shake it off. "He's tenderhearted about you because he's your daddy." Byrd felt the fatherly feeling, so powerful he was afraid she'd see it and mock him for it. He took his hand away.

"I don't like it, not one bit. Not from him, and not from you, either." She jumped up and threaded her way through the trees back to her father's house.

So she knew. She was still mad at him. He lingered for a while, so bothered that he didn't want to return to his shack. When he stood he felt all of his wounds again. He sighed as he limped down the road. He didn't want the liquor or the company of Thornton's. He wanted to see Jerusha.

She sat quietly on her steps, fanning herself. Without rising, without preliminary, she said, "What bother you, Ambrose?"

He lowered himself to sit beside her, groaning a little.

"Can I get anything for you?"

He shook his head. "Miss Bernie came to ask me if she could fight with us."

"Hope you told her no."

"Had to."

"Odd thing for a gal to be so handy with a rifle."

"She's a good gal." The fatherly feeling came back. He looked into Jerusha's green eyes and said, "Made me wish I'd gotten married after the war. Had a gal like Bernie to bring up and to fuss over."

Jerusha reddened in the face. She turned away. He touched her shoulder but she shook him off.

"What's the matter?"

"When my husband was sold away I was carrying. I lost that

baby, and I never quickened again. I reckon I'm barren. If you want a baby to fuss over you'll have to find another gal to make it for you."

He tried to put his arms around her but she squirmed out of his embrace. He said helplessly, "Jerusha."

"Go on," she said, tears streaking her face.

As he rose to go, tired and bruised, he wondered how a man like Truehart could bear to be tenderhearted. Any gal could poke a stick into the softest spot on a man's heart.

When Davey came back from his first day on the Little place, he knocked on Byrd's door and said, "I have a report, but I want to tell you and Mayor Truehart private."

It pleased Byrd that Davey had come to him first. They gathered in Byrd's shack, Byrd sitting on his bed, Truehart and Davey at the rickety table. The bed, made up, was decent enough for company. The new coverlet Jerusha had given him was still fresh, and the new pillow had been plumped. Jerusha had made him white curtains like hers to brighten the oilpaper windows, and she left him flowers from her garden whenever she visited. Today they were sundrops, their yellow petals cheerful, their green leaves fresh.

Truehart drummed his fingers on the tabletop. "What did you hear?"

Byrd said, "Let him tell it." He nodded at Davey. "A scout remember better if he tell it as he recall it."

Davey's face flashed into a smile. "First thing, I met Marse Little. He come up to us and watch us work. He say to Mr. Willis, 'Who's the boy you brought with you?'

"Mr. Willis says, 'Name of Davey. Kin to Miss Delia. Stays with the Thorntons.'

"'Why haven't I seen him before?'

"'The Thorntons just decided they could spare him.'

"'He ain't like that other boy you brought with you, is he? That fool nigger who thinks he's a sergeant?'

"Mr. Willis tell him, 'Nossuh, he's a good boy.'

"Marse Little look right at me and ask, 'Are you?'

"I recall what you told me, Mr. Byrd. I hang my head and stare at my feet. I shuffle a little, make my voice slow, talk dumb. I say, 'Yassuh, I tries to be.'"

Now, at his uncle's table, Davey reverted to his schooled manner of speech. "Can't believe he didn't see through me, acting the nigger." He shook his head. "All my life I've been afraid of Marse Little. Never realized how short he is. Don't think he's too smart, either."

Byrd said, "A cottonmouth snake ain't too smart, either, but it's dangerous. You stay wary."

"Then what happen?" Truehart asked.

"When we break for midday, I go into the kitchen to find Miss Delia and tell her I pretend that we kin. She say that's all right with her, and she glad to make a fuss over me, and she insist I set in the kitchen and let her give me something to eat. She ask after people in Willow Bend—how is Miss Niecy, how is Miss Bernie—and I tell her. Figure she'll tell me about the Little place in return if I chatter with her and put her at ease."

Byrd said, "That's right. She trust you, she tell you things."

"While I was setting there, Marse Little's butler Sam came in, with Marse Little's letters on a tray." Davey paused, warming to his report. "Sam can read. He read all of Marse Little's letters, coming in and going out. He know all of Marse Little's business and Marse Little don't have any idea." Thoughtfully, he said, "Sam says Marse Little can't imagine that a black man could read, or that he'd dare to read a white man's letters."

Truehart leaned forward, unable to bear the leisure of the report. "Did he tell you? What the letters say?"

Davey said, "I asked him. He say that Colonel Loveless go around the countryside to find men to join him. Wasn't happy about the way it was going."

"How many men?" Truehart demanded.

"Was about to ask when Marse Little come to stand in the kitchen door. Sam take the letters away and Miss Delia fall silent.

It bother me, how Marse Little stare at Miss Delia. Just like a cottonmouth, Mr. Byrd. Like a cottonmouth look at a rat for its dinner."

Truehart curled his hand into a fist and pressed it hard against the tabletop. Byrd said, "He did fine. He go back, he learn more."

As Byrd waited on the Truehart place for the sharpshooters, Bernie ambled through her father's field, past the great oak that had been struck by lightning, her rifle slung over her shoulder. She halted to lean against the rough wooden fence. Byrd said, "Miss Bernie, we'll be shooting soon, stand clear."

She grinned. "I know."

They came in a group, marching with the loose-limbed gait of a black regiment. The four veterans in front wore their Union coats, their brass buttons and decorations glinting in the hot midday sun, and the men too young for the war, dressed in their field clothes, carried their guns with the determination of soldiers. They halted before Byrd, and stood as though they were on parade, feet apart, hands on their rifles.

Eleven men. Four of them—Pete Glover, Charlie Robinson, the blacksmith's brother Asa Hood, and old William Rice's eldest, called Willie to distinguish him from his father—were Union veterans and brothers in battle from the 1st Mississippi. The rest were their sons or sons-in-law, ranging from eighteen-year-old Tom Glover to old William Rice's grandson, a grown man with children near adulthood.

"I want to see you shoot," Byrd said.

Robinson said, "Don't you trust Jim Truehart's word? That we can all shoot straight and true?"

"Ain't a matter of trust. If I'm to command you, I need to see it."

"Don't need to test me," Robinson said. "Jim's word ought to be good enough."

Bernie leaned forward, straining against the stile. Byrd said, "When you mustered into the 1st Mississippi, did your sergeant take your word that you could shoot? Or did he test you and drill you?"

They didn't disagree with him aloud. They murmured among themselves, quietly insubordinate. He raised his voice. "Where did you men fight?"

Pete Glover said, "Milliken's Bend." Willie Rice added, "The siege of Vicksburg," and the others nodded. "Don't forget Fort Blakely," Robinson said. "And Mobile." Hood said, "Some of us was in Texas, too, just after the war."

"What did you do in Texas?"

"Fought them Indians. Wasn't much of a fight. Skirmishes, mostly. Killed more buffalo than Indians. Ain't too proud of it now."

Robinson stood astride, his hands resting on his upright rifle. He said, "Heard the Indian Wars were a coward's way to fight."

Byrd thought, They act disobedient, but I can't. Isn't seemly. "How do you figure that?"

"No lines of battle. No cannon. Just hiding behind trees and rocks and bursting out at a few men when they ride by."

Stay cool, Byrd thought. "Riding into town to murder innocent people, that's a coward's way to fight," he said.

More muttering and grumbling.

Robinson asked, "Why ain't you in uniform?"

"I'll tell you. You all look fine in them coats of yours. But I can tell you that the moment the sun hits them shiny brass buttons, your enemy will know just where you are. When we fight, we wear ordinary clothes, so we can hide behind the trees."

Robinson said, "Sergeant Truehart wants us in uniform. For discipline."

They call him Sergeant, Byrd thought, irritated. "Discipline's in your mind and your heart, not in your uniform. We startle our enemy more if we look like cotton farmers but we fight like soldiers."

Robinson asked, "What was your regiment in the war, Mr. Byrd?"

Sergeant Byrd, he thought, but he said, "Fought with the 43rd Pennsylvania, United States Colored Troops."

"What rank did you rise to?" asked Robinson.

Even if he'd been ordered to command them, they'd wonder about him. Just wouldn't dare to question him like this. "Stayed a private through the war. Rose as a sergeant once I joined the 25th Infantry."

"How high?"

"Not that it matter here, but I mustered out as a first sergeant."

"Top soldier," Pete Glover murmured.

Robinson said, "I'm sorry you took a beating. But I don't know you, except as a stray and a drunk. No idea what kind of soldier you were. I ain't sure I'd trust my life to you."

A ringing voice came from the fence. A commanding voice, like her father's. "He's a fine shot."

Startled, Robinson asked, "How do you know?"

"I've been hunting with him. I've seen it."

Robinson shook his head. "That's your say so."

"Don't have to take my say so. We show you. We have a contest, right here, right now. A shooting match. You can see for yourself."

"Miss Bernie, this ain't a Wild West show. It's serious business."

"I know," she said, turning to face them, her family's friends and neighbors, men who had known her since she was too little to carry a rifle. "I'm dead serious."

One of the Willis men said, "We in danger and we waste our time on a spectacle!"

"If he can shoot, would you trust him to command you?"

"I might," said Pete Glover.

"Why not? Have the contest," Willie Rice said.

Robinson shook his head, as though he didn't like it, but he said, "All right. We have the contest. Right here. Right now."

"Three rounds. Best of three. You call them, and you measure," Bernie said coolly.

Robinson frowned. "Don't have time for that. One round,

three shots each. I mark the target and I measure." He slashed a deep X on the bark of the dead oak. "Who goes first?" he asked.

"Miss Bernie," Byrd said.

Bernie lifted her rifle and let it rest on her shoulder. She planted her feet apart—Byrd was struck at the strangeness of it, her legs in a rifleman's stance under her skirt—and sighted on the center of the X. She stood as still as a sapling and waited as though the dead tree were an animal that would startle when she fired. The spectators shifted from one foot to another. Someone coughed. Bernie ignored it. She tightened her grip on the barrel and curled her finger around the trigger. She fired. The bark splintered as the bullet hit.

She took a deep breath and sighted again. Tightened her grip again. Fired. Another hit. She unslung the rifle. Waited to quiet herself again. Rested the gun against her shoulder again. Held it loosely in her hands. Closed her eyes as though she were praying. Opened them to sight. Shot.

Robinson ran to mark her shots. He came back grinning. "Miss Bernie got a bullseye!" he said. "Mr. Byrd, you'll have a time beating that."

Pete Glover said, "Let him take his turn. Only fair."

Byrd lifted the rifle to his shoulder and felt the silkiness of the barrel against his cheek. His mind cleared like a cloudless sky and he fell into the stance that was as familiar as taking a breath. He sighted, and as he aimed, he heard the cry of the great bird above.

"Golden eagle," Bernie whispered, and he lowered the gun to watch the wings spread wide, the great body ascend, and the golden feathers gleam in the sun, until the bird soared so high that it diminished to a speck in the sky.

He readied himself again and the shot flew from the barrel, splitting the bark, missing the X. He let his anger and his calm flow through him and shot again. Without hesitating, he shot once more.

Robinson ran to the tree to check the shots. He examined the bullet holes and the notches and straightened up with a puzzled face. "I can see where two of Mr. Byrd's shots went in," he said, "but I can't find the third."

Bernie sprinted to the tree and the men followed her. They crowded around the bullet-scarred oak, looking at the splintered spots. Bernie probed the hole in the bullseye with her finger and dug in the wood with her knife. "Look," she said, holding out her hand.

Two bullets lay in her palm.

"The bullseye," Bernie said. "A draw."

"Another round?" Robinson asked.

Byrd shook his head. "Even match," he said. He held out his hand to Bernie. "Miss Bernie Truehart, you're a fine shot."

"Sergeant Ambrose Byrd, so are you." She presented him with the two bullets and he received them like a medal.

The youngest Rice began to laugh. "Man, that was some shooting! Weren't it?" The youngest Glover pummeled him on the back. The rest of younger men joined in the laughter. Pete Glover called out, "Weren't it, Charlie?"

Robinson didn't reply. He put his finger into the hole where the two bullets had hit, one atop the other. He stared at it for a long time. Finally he turned to Byrd, arms stiff at his sides, hands curled uncomfortably into attention. His voice was stiff, too. "Sergeant Byrd, we all saw that you're a fine shot. And it were gentlemanly of you to leave it at a draw."

Byrd stood at ease. He felt an apology coming.

"I can't speak for everyone, but if you want to test me at shooting, I'm ready."

Pete Glover joined him. "So am I. Boys?" he asked his sons, who came to stand alongside him. The Rices lined up, too. The Willises joined him, and so did Asa Hood.

Bernie grinned and Byrd grinned back at her. "Miss Bernie, we shoot, stand clear!"

The day after the shooting match, Willis and Davey went to work at the Little place. When they returned, they found Truehart and Byrd waiting for them in Thornton's. Willis looked shaken. Byrd asked him, "Are you all right?"

Willis said, "Don't like what happen to Davey today."

Davey looked worse than Willis. He looked ashy. He said, "Mr. Willis, let me tell it."

Truehart asked, "What happen?"

"At midday I go into the house to find Miss Delia so we can talk. I stand in the hallway because she ain't alone. There's a white man with sandy hair with her. He press her against the wall, and he curl his fingers around her throat, as though he ain't sure he want to paw her or choke her. 'Be nice to me,' he says, in a rough hoarse voice like he drunk. Delia shrink away and say, "Yes, Marse Harry.' He lean closer and tighten his grip. 'Like Mr. Little told you.' Then he laugh and let go and turn away.

"I try to pull back as he pass me, but he get a good look at me as he go by.

"Delia look ashy, so I wait a moment, let her compose herself. When I come in I ask, 'Who were that? That man grabbing you?'

"'No one.'

"'Did he hurt you?'

She rub her throat. 'I'm all right.'

"'What were that about?'

"'Nothing,' she say. 'Are you hungry? I can find something for you.' She bustle around the kitchen. She sit with me and she chatter. Ask me all about Willow Bend, how we doing, how everyone fares. But she look ashy, through all that chatter, and every time she raise her hand it shake."

Davey said, "And after dinner, when I go back to work, the sandy-haired man, the one she call Marse Harry, wander by. Had a big ruffian of a man with him. He point to me and ask Mr. Willis, 'Who's that?'

"Mr. Willis say, 'That's my new helper.'

"Then Delia come out, so she can see us, and she keep her eyes on this Marse Harry. He stare at me and laugh in a mean way. 'He don't have any fool notions, do he? Like he's a sergeant?'

Staring at me. I drop my head and look at my feet, and I mumble, 'Nossuh.'

"Still staring at me. I can feel his eyes on me. He say, 'Don't go around with a sidearm?'

"'Nossuh.'

"'What have you got in your pockets?'

"'Just a kerchief to wipe my face and a pocketknife.'

"'Empty out your pockets. Let me see.'

"I pull out the kerchief and the knife and he take them. Drop the kerchief on the ground, but hold the knife in his palm. It pain me. Just a little old worn out pocketknife, but it belonged to my daddy, and it's one of the few things I have to remember him by. I say, 'Suh, that's a pitiful little knife, it ain't good enough for you.'

"He see it pain me that he have it. He close it in his fist and grin. 'I'll keep it,' he say.

"Mr. Willis get upset and say to Marse Harry, 'Suh, leave him be. He need to help me, finish this work that Marse Little set us.'

"Marse Harry put his hand on the grip of his pistol, not like he's going to draw it, but just to remind us that he can. I feel fear all over, a chill in that hot sun.

"Marse Little come striding by. Delia watch that, too. Marse Little look at me, then he say to Marse Harry, 'Is this nigger bothering you?'

"He say, 'Yes, he is.'

"'What's he doing?'

"'He's standing there being a nigger.' And he and his friend start to guffaw, like they make a fine joke.

"Marse Little get sharp and he say, 'I know this nigger. He's a good, quiet, hardworking boy. Leave him be and let him work.' Then he get even sharper with Marse Harry. 'Don't you have business with your daddy in town? Go back there and take that friend of yours, that lazy ruffian, with you.' They stand there and guffaw some more and Marse Little raise his cane like he plan to strike someone. He say, 'You two get on out of my sight.'

"Then Marse Little say to me, 'You watch yourself, boy.'

And he give me that cottonmouth look, the one he give Delia last time. And after he leave I set down because I'm shaking so bad I can't stand upright.'"

"Where were Miss Delia?"

"Still standing there. Watching."

Truehart said, "I don't want you going there again. It's too dangerous."

Davey asked Byrd, "How do you go ahead, when you can't find out what you need to know?"

Byrd thought, Sometimes you guess and sometimes you get surprised, but he wouldn't say that, either to Truehart or Davey. "Do the best with what you find out."

Chapter 7

The Bastion

Byrd didn't like the loss of Davey's reports, but the lack of news was oddly familiar. It was like the West, where the Comanches could be far away, or they could be waiting behind the next rock, ready for a fight.

As they drank in Thornton's, Truehart grumbled, "Don't like not knowing."

"We get ready, whether we know or not," Byrd replied.

"How are the sharpshooters doing?"

"They doing fine. But we need cartridges."

"Don't every man have a stock?"

"Enough for hunting. Not enough for a battle."

"We go to talk to Mr. Levy."

They went together, and when Levy's bell jangled their arrival, Levy turned to greet them. A smile sat oddly on his lined face. "My friends from Willow Bend!" he said. "How can I help you?"

Levy's was empty, but Truehart leaned against the counter

and dropped his voice. "Hoped you might help us with some supplies."

"What do you need?"

"Cartridges."

Levy took a box of cartridges from the shelf. Truehart said, "More than that, Mr. Levy. A considerable number."

Levy lowered his voice, too. "Is there trouble?"

"We hope not, Mr. Levy."

"I hear things," Levy said, in the same low voice. "I hear there's going to be a fight."

"Mr. Levy, if there were, it wouldn't be your fight."

"I'm not so sure of that," said Levy.

From the street, a familiar voice yelled, "Shopkeeper! Hey, shopkeeper!" It was young Dixon.

Byrd asked, "Where can I hide?" Levy lifted up the counter and Byrd slipped into the back room, which was small and windowless, the floor piled with boxes, the desk piled with papers. The room smelled of cloth, flour, and cottonseed oil. Byrd stood where he could see and hear, the scout's habit.

Dixon swaggered into the store and leaned against the counter. He said to Levy, "What are you selling this nigger?"

"I don't believe that's your business, Mr. Dixon," Levy replied.

Dixon addressed Truehart. "What are you buying, nigger?"

"Just a few cartridges for hunting deer, sir," Truehart mumbled.

Dixon curled his fingers around his pistol. "It ain't right to sell cartridges to niggers."

Levy reached under the counter for his revolver, a new Colt that gleamed even in the bright light of the store. "I make my living by selling. I sell to anyone who comes to me. I sell them what they ask me for."

Dixon said, "What does a nigger need so many cartridges for?"

Levy picked up his revolver and pointed it at Dixon—not

aiming, but making it clear he could. "If you threaten me, if you threaten my customers, I'll shoot you."

"You think you'll scare me? A few niggers and a Jew shopkeeper?" Dixon said.

Levy held the gun steady.

"Mr. Dixon? What's going on?" came the voice from the threshold.

He had the soft, educated speech of a man who had been a planter before the war. He wore a black frock coat, which fit so well that Byrd couldn't see whether he had a sidearm beneath it. He was tall and slender. Under his white hat his hair was still bright, and he sported the goatee and mustache that General Lee had favored. His good eye was clear and blue, and over the other he wore a black patch.

"Nothing, Colonel Loveless," Dixon said.

Loveless said, "Leave these people alone. Don't start a fight. Not now."

Plenty of time for that later, Byrd thought, looking at Truehart's ashen face. His hand went to his hip, where his gun, Dixon's theft, used to sit.

Dixon wavered. "You watch out, shopkeeper."

"Believe me, I will." Levy put the gun down.

On the way back to Willow Bend, Truehart was silent, as though the slightest mention of Loveless would conjure up his band on the road to surround them. As soon as they arrived, he said, "We need to get that cannon onto the island."

That afternoon, Byrd sat with Willis and Truehart at the Truehart table. The day had turned overcast and muggy, so dark that Niecy had lit a kerosene lamp. She stirred a pot on the stove, raising an oppressive smell of cowpeas.

Truehart drummed his fingers on the table. "How do we manage it?"

"Have to build a road first." Willis smoothed a piece of brown paper, which crackled under his fingers.

"Like you told me," Truehart said, clenching his hand into a fist and forcing himself to release it. "Straight up the hill."

Willis picked up his carpenter's pencil. "Can't just slap it together," he said. "Have to figure it." He began to sketch. "Where to put it through the trees."

Truehart said, "Use the path Bernie made."

"That path snake all around. Won't help us." Willis sketched some more. At the stove, Niecy stirred the cowpeas so violently that the spoon clattered against the pot. Willis asked, "How much do the Napoleon weigh?"

"I told you," Truehart snapped. "Two thousand pound."

Willis said, "Not more than four bales. A team of mules can pull that. Harness up those mules and pull it up the path, little by little."

Truehart pushed his chair away from the table, a raw scraping sound on the planks of the floor. "Just tell me how soon we can get it done."

"Man, you jumpy," Willis said. "Not like you. What bother you?"

Niecy clanged her spoon against the pot, making it ring like a tocsin. "Tell him!" She glared at her husband. "If you don't, I will."

Willis set his pencil down. "Tell me what?"

Truehart stood so swiftly that his chair fell to the floor. "We saw the one-eyed man in town yesterday."

Willis' face turned ashen, as Truehart's had. "Where?"

"He come into Levy's to tell young Dixon not to start a fight. Not yet."

Willis rose, his whole body trembling. "He close by and you didn't tell me? Could be here any moment and you didn't tell me?" He grabbed Truehart by the arm. "Could come into town with his men and you didn't tell me?"

Byrd said coolly, "He tell you now."

"Could be here like the devil with all of his demons on horseback!" Willis cried out.

"This man Loveless. I saw him," said Byrd. "He's just a man, and he's a soldier."

"How do we defend ourselves against that?"

Byrd said, "I fought against the odds before. If you scout, and plan, and prepare, you can win a battle against the devil himself. Which he ain't." The smell of cowpeas was hateful to him, but he said to Willis, "Set down and pick up that pencil. Can't slap a road together, and can't get the cannon over without the road."

Byrd perched in Willis' skiff as Willis rowed to the island. So soon after sunrise, the slightest haze hung over the river. The gnats hovered over the water in a glimmering cloud and the sun smiled tenderly on the rippled water. The last of the night-blooming flowers scented the air with a fragrance that overwhelmed the smell of silt. The beach gleamed white, and the willows on the island trembled in the breeze, their branches caressing the ground. Byrd thought that Willow Island had never looked so beautiful.

Two skiffs danced alongside then, one bearing the Willis boys and the other the Glovers. The Rices, aided by Robinson, pulled at their rowboat. Behind them, Truehart's heavy boat plowed through the water. At the rear, the Hood brothers, who rarely went on the water, poled their cobbled-together flatboat.

Willis landed his skiff on the beach, and the other skiffs followed, barely scraping the sand. Truehart's rowboat gouged the sand as it landed, and the flatboat bumped the shore.

Truehart clambered from his boat. Hand on his rifle, he turned to keep watch as the rest of the men alit. Byrd climbed out, still careful of his bruised ribs. He slung his rifle over his shoulder.

Willis reached for the axe and passed Byrd the two-handed saw. "Careful with that," he cautioned, as he picked up his rifle. Willis' sons, also armed, also carrying axes, crowded around their father. Robinson, who had brought a knife big enough to cut canebrake, stood with them. The rest of the men huddled around Truehart, the gang around their old driver, awaiting their instructions.

Truehart said, "Today we build a road, but we do more than that. We build a bastion." He scrutinized the group, then shifted his gaze to the beach and beyond it, the river. "While some of you work, some of you keep watch. Four men on the beach on guard. And everyone keep his rifle handy."

No one spoke. There were nods and murmurs. Byrd thought, They talk a lot about being soldiers, but they ain't quite ready yet. It bother them to get so close to it.

"Dan explain where the road go and where the trees to need to come down."

Truehart set Byrd and Robinson to work together at the base of the hill. Still the driver, Byrd thought, making sure we get along with each other. Robinson had pouches of fatigue under his eyes. He hefted his axe, groaning as though it were a heavy burden.

"We start with this one," Robinson said, pointing to a cypress at the base of the hill, nearly a yard in diameter. Underneath it grew marsh grass, the old matted under the new, and tough, twiggy brush. Robinson found a knife for Byrd, and they worked together.

Robinson began to hum as he cut away the brush. Byrd knew the song: "Trouble So Hard." Robinson began to sing, his knife coming down in a rhythm with the word "trouble." Byrd felt the rhythm in his bones: the swish of the grass, the slash of the knife, and trouble. Hard trouble.

Willis called out, "You quit that!"

"Sing to make the work easier!" Robinson called back.

"It don't! Hush!"

Robinson fell into silence. Around them, no one spoke and no one sang. Byrd had never known a group of black men to work without singing, and it made him uneasy.

When the ground was clear, Robinson said, "I fell it. Stand behind me." He picked up the axe and notched the trunk. A chip of bark flew through the air and the wounded wood released its smell of skunk. The blow sent a tremor through the tree and the earth around it. Birds swarmed into the air, chattering with alarm, and a white tail flashed as a frightened rabbit bounded to safety in the thicket.

Robinson hewed the axe, grunting with the effort. The notch grew bigger, a deeper hurt on the trunk. He stopped to wipe his face, slick with sweat, as though he had a fever. He hoisted the axe again, chopping and chopping until he exposed the heart of the tree. He pressed his hand against the trunk and the tree wobbled. "Stand back!" he warned Byrd. The tree toppled, the trunk thudding against the ground, the crown brushing the dirt. Emerging from the leaves, a snake hissed, opening its cotton-colored mouth in fury. Above, the great hawks circled and soared, hungry for the creatures disturbed by the tree's fall.

Byrd stared at the stump and was surprised by the notion that felling a tree was not so different from killing a man.

Suddenly Robinson dropped the axe, grabbed his middle, and ran into the thicket to vomit up his breakfast. Truehart came running to ask, "What's wrong?"

"Robinson sick at his stomach."

Truehart retrieved the water bucket as Byrd waited. The rest of the crew returned with Truehart. When Robinson appeared, ashy and faint, he sat down heavily in the shade in their midst. He raised the dipper to his mouth with a shaking hand. He said, "Suddenly I thought that we might be building our graveyard."

Truehart said sharply, "Charlie, you can't think that."

He cried out, "How can I think otherwise? Don't all of us lie awake of a night, thinking it?"

Byrd put his hand on Robinson's shoulder. He said quietly, "We all afraid."

Truehart said, "Sergeant Byrd, don't say so."

Byrd said, "Why not? Since we all feel it, so bad we can't sleep and can't keep down our food?"

"Because it ain't seemly to say it."

Byrd turned to survey all of the men, who watched him

quietly, waiting for him to reply. "Sergeant Truehart, have you forgot? That a good soldier isn't the one who never feels fear? He's the one who feels fear and acts brave anyhow." His eyes swept the group, in the commander's look he had learned from Sergeant Shaw, regarding each man as though the words were for him alone. "All of you were soldiers and you all recall it. Feel fear, and fight despite it."

The men nodded and murmured. Their faces lightened a little. Robinson drank more water and wiped his mouth.

Byrd said, "Take it easy, soldier."

Robinson rose slowly and looked at his fellows. "Know I left my axe here somewhere. Do anyone see it?"

When they returned to work, no one sang and no one spoke. The island filled with the sounds of the human battle against the wild growth of the island: the hack of knives against the cane and brush, the chop of axes into the heart of cypress trees, and the rasp of saws, roughing the trees into logs for the road.

By the end of the day the road was done. It ran from the base of the hill to the glade, straight up, six feet wide, an invitation to overrun the hill. On either side, the thicket remained undisturbed, full of hiding places for the sharpshooters.

Byrd walked slowly up the hill, the logs rough under his feet, missing the shade of the trees on the open path. He glanced at the thicket. He would come back later to confirm the spots for his sharpshooters. Now he wanted to stand in the glade once more, before it was readied for battle.

He saw her while he was still on the hill. Today, she had come without her rifle or her game bag. Not a wild creature. Not a hunter. A girl in a faded calico dress, her hat pulled low to keep the sun from her face. She contemplated the glade that had been her refuge and her bower. "All them trees gone," she said.

"Had to do it."

She gazed down the hill, her face full of sadness. "Spoiled for hunting."

"No hunting here for a while, Miss Bernie."

She stared at the gash the corduroy road had made in the wilderness. "Won't ever be the same here."

He heard something that didn't belong to the thicket, or to the crew below, their voices faint so far away. "Do you hear that? On the swampy side?"

She turned to look. "Sounds like a boat. Traveling slow."

He scanned the river. Whoever rowed it wore a hat, pulled low against the sun. "Taking a good look at us."

"Could just be fishing," said Bernie, talking over her fear.

"Or spying."

He flew down the hill. Breathless, he panted out the news to Truehart, and Truehart panted behind in up the hill to the glade Bernie had gone. Truehart strained to look, but the boat had disappeared somewhere down the river.

When Byrd returned to Willow Bend, it was still too hot to sit in his windowless shack. Byrd eased himself into a chair on the porch of Thornton's. Buster lay at his feet, head resting on his paws. Byrd stroked the dog's head and thought about Jerusha.

The last time he visited, he had refreshed a wound as bad as the loss of her husband. He was ashamed that he'd hurt her, and he didn't know how to make it right. A handkerchief wouldn't be enough. A few days ago Robinson had humbled himself be contrite to him. He could be as good a man as Robinson. He could bring Jerusha an apology.

He rose—whenever he sat, he still felt stiff—and hobbled down the steps. Buster came after him, wagging his tail. Buster thought they were going back to the shack, where he had taken the habit of jumping on Byrd's bed and sleeping on Byrd's feet.

Byrd sighed. "We go see Miss Jerusha together."

He found her in her front yard, where she knelt, yanking weeds from a flower bed. He called out her name and she rocked back on her heels. Before she could say, "I'm still mad at you," he said, "I'm sorry for what I said before. From the bottom of my heart."

"Sorry's cheap."

"Hard work ain't. You have anything you need done? Anything that requires a strong back? I'll do it."

"You too bruised up for hard work."

He touched her shoulder. "Jerusha. Trying to be tender. Don't like that I ain't good at it. Help me out."

Buster nosed her cheek and she laid her face against the dog's. Buster licked her, close to her mouth. Softened, she said, "Don't you try to kiss me, you old hound." She sighed and rose. "Come into the house. There's fresh buttermilk." She rubbed Buster's head. "I give him some, too."

Buster lapped at his buttermilk from a dish on the steps while Byrd waited inside. Today the glass vase on the table was filled with wild roses, which were fragrant with little pink blooms and fierce with thorns.

Before she could fetch the pitcher for him, he embraced her and murmured, "Why are you so sharp with me?"

"Don't know. You spark it in me."

He tightened his embrace and kissed her gently on the cheek. "Don't mean to."

She wrapped her arms tightly around his back. He started away. "No," he said.

She loosed him but didn't let go. "How can I love you if I can't put my arms around you?"

Shame and desire warred fiercely in his chest. He craved her touch and he couldn't bear for her to feel his back and he had a devil of a time with himself. "Scars are all healed up."

She stroked him through his shirt, lightly and tenderly, as no one had since the scars were made. He stiffened. "No, let me," she said. Tensed against her touch, he let her. "What are you doing?"

"Trying to feel how bad the scars are."

"Can't fix them now."

"Let me see them," she whispered. She traced the scars— not with a healer's touch, but a lover's.

He didn't move. The feel of her fingers was gave him pleasure, even on the ridges of scar that didn't feel right, that had never felt right, since the flesh was flayed and made to heal wrong.

Very low, she said, "If you take off your shirt I can see what I might do."

To touch his naked flesh. To see it, scarred and ruined, the reminder of everything about slavery days that hurt and shamed him. He pulled away. "No."

She let her hand linger lightly on his face. "Sometime?"

He turned away and she brought him back with the lightest pressure of her fingers. If he bent his head he could kiss her. He broke away. "Don't know," he said.

The next morning, Truehart summoned Byrd and Willis. Truehart's face was tired and drawn and he was too restless to sit. "Follow me," he said, striding off his nerves, and he led them to his fallow field, where Byrd had tested the sharpshooters. He paced as he spoke. "Need to take over the cannon right away."

Willis said, "Been thinking about it. How much it weigh. Josiah have a good flatboat, but it won't carry such a weight."

Truehart pressed his hands together. "How do we carry it, then?"

"Barrel and carriage come apart. Take it over a piece at a time. Put it back together once we're on the island and harness up the mules to pull it up the hill."

Truehart's eyes glittered. "No. We do it by stealth. We take over the cannon by night. No mules, they bray an alarm. Use a team of men to pull it up the hill."

"A team of men to pull that thing uphill? Are you crazy?"

"Two thousand pound the same as four bales. How many men to carry four bales?"

"At night? In the dark?"

"Someone watching, we know it."

Truehart and Byrd crowded inside the shed. Willis flourished his biggest wrench. He applied it to the bolts on the Napoleon but they didn't move. "Get me some oil," Willis said. "Any kind of machine oil." Truehart brought some and Willis poured it over the bolts. He struggled again with the wrench and made no progress.

"What now?" Truehart snapped.

Willis said, "Get Josiah. He help us."

Byrd fetched his landlord, known to be the strongest man in Willow Bend. Josiah torqued the wrench. "Man, them bolts are tight."

Willis said, "No one touch them for ten year or more, since they were made."

"Pour on more oil," Truehart commanded.

Josiah tried again. In the heat of the shed, his forehead beaded with sweat, and his great forearms bulged with the effort. Grunting, he yanked on the wrench, and the bolts cried and complained and broke free.

Truehart stared out the door. "It just occur to me," he said. "What if them canisters don't fire?"

"Why wouldn't they fire?" Willis burst out. "Set in here where it's dry for ten year. Gunpowder don't go bad like flour. Plenty to worry about, don't need anything extra." He said to Josiah, "Stop. We loosen them now and undo them tonight, when we take the cannon across."

"Tonight?" Josiah asked. "Feel like a storm coming. We go tonight?"

Truehart's face was as hard as iron. "We go tonight, whether it storm or not."

At twilight, they gathered at Truehart's shed. Truehart, to oversee, and Thornton to help him. Byrd's riflemen and Byrd, to direct them. Willis, to explain the task. Josiah, for his strong arms, to provide what help he could.

The day had been hot and humid, and as the sun set, the air grew hotter and wetter. The day's sky, gray and overcast, began to darken. A storm ached in the air.

Truehart said, "We take the Napoleon over tonight." He

gestured toward the river and the island. "We don't know who wait, and watch, and lurk. We do it stealthy by night."

Glover asked, "Do we take a lantern?"

"No. No lantern."

Robinson said, "We steal away. Starlight if we lucky. Darkness if we ain't."

Byrd tamped down his memories of stealing away.

Truehart said, "I lead you and I take my rifle. Sergeant Byrd, you follow behind, armed." He gazed at the rest of the men, his eyes hooded and pouched with weariness. "The rest of you, you carry. Think on this. You don't carry a load that pull at your shoulder and hurt your back. You carry the weapon that defeat the ruffians and the one-eyed man. The weapon that save Willow Bend."

Willis released the barrel's bolts. He said, "Take this down to the shore, but don't load it."

"Why not?" Robinson asked.

"We get the carriage over first, since it weigh more." Willis sighed. "Because if it don't sink, we know it can take the barrel."

Robinson asked, "Do you doubt?"

"God know. A man who builds, he can only guess and try."

There were fourteen men to lift the barrel once the bolts were unloosed. They inched to the shore where the flatboat waited. A younger Willis cried out, "Damn these skeeters, they try to eat me alive." The gentle slope down the shore slowed them. They set it down on the shore, grunting.

Willis said, "Now we take the carriage."

The carriage had two big metal wheels and a long metal pole behind. In the war, the pole was attached to a wheeled box called a limber that four horses were hitched to. They had no limber and no horses. Eight men would pull on the pole and another four push on the wheels.

The men grunted as they tried to move the carriage, which was much heavier than the barrel and more complicated, with the pole in front and the moving wheels behind. "Men? You all right?" Willis asked. Someone groaned. "Hush!" Truehart said.

Willis ran to the river's edge to direct the men in loading the carriage onto the flatboat. He fretted, "Hope that boat can carry the weight."

Byrd said, "What if it don't?"

"Then we sink like a stone with it."

The men heaved the carriage onto the flatboat. Willis and Byrd stepped gingerly onto the boat and tried to steady themselves as the rest of the men pushed the boat from the shore. Byrd picked up his paddle. He thought of the negotiating the river in the dark and felt deeply uneasy.

Willis said, "We riding low. I can feel it." He called to Truehart, who watched from the riverbank, "Can you see? Are we low in the water?"

Truehart whispered hoarsely, "Can't tell. Keep your voice down."

The sky was deeply overcast, and the black sky blackened the river. Willis cursed softly. "Can't see a thing."

Byrd bent to check and the raft pitched from side to side. Willis forgot Truehart's admonition and shouted, "Damn you, don't rock this thing! Stand steady!"

Byrd stood still. Willis lowered his voice. "Paddle like I do." Byrd worked to match his rhythm, and as he made the effort, the flatboat shook in the water. Riding low.

Willis shivered with worry and snarled, "Damn you, match me!"

"I try."

"Do better! Otherwise we tip and send the carriage to the bottom of the river."

Byrd watched Willis and equaled his strokes. The boat steadied, and they paddled in unison. Nearly halfway across. Byrd let himself breathe. Let some of the knots in his shoulders unknot.

Something splashed nearby the boat, and something broke the river's surface. Byrd couldn't see what, only a roiling in the water in the darkness.

The boat collided with it and it reared up, disturbing the water. A dark scaly head and tiny glinting eyes.

Willis whispered, "Gator."

"Never saw a gator here before!" Byrd hissed, frightened and furious.

"They hunt at night."

The gator thrashed its tail next to the boat, making a sound halfway between a rattle and a hiss. It opened its maw, showing rows of sharp jagged teeth. In its wake, the boat rocked wildly.

We scared to death of that one-eyed man, Byrd thought, as the boat yawed back and forth. And we die tonight because a gator swamp us and tear us to pieces.

Willis paddled frantically, as Byrd was too upset to match him, and the boat rotated in the water, colliding again with the gator. The gator tried to sink its teeth into the edge of the boat. Willis cried, "Match me! Quick!" and the boat began to pull away. The gator released the boat and lifted its head, hissing in rage. Willis and Byrd poled the boat as fast as they dared, straining their eyes in the dark. Byrd thought, If Loveless is out there, this moment, we too worried to care.

The gator submerged and disappeared from sight.

Shaking, dripping sweat, Byrd paddled. When the flatboat bumped onto the beach, he muttered a prayer: "Thank you, Lord."

Willis and Byrd staggered onto the beach and fell to the ground, panting with relief. Byrd murmured to Willis, "Can't believe I ain't dead."

Willis laughed, his nerves strung too tight. "The night ain't over yet."

Bringing over the barrel was easy in comparison. The boat didn't ride low. Byrd knew to stand steady and paddle steady. No alligator raised its head.

When the men gathered again on the island, the air was even hotter than before and the sky was blacker. Lightning lit the distant sky, and thunder rumbled, still far away.

The men came together to drag the carriage, eight men to pull on the pole, four behind to push on the wheels. The carriage slid over the sand like a child's toy, and the men sighed with the hope that the journey up the hill would be as easy.

On the corduroy road, the wheels caught on a log. The men in front raised the pole, straining with the effort, and the men behind pushed with all their strength. The carriage moved slowly but steadily over the first few logs, but as the road slanted upward, their progress stopped. The men in front lifted the pole and the men behind pushed. The wheels caught again. Willis said, "Have to drag it one log at a time."

The frogs were undisturbed by the men and the cannon. In the swamp the bullfrogs boomed. The air was thick with skeeters. Robinson cried out, "Damn these skeeters on my face!" and let go the pole. Several angry voices yelled, "Don't drop it, damn you!"

His voice tight with agitation, Truehart said, "We ascend a log, we stop, we rest, we slap the skeeters away. Then we start up again."

Underneath the frogs was the sound of slithering. Beyond the path, cottonmouths lurked in the thicket. Byrd thought of the gator's maw, also cottony, and under the sweat that poured down his face and his shirt he was cold with the memory.

It was an agonizing dance, to lift the pole, let the front wheels clear the log, and to push the back wheels up the hill. Then to rest, to try to wipe away the sweat that ran stinging into the eyes, and to brush the skeeters away.

All of the men grunted with the effort, even though Truehart whispered harshly, "Quiet!"

When the carriage was halfway up the hill, they all heard it. The crashing sound in the thicket, loud enough to be a man. More than one man. If it was a scout for Loveless, he was a fool to make so much noise. Or careless. Or both.

Byrd thought, Of all God's dangers I've seen in my life, I don't want to die tonight. Not toting a cannon up a hill.

Byrd tightened his grip on his rifle and strained to see in the darkness. The crashing came closer. Through the trees. Onto the path.

Byrd froze. He raised his rifle. They emerged, stopping to gaze at the men and the carriage.

They dropped to all four feet and crossed the path, their bodies fat, their gait a waddle, their ringed tails faintly visible in the darkness. Raccoons.

The men began to laugh, the high ringing sound of fear. "Afraid of a bunch of raccoons!" they said, slapping each other on the back. "Maybe Loveless turn into a raccoon to spy on us!"

"Quiet!" Truehart hissed.

Back to the agony of pulling and pushing, a log at a time. But every log brought them closer to the top of the hill and the glade.

When they finally dragged the carriage into the glade, they laughed weakly with relief. As they rested, the wet air turned to drizzle, a pleasant patter on the glade's leafy canopy.

Truehart said sternly, "Ain't done. Still the barrel to fetch."

"Barrel weighs less than the carriage. Shouldn't be such a task," Willis said.

As they descended the hill, the drizzle turned to a needling rain and the black sky flashed yellow with lightning. Byrd counted until the thunder pealed. Not close yet. The air stirred.

They had fourteen pairs of hands to carry a barrel that weighed eight hundred pounds. Byrd thought, It's like carrying a sack of flour. Even a tired man could manage that.

On the beach, fourteen men slowly bent to lift the barrel; they slowly straightened their knees; they slowly unbent their backs. Byrd called out, "You all right? You need me to help?" even though he would be hampered by the rifle over his shoulder.

"We all right," Willis said. "You stand guard behind us."

As they carried the barrel across the beach, the lightning flashed brightly over the river, and the thunder swiftly followed. The wind became persistent and pressing, and the needle-like shower turned into a pelting rain.

At the base of the hill, Willis said, "Set it down. We rest for a moment." The rain fell hard enough to be a soaking downpour. It ran down Byrd's face, sending the last of the sweat stinging into his eyes, no matter how hard he blinked. At least the skeeters were gone. A downpour drove them away.

"Ready?" Willis asked. The men braced themselves to lift the barrel. But it was so slicked with rain that the men had trouble getting a grip. "We all right?" Willis asked, but the barrel slipped from more than one pair of hands, and more than one man yelled, "Damn! Watch it! Get ahold of that thing!"

Willis said, "Grab it from the far end and tilt it. Get ahold of it from the bottom, where it still dry." The men closest to Byrd, Willis' sons, two pairs of hands, one on each side, lifted it, grasped it, and held it secure. "We all right," said his eldest, his namesake Danny. Then the next two men. Then another. The rain lashed their faces and soaked their clothes. Byrd was as wet as if he'd been swimming in the river.

At last, all fourteen men lifted the barrel. Truehart went ahead, stepping cautiously onto the corduroy road. "Damn, it slippery here," he said. "Slicked with the rain."

They moved even more slowly than they had with the carriage, as they tried to find their footing on the wet logs and creep upward. Danny Willis cried out, "Have to let it down," and everyone groaned, knowing the effort to pick it up again.

The rain came down in sheets, swift and so angry that it was impossible to see into the darkness. The men inched forward. The lightning flared over the river, and the thunder immediately followed, a sharp whiplike crack.

They paused. "Don't set it down," someone pleaded.

A bolt of lightning hit so close that the thicket was momentarily full of blinding light, and thunder boomed overhead, sounding like God's own cannon fire. Every man startled and the barrel slipped from every pair of frightened hands.

In the thicket a cypress tree, too wet to catch fire, smoked and sizzled. The mud began to smell of everything that had died last winter and that had rotted as the weather warmed. Byrd tried not to think of the last time he had fought in a thicket full of smoke and mud.

"God damn!" Truehart roared, not caring about being quiet while Nature made such a din.

Willis said, "Shut up! You ain't sergeant over the weather. Could have been us hit by lightning."

The men laughed weakly. The two Willis boys tilted the barrel, intending to start the long process of lifting and grasping to be able to carry. Danny Willis' voice was startled and plaintive. "Can't get a grip. The bottom as wet as the top, and muddy, too."

Willis was too irritated to speak kindly to his own boy. "Don't care how you do it. Pick it up and tote it."

The rain lashed against them, beating their skins, obscuring their sight, creating a waterfall down the hill, so that every log was as slippery as glass. They moved so slowly that Byrd could scarcely see that they were moving.

Byrd's arms ached and his legs burned. All of the wounds and bruises from his beating, which he thought were healed, troubled him again. It was like the war, when the anticipation and the fear and the shock were as exhausting as any effort in battle. He felt tired, sick tired, as he had in the Battle of the Wilderness, three days of fighting in a state of rage and fear, until he was so tired that he thought he had died and God was talking to him.

Someone screamed, the high thin scream of a young man pushed beyond his strength: "I can't go on!" and fell to the ground. "I can't move!"

Willis shouted, "Set this thing down! Danny ain't all right!"

Byrd ran to Danny Willis, who lay in the mud. Willis bent over him but Byrd knelt down, pushing Willis aside with a firm hand. "Man, how are you?"

Danny curled up like a baby, sobbing. "Can't do it."

Byrd lay his hand on Danny's shoulder, the gesture of comfort that Sergeant Shaw had offered to his broken young recruits. "It's all right, soldier. It's all right. Catch your breath."

As Danny breathed and calmed, the sobs slowed. Byrd waited. "I'm so sorry, Sergeant Byrd."

"It's all right. Can you set up?"

Danny sat upright, snuffling like a little boy.

Byrd said, "You take your time, soldier." The snuffling gave way to a grown man's sniff. "Better, soldier?"

A surprised tone. "Yes." Danny flexed his arms. "I try it."

Byrd called to Truehart, "We all right here. Ready when you are."

Byrd rose. His pants were filthy with mud that stank like a swamp. But he felt better, his sergeant's second wind. They inched upward, a slow, slippery step at a time. When they stopped to rest, Byrd fell to the ground. His clothes were soaked and so thick with mud that they might never be clean again. He wiped his face with his sleeve only to smear it with reeking mud.

When they reached the top of the hill, and set the barrel down in the glade, Willis said in a ragged voice, "We put it back together before we go."

"Oh, man!" "Can't lift my arm to do another thing!"

Truehart said, "We ain't coming back in broad daylight tomorrow to do it."

Byrd put down his rifle and joined the last effort to lift the barrel and set it in place. Willis fumbled for the bolts in his pocket. "Can't see where they go," he said.

Byrd said, "Feel for them. Like a blind man."

Willis found the bolt holes. Slipped in the bolts. Tightened them. "You can let go," he told the crew, and they slumped to the ground in exhaustion.

Willis dropped his wrench and fell against the secured barrel, too tired to speak, his breath as ragged as a sob.

The rain slowed. As they descended the hill on wobbly legs, it diminished to a drizzle once again, a cloud of mist over the black still water of the river.

Byrd accompanied Willis to the island to make sure that the cannon was hidden in the foliage of the glade. The sun was out and the river was as smooth as a mirror. The daytime birds, ducks and their ducklings, geese with their goslings, were the only creatures to swarm around the skiff, quacking and honking as the men sculled past.

They beached and loitered their way up the hill, where the logs squelched a little under their boots and the road was littered with leaves and twigs from the storm. Byrd gazed upward at the glade. He said with satisfaction, "Can't see a thing. Anyone who don't know will be mighty surprised we keep a Napoleon up there."

Willis wanted to survey the other side, which he had never seen. They descended the hill, Willis following Byrd through the trees, and Byrd said, "We could put the camp here. Flat and open. Have a stream here, too. Fresh water."

Willis stared into the thicket.

"What is it?"

"A lot of trees down in there," he said. "From the storm?"

Byrd's skin began to prickle. "Let me look." At Willis' look of protest, he said, "I scout it, then come for you."

Byrd edged into the thicket, his feet squelching in the dirt that the storm had turned into mud. Willis was very likely right. Lightning had hit the island more than once during the storm. But there was no smell of scorch in the air. The small birds that nested in the cypresses chirped and trilled, and the small animals that lived on the ground scurried undisturbed through the grass.

No one had camped here, unless they had left the place as undisturbed as the Indians used to. He breathed a little more easily as he slipped deeper into the thicket.

And saw the clearing—the trees and the brush were gone— and the ramshackle lean-to that had been built upon it.

No evidence that anyone was there, and as he edged closer, no evidence that anyone had camped there. He sidled up to the lean-to and peeked into the doorless opening.

There were barrels inside.

Still cautious, he slipped within to look. They were ordinary wooden barrels, like the ones in Thornton's. The lean-to smelled of smoke and salt, and when he removed the nearest cover, he found that it was full of preserved meat. He opened the other. It was filled with flour.

It reminded him of slavery days, when Massa's white bread and Massa's ham found itself beneath the aprons and shirts of house servants, whose mouths watered for the food that Massa and Missus never allotted to slaves. Someone was stockpiling. Someone in Willow Bend, worried and full of foresight, had brought provision to the island.

Just like slavery days, he thought. Stealing away.

Byrd hastened back to the shore. At the Trueharts', Truehart sat wearily at the table, as a smiling Niecy poured coffee for their visitor. "Delia come to see us! Marse Little give her the afternoon so she can see us."

He said to Truehart, "Come outside. I have something to tell you."

Irritated, Truehart said, "Tell it here."

Delia had the ashy look of a woman whose nightmares woke her. She clenched her hands in her lap and unclenched them and clenched them again. Her eyes darted over the room, unable to settle on anyone's face, unable to meet anyone else's eyes.

Too upset to watch today, Byrd thought. "Can I trust her?"

"Of course you can! My cousin Delia!" Niecy said, startled.

Byrd scrutinized Delia. He said coolly, "I think you spy for that man Little on his say-so."

Delia burst into tears and wept into her hands, as inconsolable as a widow. "Niecy, I'm so sorry."

Niecy asked, "Delia, sugar, what's the matter?"

Delia raised a swollen face and forced out the words. "Marse Little tell me to find out what I can and tell him." Hands to her face again. "He tell me if I don't, he let those ruffians have their way with me."

Niecy cried out, "Delia, come to us, stay with us, we protect you."

"Niecy, then they come for you, too." She cast her tear-stained face toward Truehart. "All of you."

Truehart broke the horrified silence to address Byrd. "You was a scout."

"I was."

"Was you a spy, too?"

"Sometimes."

"Can you help Miss Delia?"

Byrd said grimly, "I might. If I can trust her." He asked Delia, "Can I?"

Delia raised her head, her face still wet, but no more tears came. "I tell you what I know."

"If you lie to us, if you betray us, you find that a white man ain't God's only danger to you."

She wiped her face clean. Her eyes were deep dark pools. "Born in slavery and raised in slavery. In God's danger every day of my life. I recall that, Mr. Byrd."

"Tell us about Loveless."

She nodded. "Sam read it in a letter. Loveless have eighty men. They gather at Marse Dixon's place."

"When?"

"Don't know. Soon."

After Byrd gave Truehart his news about the shed and the barrels, Truehart called all of Willow Bend together. They filed into the church that afternoon, dirty and sweaty from the morning's work, worried that he had summoned them. Truehart took the pulpit. He looked as though he slept badly every night, dragging all of Willow Bend with him in dreams. He spoke in his coaxing voice. "Someone build a lean-to on the island. Someone bring provision there. Who were it? If you know, tell us. If it were you, tell us." His gaze rested on each face, and they all stared at their hands or out the window, like bad children who were thinking, Weren't me!

Truehart sighed. "Loveless could be here any day. Someone watch us when we build the road on the island. Someone care what we do. Need to know. We do one thing if it were one of you. We do another if it were Loveless."

A painful silence, like the moment when the Reverend asked the congregation to search their souls and think about their sins. Maggie Willis raised furtive eyes to her friends Niecy and Bessie. Bessie knotted her handkerchief in her lap, uncharacteristically silent.

Truehart asked gently, "Do anyone have anything to say?"

Outside, a bird broke the human silence: Pee-wee-wee-wee! A bird that no one noticed, or cared about.

Pete Glover raised both his hands, a man surrendering, and said shame-faced, "It were me. I did it."

"Why?" Truehart asked.

"My wife wanted to bring some provision over to the island by stealth and she need a place to put it."

"Why would you do such a thing?"

Bessie Glover rose to her full majestic height, her starched apron snapping like a banner on the battlefield. She put her hands on her hips and hectored Truehart as if he were one of her badly behaved young sons. "All this fuss about getting that fool cannon over to the island! What about the rest of us? Where are we going to stay? How are we going to eat? What are we going to do for water?" She glared at Truehart. "A hundred people who need to use the privy—how are we going to manage that? Do we take that by stealth?"

Her husband added, "What about my mule? Can't put her in my skiff and take her over the river by stealth. Can't leave her behind!"

Miss Louisa's face twisted with worry as she clutched her husband's hand. "What about us women and children? Do we go by stealth? Steal away to the island at night?"

At the words "steal away" Byrd recalled the tobacco-scented air of a hot summer night in Virginia. He heard the sound of the dogs that panted to find him and drag him back into slavery. He burst out, "We won't steal away! We ain't slaves! We do this proper in broad daylight, like free men and women."

Truehart said, "What if Loveless and his band surprise us, while we stand on the shore?"

Byrd rose to make his point and project his voice. "Out West, when settlers traveled through Indian country, they didn't go alone by stealth. They banded together, in a long train of wagons, under the escort of an armed guard. My company guarded many a wagon train. We protected them and kept them safe. We do that here."

"I don't like our chances."

"Our chances better with all our riflemen around us to defend us."

"Still don't like it."

"I don't either. We could ask them Federal marshals to come back to help us. Maybe the Angel Gabriel come down with his host to help us. Just as likely."

The room filled with nervous laughter.

Truehart rubbed his face. "Don't like it, either way. But we do as you say, Sergeant Byrd."

After Delia brought her news, it spread through Willow Bend more swiftly than President Lincoln's telegraph had sent a message to every officer in the field of battle. The women figured the provision and it came by stealth in little boats, day and night. Josiah Hood lent his flatboat to carry provision and to ferry mules, two at a time, a run every hour, even if they brayed with distress as they crossed the water. Jerusha's cow had balked about getting on the boat and bellowed louder than a mule all the way across the river. If Jerusha didn't cherish that cow so much Byrd would have pitched her in for the alligators to eat. Within days, the people of Willow Bend were ready to cross the river.

Truehart gathered them in the church. The Reverend blessed them, but Truehart gave the sermon. "We know that Colonel Loveless and his band of ruffians are ready. That they're close by. But we're ready, too. The Napoleon is on the island. The sharpshooters know where to stand and how to shoot, thanks to

Sergeant Byrd." Byrd flushed to hear Truehart call him sergeant. "We have our provision and a safe place to make our camp."

Truehart said, "But that ain't enough. We need to be ready in our hearts and our minds and our souls. Need to act like soldiers, all of us, whether we hold a rifle or not." He cast a stern look at Bernie. "We need to act brave, even though we might feel afraid. We need to stand and fight, and we need to stand together."

They murmured among themselves. They nodded. Byrd wanted to stand and call out. But he held back. The mood was too somber.

Truehart said, "The island ready for us. Today, we pack up. Tomorrow, we move. We cross over."

The words gave Byrd a chill. Cross over to freedom. Cross over to death.

"How long?" someone asked, wanting to know how much to pack, but Byrd's mind was still in the past.

Truehart said, "We plan on a few weeks. Two or three. Should be over by then."

Suddenly the room was silent as the thought echoed through it: Or we'll be dead by then.

Jerusha caught Byrd by the hand as they left the church. "Come for supper tonight."

Byrd sat at Jerusha's little table. The evening sun glowed golden through her oilpaper. On the table was a vase of flowers that didn't really belong in a vase, even though they were a pretty color. Forget-me-nots.

She served him cowpeas and cornbread—he had yet to tell her he didn't care for them—and it didn't bother him much, since he was too keyed up to eat.

"Ambrose, you haven't finished your supper."

His excitement for battle rose in him. "Jerusha, this is the last time in a long time that we'll be able to be alone."

"Ain't there anywhere to slip away?"

"We'll be in camp. Ain't no place to be private in camp."

She teased him. "What do we need to be alone for?"

"No, be serious." He twined his arms around her waist "Don't know what's going to happen."

"You been a soldier all your life. Been in battle many a time Still here."

"Always a chance to die, in battle." He sighed. "Want to hold you in my arms first."

"Is that what soldiers say? How they beguile?" she asked, grinning.

He laughed. "Yes."

She wove her arms around his neck and whispered, "If you take off your shirt and let me look at them scars, I'll do it."

He raised his eyes to hers. Clear green eyes like river water. She kissed him, the softest brush of lips on lips.

He shucked off his jacket and raised his hands to the top button of his shirt. His hands were shaking, but she didn't move to help him. She was going to leave shedding his shirt up to him. Slowly, he unbuttoned the top button; slowly, he unbuttoned the rest. As he unbuttoned his cuffs, the shirt fell open. There was nothing wrong with his chest. The gals in the bawdy houses had often said so. It was light brown, ribbed with muscle, and sprinkled with fine dark hairs. Handsome, they told him. He stood like that for a moment, half-dressed.

His hands were still shaking as he slipped off the sleeves, one at a time. He let the shirt fall from his shoulders to the floor. His naked chest was all over gooseflesh. In the warmth of a spring night, he was goosefleshed with fear.

He raised his eyes to hers, looking as resolute as if he were going into battle, and turned slowly to give her a clear view of his back.

The pale brown flesh was crisscrossed with welts of darker brown scar. From his shoulder blades to his waist, the wounds had healed in lumpy ridges. She touched one of the scars. He'd felt them himself, with some difficulty. They felt like the bark of a tree, scaly and dry and not entirely alive, but it was feeling flesh. He started at her touch.

Ten lashes the first time. Twenty-five the second. She traced the scars with her fingers as though she could count the lashes he'd received in the pattern of the ruined flesh. She pressed her cheek to his back and let the salt of her tears slip over the healed wounds. She kissed the scars that were wet with her tears.

"Jerusha, quit." His breath came ragged.

Her voice was muffled by his skin. "Quit what?"

"Can't do it." He pulled away and reached for his shirt.

She wiped her face with her hand. "Didn't think that trying to lie with you would be my life's work."

Shirt still unbuttoned, back safely covered, he said, "Not that long. Just not yet."

Byrd slept fitfully and woke when the light outside his oilpaper windows was still blue with night. The earliest birds cheeped and chirped in the trees. He forced himself to wait for the first rays of sunrise. He sat up, disturbing Buster, who opened his eyes and snuffled. Byrd rubbed the dog's head. "Today we go over to the island," he said, and jumped out of bed.

Buster sat on his haunches and watched as Byrd packed. There wasn't much to pack—his clean shirt, his Western coat, and a blanket to roll everything into. It fit into the carpetbag he carried when he arrived in Willow Bend. He still regretted the loss of his sidearm.

When the oilpaper glowed a soft yellow, Byrd slung his rifle over his shoulder. Buster rose to his feet, his tail wagging, his eyes bright. In a fierce rush of affection, Byrd hugged the dog. "Today you come with me, old boy. We stay together."

The air had yet to lose the cool of nighttime, and the crickets sang one last nighttime song as Byrd closed the door of the shack, Buster at his heels. Byrd paused before he turned to take the path down to the river. The sun cleared the treetops, turning the sky the color of gold, painting the dirt road and the wooden buildings of Willow Bend with the same otherworldly glow. He beheld it, the speck of a place, the store, the blacksmith's, the school, and the church, and he felt his chest ache. He thought, Don't know when I'll see it again. He wasn't going far, just across the river. But he might never be able to return.

As Byrd emerged from the thicket, the sun gilded the river, giving the muddy water a fleeting, dazzling beauty. Byrd shaded his eyes against it and descended to the shore, where the flatboat was moored and readied to ferry the people of Willow Bend across the river. At the riverside, the sharpshooters had gathered, unusually silent, waiting for Byrd. Robinson waved wordlessly and Byrd waved back.

Robinson's family huddled together on the shore next to a mound of boxes and bundles tightly fastened with twine. Miss Louisa had packed as though they were leaving forever, like the Exodusters.

Miss Louisa clasped her Bible in her hand. The younger daughter clutched a doll to her chest, and the littlest boy, past such things, sucked on a blanket for comfort. Robinson broke ranks with the sharpshooters to embrace his wife. Miss Louisa wept and clasped him tightly as he stroked her hair and murmured, "You take care." He released her and hugged Little Lou and her sister together in a big fatherly grip, saying, "You help your mama." He enfolded his elder son, a boy of an age to hate being dandled, but who didn't pull away. He bent down to cuddle the littlest boy, just able to walk, and gently took the blanket away. "Give me a kiss, sugar." He pressed his cheek to the baby's downy head.

His voice throaty, he opened his arms, as if to embrace them all one last time, and said, "I see you again after we cross over."

Chapter 8

On the Island

Byrd stood at the bottom of the hill with Little Pete, the eldest Glover son. The day promised heat, and it was good to be in the thicket's shade. Little Pete held himself tense, his rifle slung over his shoulder. "At ease, man," Byrd said, and Little Pete set the gun down, balanced on the ground between his feet, his hands keeping it upright.

"How are you, soldier?" Byrd asked him.

"I'm all right." A muscle in his cheek twitched and he raised his hand as though he were brushing away a skeeter. He looked through the trees at the river, glittering in the sun. "Sergeant Byrd, when will they come?"

Byrd's eyes followed Little Pete's, as though the light on the water would tell him. "Just have to wait until they do."

Little Pete hesitated. Byrd asked, "What is it?"

"Hope we'll be all right."

In the camp, a baby began to cry, and several others joined in. Jerusha's cow lowed, not liking the human noise, and the mules brayed in response. The sound of animals was familiar. Animals had always been part of the Army, out West and elsewhere. But the babies' cries took Byrd back to his Civil War days, when women and children followed the Army as contraband. He had fought for President Lincoln and the Union, but he had also fought for those women and children, so recently slaves, just behind the lines.

He shook his head to clear it. The men were already jumpy. A commander had to stay calm. He shaded his eyes against the glitter of the sun on the water and listened for any sound across the river.

Then he heard it, the familiar sound of a horde on horseback: galloping hooves, gunshots, and the Confederate war cry, the Rebel yell. "Get them niggers!" someone cried out, and Byrd was startled how well the sound carried from a hundred and fifty feet away.

Byrd felt the excitement of battle rise in him like sap in spring. "They're just across the river," he told Little Pete. "Run! Get the rest of the men and tell them to get into position. And tell the Napoleon crew to stand ready, too. Hurry!"

"Yes, sir!" Little Pete grabbed his rifle and dashed up the hill, calling out, "It's started! They're across the river!"

The sharpshooters raced down the hill, whooping with excitement and fear. As they passed them, Byrd called out, "Get into position and hush! We surprise them. And remember the line of fire, like we drilled it!"

Robinson laughed. "Don't want to shoot each other!" he said. Byrd felt his heart race and his blood run more swiftly as each man slipped into his spot in the thicket and disappeared into its vined and leafed darkness.

Across the water the horses halted and the men began to shout. "Run off already." "Scared them niggers away before we come here!" "Not even a thing to take." "Not even a chick or a shoat!" "No gals, damn it all!" A single cry rose up. "Burn the place! Burn it to the ground!"

On the island, a mule brayed, and the other mules began to bray in response. Across the river in Willow Bend, someone shouted, "They're on the island!"

Byrd sweated in the thicket's shade as he waited for Loveless' men to decide what they would do.

He squinted against the dazzle of light on the river. As he watched, a single mounted man drove his horse down to the shore. The horse neighed and balked, and the man beat its neck with a crop, yelling, "Go on, damn you!" The horse splashed into the river, and as the rider continued to goad, it panicked and swam into the water in a frenzy, nearly throwing the rider. Unable to beat the horse onward or control the reins, his shouldered rifle throwing off his balance, the rider clung to the horse's neck, captive to the horse's fear.

Rifle in hands, Byrd thought, Is he a scout? Or is he a picket, with the rest behind him?

Once on the island, the rider tried to get his bearings. The horse lowered its head. The rider pulled on the reins, and when the horse didn't settle down, he struck it with the crop. The horse whinnied and tried to buck. Byrd knew why the rider didn't dismount. The horse would bolt. Would the rider dismount, despite the horse's agitation? Try to run up the hill?

The rider tried to grab hold of his rifle, but he couldn't control the horse and aim his rifle at the same time. He dismounted and the horse wheeled around, looking for a spot to bolt to. The agitated horse turned and turned, getting in the way of the unhorsed man. He slapped the horse on the rump. "Damn you, I'll shoot you!" he yelled, and he ran free of the horse to the edge of the beach where the trees began.

Byrd raised his rifle. Training his gun on the rider, he thought of his battle days, when he hid to shoot his Indian adversaries, sighting on the chest. One careful shot to fell a man. Closer to murder than any other kind of fighting. Too close to murder for comfort.

The man found his way across the beach and through the opening in the willow trees. He made his way to the path and stared upward. He hesitated, looking into the thicket, listening for anything unusual. Nothing but the low whine of skeeters and the call of a bird on the other side of the island.

On the beach, the panicked horse whinnied, and on the other side of the island, a mule brayed. Another neighed in response, and the man began to shoot wildly. He shot up the hill and into the thicket. Wild shots.

Byrd thought, He's trying to smoke us out. Or he's a fool. Don't matter which. He fired into the air, the signal for the nearest sharpshooter. Robinson.

Robinson fired and the bullet caught the man in the arm. He cried out in surprise and pain and dropped his rifle. As he looked around for the source of the shot, Robinson fired again. The bullet hit the man in the chest and he fell to the ground, groaning as he bled. Robinson shot again, and this time the man was still.

On the beach, the horse panicked, rearing and screaming on the sand, too frightened to bolt into the river to swim to safety. Byrd hated to kill a horse, but he couldn't let a fear-crazed animal tear through the island. He fired, and the horse gave a final, awful scream—every man who had been in battle remembered that sound—and fell dead on the beach.

Byrd looked over the river, over the sparkling water with its cloud of gnats, and strained to see. Strained to hear. There might be a troop behind the dead man, set to swarm onto the beach.

Byrd clenched his rifle. As he slipped down the hill, he hissed at each man he passed, "Stay quiet. Don't move. Ain't over yet."

There was no one on the shore, neither man nor horse, but the sound of shouting came through the trees just beyond the water's edge. A roar so loud it was hard to hear the words, except for "kill" and "nigger."

Byrd threaded his way through the thicket again, whispering, "Stand ready." He found his own spot, high up on the hill where he could see the river and the beach and the path to the glade.

Across the river sounded an ear-splitting whistle, and another voice, the voice of command. "You're a damn shame, all of you! Cowards, every one of you!"

Loveless, exhorting his men.

"We ain't cowards!" rose the shout from the unseen crowd. They hooted and howled and let out the Rebel yell again.

A pistol shot rang out. Someone screamed, and the crowd was silent. Had Loveless just shot one of his own men? "As I command!" Loveless cried out.

"Ain't staying here to be shot!" someone else shouted. "Not by niggers and not by him!"

Horses began to whinny, as they did when riders pulled on the reins. Byrd listened as the men rode away, whooping and yelling as they had when they came. Byrd waited until the sound of hooves faded, and he could no longer hear horses or men.

Byrd said to Robinson, "They gone. For now."

Robinson asked, "Should we stay put?"

"No. Just the usual watch."

Panting, Truehart raced down the hill, where Byrd and the men clustered around the body. "They gone?" he asked.

"For now."

Truehart bent down. "Who is he?"

Byrd rolled him over. He was lined and grizzled, a hill country man aged by not enough to eat and too much to drink. He had died of a shot to the chest, and his shirt was soaked with blood. The men stared at him and murmured, "Never saw him before."

"What do he have in his pockets? Any letter, or card of business?"

Byrd rifled the man's pockets to find a dirty handkerchief, a twist of tobacco, and two dimes. Truehart said, "Leave it all. When they find him, we want them to know we ain't thieves."

"What should we do with him? Should we dig a grave?" Byrd asked.

Truehart looked grim. Byrd had never seen him like that, icy. "We dump him in the river. The horse, too."

Byrd grabbed the dead man's feet and pulled the corpse down the path. The man's head bumped every log, and on the beach, his head lolled to the side and sand filled his mouth. Truehart helped Byrd drag the dead horse to the water. As its blood painted the sand, a buzzard flew low to investigate, making a deep hissing caw. Together, Byrd and Truehart heaved the dead man into the river, and after him, the horse. As the buzzard circled, and they watched the blood plume in the water as the river carried the bodies away.

When the sharpshooters returned to the camp, they were greeted with a crowd of women and children, who fired questions at them like bullets. "Did you shoot him? Is he dead? Is they coming back?" The two half-grown Glover boys crowded around Byrd. "Can we fight?"

Byrd laughed. He said, "No, you boys can't fight." To the rest of them, he said, "Just a skirmish. One man. We dispatched him." He put his hand on Robinson's shoulder. "Mr. Robinson did."

Miss Louisa scolded her husband in her relief. "You put yourself in danger!"

In full view of everyone, he grabbed her around the waist and hugged her tight. "I'm all right, sugar." He kissed her right on the mouth, and when he let her go, she said, "Charlie!" and burst into tears.

Jerusha edged close. She rested her hand on his shoulder and asked softly, "Are you all right?"

He covered her hand with his own. "I surely am," he said, smiling at her.

Maggie Willis took his hand. She said, "We make a special midday dinner for all of you. Brave men. Heroes."

Byrd thought of all the fighting still ahead. He replied gently, "It's a kind notion, Miss Maggie, but don't trouble yourself. I ain't a hero yet."

After midday dinner, Byrd and Truehart, Willis and Thornton sat at the rough table Willis had made, on his rough camp chairs.

Willow Bend had re-established itself on Willow Island in two neat rows of little canvas tents, like the ones Byrd lived in as a soldier. Between the tents, at one end of the table, Niecy had set up a cookfire. Cookfire and table were shaded by a canopy, also made of canvas.

Around them, the camp was full of activity, something that Byrd recognized from his Army days. When battle loomed and fear stalked a camp, everyone found a way to keep busy. Miss Lizzie did the wash and Miss Carrie nursed her baby. Bessie Glover and Maggie Willis sat on the ground with a pile of mending. In the thicket, the bigger Willis boys chopped firewood, and Robinson, relieved of guard duty and resting as befit a hero, whittled a whistle for his littlest boy. Miss Octavia, aided by Davey, schooled the children under a tree. She had brought her slates and spellers with her, and today her scholars were reciting their multiplication tables.

Nearby, next to the cookpot, within earshot of whatever the men were about to say, Niecy and Jerusha washed the dinner dishes, and Bernie dried them. Bernie worked slowly, carefully drying each tin plate and cup, setting them down on the edge of the table in good order. She wore an apron, the badge of her mother's command, kitchen duty. She stole a look at Byrd. Since they came to the island, she had been quiet and dull, but he was glad to see the hint of a smile on her face.

Byrd thought, She hates drying them dishes. She's lingering to listen to what her daddy says. It cheered him as though he'd heard her laugh.

"What happen today worry me," Truehart said.

"The sharpshooters do exactly what we ask them to do."

"Just one man and he cause all kinds of havoc. They have a troop behind him. Eighty horsed men. Have to plan for that."

"The sharpshooters know what they have to do. Sight on whoever come up and aim true."

Truehart frowned. "Want it to be orderly," he said. "Want to wait and draw them up the hill so we have the advantage. The sharpshooters, and at the right moment, the Napoleon."

Byrd said, "Ain't smart to wait. We hidden, we see them and they don't see us. We have the advantage. We fire on them while they stand on the beach. Sow confusion."

"Then we fight two battles at once—on the beach and on the hill. Don't have enough men for that," Truehart said.

"We talk about this, more than once. A dozen sharpshooters do damage to a troop."

"What keep them on the path? What if they run off into the thicket?" Willis asked.

Byrd said, "They make a racket and we know where they are. We still have the advantage."

Truehart looked upset. "How do you know how many run into the thicket? How do you know if you've shot them dead?"

"You don't," Byrd said. "But you do your damnedest."

Truehart struck the table with the palm of his hand, startling the women. "That's a mess of a battle!"

The Glover boys ran by, the elder chasing the younger. They were too young to fight and too keyed up to sit in Miss Octavia's school. Yesterday, full of restless energy, they had taken a skiff to go fishing, in full sight of anyone on either side of the river. When they came back their mother had scolded them for all the camp to hear. "Lead them ruffians right to us!" she cried out, smacking their faces. Their father, fear fueling his rage, had whacked them across the rear with a stick.

Today, still mad at them, Glover said, "Quit that! Go off and do your chores!"

"We done our chores!"

Glover said to Truehart, "They fool enough to put themselves in danger. And the rest of us in danger."

Willis said, "Give them something soldierly to do. Let them stand on the crest and watch. Be our runners to fetch the sharpshooters if we need them."

Bernie set down a cup too hard on the table, making all the dishes rattle. Truehart looked at Bernie and spoke to Byrd. Stern, and not at all clear who he was being stern with. "Sergeant Byrd, we talk all this over more than once."

Byrd said, "You in charge of the Napoleon. You put me in charge of the sharpshooters. I give you my estimation, and you naysay me. Am I in this fight or not?"

"Just want a proper battle."

Bernie listened closely. Byrd felt her attention, even though he answered her father. "But it ain't a proper battle, just like they ain't proper soldiers. Sow confusion and they won't know whether to shoot back, go up the hill, or turn tail and run. Pick them off as they try to come up the hill, and be ready to stalk them if they go into the thicket. Ain't the least like fighting a troop of soldiers. Like hunting. Something wild and dangerous."

"Like hunting bear," said Bernie. Her voice, calm and low startled everyone more than her father's outburst.

Truehart turned to his daughter and said sharply, "You go on and help your mama, Bernie."

"Daddy—"

Niecy said, "Don't pester these men, they planning how to fight. Go fetch me some eggs." When Bernie hesitated, her mother said, "And don't naysay me. Go on and don't dally!"

Bernie bit her lips. Shoulders slumped, head down, she trudged away.

Willis said, "Jim, won't be orderly. Don't matter what we do."

"We wait. See how they act." He looked at Byrd. "Can you agree to that, Sergeant Byrd?" Truehart asked.

Byrd nodded. "Don't like it, but I'll ready the sharpshooters for it."

"I check on the Napoleon." Truehart rose and the others rose too.

"I'll be along soon," Byrd said. He walked toward the barn. He wanted to go into the thicket behind it, where he could think in private for a moment.

But someone was right behind him. It was Jerusha. She said, "It's Miss Bernie, ain't it?"

The ground underfoot squelched when he trod on it and released the smell of rot, like the swamp. The trees were old cypresses, tall and twisted and hung with Spanish moss, which shut out the daylight and made even midday feel like dusk. The space between the trees was a natural clearing about the size of Byrd's armspan, too small to feel like a room. Byrd was as close to Jerusha as if they were lying together.

Ill at ease, he said, "She miserable and everyone can see it."

"Never saw a gal pine because she couldn't hold a rifle," Jerusha said. "It eat her up."

"Thought you didn't care for Miss Bernie."

Jerusha moved close to him, close enough so he could smell her, sweat and woodsmoke and the roots she used, aromatic and bitter at the same time. She said, "Give her something soldierly to do or she'll shoot somebody with that rifle. Might be herself."

"Her daddy won't let her stand on the hill and I won't, either."

"Her daddy give them Glovers, them imps of Satan, something soldierly to do. Surely we can find something for her, too."

Byrd frowned.

Jerusha moved closer. Intimate. "Don't we women need to defend ourselves? Let her plan how we do it. Ain't that soldierly enough?"

Byrd found Truehart in the glade with the Napoleon crew. He explained Jerusha's suggestion, and Truehart replied with exasperation. "Don't want her fighting."

"Ain't fighting. Planning." Truehart frowned. "Ain't likely to need such a plan, but it aid us if we do."

"Don't like it."

Byrd, who had commanded many a rebellious youngster, said to Truehart, "She just like the Glover boys. Need something to keep her out of trouble."

Truehart and Byrd took Bernie aside and described Jerusha's notion. Truehart said, "We entrust you with keeping the women and children safe. With getting them off the island if the ruffians break through."

Byrd said, "It's a job for a soldier."

At the word "soldier," she straightened up a little. Truehart said, "We trust you to figure it and explain it."

Byrd watched as Bernie paced through the camp. As she gazed over the mucky shore. As she sat at the table, a piece of Willis' brown paper before her and one of his pencils clenched in her hand. Byrd watched as she drew, her forehead creased with concentration. He didn't offer to help her. She'll manage by herself, he thought, proud of her.

That afternoon, before the women began to prepare supper, she asked them to gather around the table. Truehart had taken his usual spot with the crew of the Napoleon, but Byrd, curious, lingered to listen to Bernie. Miss Maggie brought a basket of socks to darn, and Miss Bessie mended a shirt. Miss Carrie, who never set little Isabella down, cradled the baby.

Bernie stood tall as she explained what her father had asked her to do. "Keep us safe, us women and children."

Despite their homely tasks, their ears were cocked for any sound from the other side of the island, any sound that might mean battle. They listened with little attention, focusing on the work in their laps. Looking puzzled, Maggie interrupted. "The men protect us."

"Don't know about you," Jerusha said tartly, "but I brought my butcher knife, and I'll use it if I have to."

"God help us!" Maggie said.

Miss Bessie said tartly, "Whose notion were it for you to figure such a thing?"

"My daddy's. And Sergeant Byrd's."

Bessie spoke loud enough to address a crowd. "I don't care if it were your daddy's notion. It's a fool notion." She looked at the rest of the women, daring to say what all of them were thinking. "I ain't about to take orders from a half-grown girl who's playing at soldiering."

"Miss Bessie, she's handy with a rifle and she has a good

head on her shoulders. We can listen to what she has to say," Jerusha said.

Bessie said, "So it were Mr. Byrd's fool idea, too. You'd say yes to anything he suggest, since you sweet on him."

Jerusha blushed bright red. She said sharply, "Miss Bessie, you full of things that ain't any of your business."

Bessie rose and Maggie rose too. She said, "I have work that needs doing. Don't have time for this." Bernie's audience deserted her.

Bernie sat unmoving, too upset to speak. Jerusha rested her hand on Bernie's arm but Bernie shook it off. Bernie said, "They won't do a thing I ask. Won't even listen to me." She limped away and crawled into her tent like a little girl burrowing into her bedclothes.

Jerusha gave Byrd a pointed look as sharp as her tongue. He sighed and rose. At Bernie's tent, he knelt. "Miss Bernie."

She pushed aside the blanket that served as a makeshift door. A girl with less spine would have been crying, but her eyes were dry. She didn't waste her misery in tears. "What is it, Mr. Byrd?"

He said firmly, "Come with me. We talk about soldiering."

She emerged from the tent and stood up. Still unhappy. But she followed him to the quiet spot in the thicket, where it was dark and cool in the middle of the day, and where she had to stand so close that he could smell the starch in her dress and the soap on her hands and her natural smell of green apple. It was even more intimate than the glade, and he was suddenly uneasy to be in seclusion with her.

He said sternly, "Miss Bernie."

She stood with her head lowered and her fists clenched into the skirt of her dress.

"Miss Bernie. Look up at me."

She shook her head. "They make fun of me."

"If you command, you need to earn their respect. Can't just walk in and tell them." She looked up. "Being a soldier, you start with doing as you're commanded. There are lots of ways to fight." She didn't reply. He said, "Davey do a fine job as a scout. Didn't touch a rifle."

She burst out, "Davey do something brave and important! It ain't fighting to stir a pot of cowpeas!"

"Sometimes a soldier carry a rifle. Sometimes a soldier dig a latrine. Sometimes a soldier stir a pot of peas. A soldier do as he commanded."

She was still upset.

"A soldier can't be willful. Can't get upset and storm off. A soldier have to be calm and brave, whatever the task a soldier set to." He was firm with her. "Firing a rifle or making dinner."

She turned away. He grabbed her by the arm, more roughly than he intended. "I ain't excused you yet."

"Let me fight."

Still holding her arm, he said, "Can't. Won't."

She didn't move.

He said, "Behind the lines ain't easy." She was silent. "Ask your mama. What she do is part of fighting, too." He pressed his point. "She brave and calm, just like a soldier."

She stared behind his head. He loosed his grip on her arm and against his better judgment, clasped her hand. He meant it for a handshake, but she curled her hand in his. Like a daughter's. Like a wife's. Feeling roiled in him. Holding her hand, he said, "Can you do that for me?"

Her hand still curled in his, she said, "Don't like it, not one bit."

"Can you try?"

She nodded. "I reckon I can try."

He let go her hand. "Under my command, you do better than try. You do your damnedest."

She was fully attentive. Not pouting any more. "Yes."

"You have your orders, soldier," he said.

She looked at him, a thoughtful look. "Yes, I do, sir," she said. She straightened up, and as she left to go back to the cookfire, her step was quick and determined.

Byrd stared after her and shook his head. What had he done to change her so? He hoped her lightened mood would last.

That night, Byrd couldn't sleep. He reached out to pet Buster to reassure him, and the dog sighed, rolled over, and didn't wake. Byrd stood. His bones ached. He sighed too, and walked slowly up the hill to the crest, where the Napoleon stood. He would sit where he could see the river, and he would recall the quiet he'd felt in the glade, when it was undisturbed.

He wasn't alone. Truehart waited there, his eyes on the hill.

"Didn't mean to disturb you," Byrd said.

"You ain't. Couldn't sleep."

Byrd thought of the times he lay here at night, the trees sheltering him, the breeze lulling him to sleep. "It's a good place to set."

As the air filled with the sound of crickets and the songs of frogs and the cries of birds that hunted at night, Truehart and Byrd watched the light of the fireflies flashing over the water, casting their faint greenish light.

His voice low, Truehart said, "Never slept well or felt right before a battle."

"Ain't unusual." In the dark, it was hard to see Truehart's face, but his voice made it plain. It wasn't seemly to say so, but Truehart was afraid, just like his men.

Truehart said, "Don't think you've ever been afraid, Sergeant Byrd."

Byrd was startled into laughter. And into the truth. "When I was younger I was a damn fool who was never afraid. Mad, and wild, and called it courage. I've been in battle so often I've forgot what it's like to feel afraid. Ain't a good thing to forget."

Truehart stared at the river. He said, "I worry about Bernie."

"She seem all right. For now."

"Changeable. In a misery, and after you speak to her, she better. What did you say to her?"

"Told her to act like a soldier and do what she told to do. Don't know why that cheered her."

Still looking out at the water, Truehart said, "Don't understand it, and it trouble me."

Byrd looked at Truehart, even though all he could see in the dark were the whites of Truehart's eyes. In a low voice, he admitted, "It trouble me, too."

Chapter 9

On the Hill

Byrd slept fitfully in the camp. He never took his boots off, wore his clothes to bed, and kept his rifle within reach. He woke more than once every night, startled into wakefulness by his own worry.

Tonight he was torn from sleep by the sound of screaming. A woman screaming.

Only half-awake, he grabbed his rifle, rolled from his tent, and raced outside into the darkness. It was Miss Louisa, Robinson's wife, and she was screaming like a woman gone mad.

The Glover children swarmed from their tent like frightened ants, and their mother followed, her nightdress wrinkled, her uncovered hair mussed with sleep, her face filmed with sweat. "What happen?" she whispered. The Willis families shot from their tents, as did the Rices and the Hoods. They crowded together, forcing themselves awake.

The sound of running feet alerted Byrd and he gripped his rifle. But it was a familiar voice, Thornton's. "What go on?"

Louisa crawled from her tent, her hair wild, her nightdress

hiked up, her face streaked with silvery tears. Jerusha ran to her and cradled her, saying, "Hush," as she'd calm a child. Louisa sobbed in Jerusha's arms. Jerusha stroked her hair. "Hush now," she said.

Louisa continued to sob.

Jerusha said, "It's all right. You all right."

Still sobbing, Louisa broke free of Jerusha's embrace. "Dreamed that my husband was dead, shot dead, and they were coming for me."

The crowd was silent, because all of them, sleeping and waking, had the same thought.

The eldest Robinson girl held out her arms to her brothers and sisters, who stood as though rooted to the earth while their mother wept. "Come here," she whispered. Her brother, old enough to disdain comfort, put his arm around her shoulders. Her younger sister hugged her around the waist. The littlest, who could barely stand, buried his face in her skirt, too frightened to cry. She embraced them all and murmured, "Mama's going to be all right. We're going to be all right."

Shamed by her example, Maggie Willis bent to embrace all of her younger children, murmuring "Hush. Miss Louisa just had a bad dream." And even Bessie Glover, her children momentarily subdued into silence, gathered them in a rough hug and admonished, "It all right now. We go back to sleep." Byrd watched them and felt an unfamiliar lump form in his throat. An unfamiliar pressure behind his eyes. As he tried to blink the feeling away, he saw Bernie, tall and straight in her white nightdress, standing alone. A peculiar expression on her face. Fear and resolve, just like one of his sharpshooters.

Jerusha slipped in beside him. "Miss Louisa quiet enough," she said. She grinned. Fear did that sometimes, he knew. She said, "Do you want a little sugar?"

Damn. No. He'd bust out crying like the littlest Robinson. "I'm all right," he said stiffly, moving away. "Got to check on the men on watch."

As he left the camp, swallowing hard, he felt Bernie's eyes on him.

On the hill, he stopped to talk to Robinson, who stood watch, looking worried and drawn. "Heard my wife crying out What the matter?" Robinson asked. Byrd told him. "She troubled by her dreams," Robinson said. "Always." Somberly, he added. "Do you think we'll be all right, when they come back?"

"We'll do our damnedest," Byrd said.

He was too restless to go back to his blanket. He remained unmoving on the hill, scanning the water. At the sound of footsteps, he turned to see Truehart, who asked, "Everything all right?"

Byrd nodded.

"Go on back to sleep, Sergeant Byrd."

"Don't think I can, after that."

They stood watch together as the air filled again with the ordinary sounds of night, the rasp of crickets, the roar of bullfrogs, and the whine of skeeters. From this part of the hill, the half-moon gleamed in the inky sky, shedding its light on the bats, with their crabwise, swooping flight. A horned owl swished somewhere in the trees, calling out its haunting cry: *Whooo? Whooo? Whooo?*

The next morning dawned hot and still, early summer in May. The men on the hill, hidden in the trees, sweated in their long-sleeved cotton shirts. Byrd remembered wearing his army tunic, heavy wool, in the heat of a Virginia summer during the late war, and in the dry desert heat while he fought the Indians.

This was a different heat from any other place he had lived or fought. The Delta's heat was like a blanket that had fallen into a river and had never dried. It was heavy, dense, muddy, and full of the itch of tiny insects. His nose and his neck and his head itched all the time, no matter how often he tried to scratch.

Byrd stopped to talk to Robinson. "How are you, soldier?"

"My wife's dream. Can't get it out of my mind."

"Just a bad dream."

"I know. But it rattle me."

Byrd inclined his head, feeling more than he wanted to. "Bothered us all."

Robinson's face glistened with sweat. "If any harm come to my Louisa—"

Byrd thought of Bernie, and with a rush of contrition, of Jerusha, too. "We all feel that way about someone."

All of the men on watch were jumpy. "Keep thinking I hear them horses," young Glover told him.

Byrd said, "Keep listening, soldier."

Byrd was jumpy, too. Last night's upset—Miss Louisa's nightmare, and her daughter's bravery with the little ones—had rattled him more than he wanted to admit. He was full of feeling, and not much of it was useful to a soldier.

Byrd roved the hill. He settled in the glade, where Truehart and Willis watched over the Napoleon. The sky was bluer than he had ever seen it, and the azure reflected into the river. Byrd shaded his eyes against the blaze of the sun on the water.

Truehart drummed his fingers on the cannon's barrel, a jumpy tattoo. Willis, coiled tight, would have paced if the glade gave him enough room.

"Do you hear that?" Truehart asked.

The drumming sound of hooves and a distant prolonged yell. And rifle fire, with no screams of agony to accompany it. A horde of men in horseback, firing into the air. Loveless and his ruffians, riding again into Willow Bend, racing their way to the shore opposite the island.

Byrd nodded. Willis said, "I fetch the sharpshooters," and he sprinted from the glade to alert the riflemen. As they ran past, Byrd called out, "Get into position like we drilled. And stay put! Stay hid! We surprise them."

"We whup 'em!" Danny Willis called back, grinning and raising his rifle high.

"Hope so!"

Byrd scanned the shore across the river, where the horsed men had begun to cluster. The horses neighed and snorted and tossed their heads. A cultivated voice, a planter's voice, rang across the water to the island. "Wait until I give the order. And hold your fire! The horses will bolt."

A rough voice jeered, "I reckon I can handle my own horse."

He wore the white hat he'd worn in Levy's, and he sat easily on a white horse like the one General Lee had surrendered on. The white hat caught the light and gleamed wherever he stood. Easiest thing in the world to sight on that hat, Byrd thought. But Loveless wasn't in front, where Byrd expected a commander to stand. He was in the midst of a mob.

Without waiting for the order, the riders urged their horses into the river. The horses neighed and complained and shook their heads and refused to move. One of the men raised a crop and brought it down hard on the horse's neck. The horse screamed in outrage, but it thrashed its legs in the water and moved forward. The other horses followed in a watery stampede.

Like the scout, these riders were unused to riding in water. They struggled to keep their rifles slung on their backs as they fell on the horses' necks and held on like little boys who were just learning to ride. As the horses swam, the men were submerged up to their waists. One man dropped his rifle in the water and cursed. He slipped from the horse to retrieve it and poured water from the barrel as if it were a spigot.

The horses ran the men. They shook their heads and the water from their manes soaked the riders. They pumped their legs underwater, bobbing as though they were trotting, forcing the men into a rhythm of into the river, out of the river. The horses churned the silty river water, releasing a deep dank smell of waterlogged vegetation and dead fish and mud.

Byrd felt the excitement rise in him, better than the surge of desire on the steps of a bawdy house. We'll fight a battle today, he thought, and by God's grace, we'll win it.

The first group of men splashed toward the shore. The horses found their footing on the sandbar and the riders hollered in their glee. A short, stocky man whipped his horse forward and it nipped the flanks of the horse nearest it. The horses began to whinny and move in the crablike motion that signified an intention to rear. The riders grabbed the reins, shouting, and the horses bunched together, turning and lifting their front legs and nipping any flank within reach.

Byrd wondered if Loveless had assembled eighty men. He couldn't count in the melee that crowded onto the sand. They overran the beach, a disorderly band, streaming wet, slippery on their saddles, cursing.

One of the men raised a flask to his lips. Another man did the same. And yet another.

In the midst of the throng, Loveless sat unperturbed on his white horse. The white hat was still dry, still unsullied. His voice rang out. "Hand me that flask."

The nearest man stared at him. "Who has one?" he asked. "Give it to me." He put his hand on his pistol.

The man said, "Ain't worth getting shot over," and the flask went to Loveless.

Loveless uncapped the flask and poured the whiskey onto the sand. Someone said, "Damn shame."

Loveless dropped the flask on the sand. "You're a damn shame, all of you. You call yourself soldiers? You're cowards, every one of you."

"We ain't cowards!"

"Yes, you are," he said. "Getting drunk before you fight! You're afraid of a bunch of niggers."

"We ain't afraid of a bunch of niggers!" someone yelled. They hooted and howled and let out the Rebel yell. Someone called out, "We'll kill them niggers!"

A familiar voice. Young Dixon. Dixon raised his rifle high and bellowed, "Who's with me? To kill them niggers?"

Byrd thought, Worse than the Comanches. No command, no order, drunk on the field. They ain't soldiers. Act wild, fight wild. We have a brawl on our hands.

Byrd knew how to fight a battle that was like a brawl. You ducked and dipped and scrambled to confuse your adversary. He hoped with all his strength that his sharpshooters could bend to the dance that Loveless' ruffians would lead them. He prayed that they would lend their skill as lifelong tricksters, Br'er Rabbit dancing with Br'er Fox, to fight these men and win.

It was time to wait, to gather strength, and to see what the adversary would do.

Loveless said, "You want to kill niggers? Go up the hill and find them."

Someone else said, "They killed that scout right dead."

"Are you cowards? Up the hill."

A man dismounted. He moved with difficulty and he stood crooked. He said, "Reckon I'll earn that money Little promised us. Up the hill. Who's with me?"

One man slid from his horse, then another. None of them were tall or straight or young. Byrd wondered what kind of band Loveless had put together. "We'll go with you," one of them said quietly. The crooked man limped toward the willows that separated the beach from the hill, and the rest followed him in a cluster, moving as carefully as hunters. The crippled man's fellows looked upward. They were like hunting dogs, sniffing the air.

Young Dixon pushed himself forward. "Follow me!"

Byrd was two men at once. He was dead calm, as a soldier should be, and he was full of murderous rage. Without the discipline of twenty years of soldiering, he would raise his rifle and shoot Dixon dead on the spot.

But he would not. He would wait. He would let the enemy dance itself into death, on the path and up the hill.

Dixon yelled, "Let's go kill some niggers!" His band ran with him, brandishing their rifles and hollering out the Rebel yell. They ran across the beach, past the willows, through the opening Willis had made for the path uphill.

And they paused, confused by the corduroy road.

Dixon yelled again. "Up the hill! They're up the hill!"

His horde came with him, their boots pounding on the logs, their rifles held like torches, firing into the air. The smell of black powder drifted toward Byrd and his whole body rose to it.

Now, Byrd thought. He fired into the crowd, not caring where he hit, giving the signal.

He slipped into the protection of the thicket. Around him, rifle fire sounded. Thank God, he thought. Good men, sighting and shooting just as we drilled it. Fire and fire and fire and reload to fire again. Hit whatever you can. Keep firing. The bullets hissed and burst like deadly popcorn. The air in the thicket filled with the smell of black powder, overpowering the smell of black mud. Byrd's two selves twined together, one dead calm enough to aim true, the other full near to bursting with rage as explosive as gunpowder.

The men on the path began to fall. "Damn, I'm hit!" someone yelled, as though he were surprised that a black man could fire a bullet to wound and kill. Men fell with a thud, and shrieked into the thicket's depths. Someone shouted, "Help me! Damn you, help me!" And someone else screamed, "I'm dying! I'm dying!" Byrd saw a man hit in the throat, bright blood spurting, fall to the ground, his blood running in rivulets onto the logs. He had no speech. He stretched out his hands, gurgled, and died.

The sharpshooters never spoke, never showed themselves, and never stopped. They fired and fired and fired and reloaded to fire again. The men on the path screamed and fell, cried out and died.

A man detached himself from the pack under fire and fled into the thicket. Several others—Byrd couldn't see how many— followed him. They crashed through the thicket and stopped. Getting their bearings, Byrd thought. He couldn't see where. The faint light that helped the sharpshooters also aided the men who deserted the battle on the path.

Byrd waited. They would betray themselves soon enough.

He couldn't see through the trees, but he could hear the thud of feet on the wet dirt and the crashing sounds as men tore through the thicket. It came from somewhere down the hill. Damn, Byrd thought, it's worse than tracking a deer. At least a deer has the sense to freeze when it knows it's in danger.

He didn't move. He had warned the sharpshooters again and

again about leaving the safety of their hiding places. About the risk of shooting each other. He would stay put, just as he had schooled his men, until he knew where the intruders where, and where the shots came from.

The sound of rifle fire was like a light in the darkness: a single shot, meant to flush out a hidden man. The call of the bullet brought forth a crack of response from a sharpshooter. There was another shot from the first gun, Loveless' man, and another. There was no cry of pain or scream of death, but there was no answering fire from the sharpshooter, Willie Rice.

Byrd ignored all the advice he had given his men. He ran. As in a fight with the Comanches, he ran as silently as he could, slipping from hiding place to hiding place, ready to duck at the sound of a shot. The trees were old growth here and the sun never hit the ground. His boots squelched into mucky dirt.

Whoever had shot called out, "Where are you hiding, nigger? Come out and show yourself, you coward!"

The sharpshooter's shot reached its target. The man cried out, his voice choked with blood. The second shot rang out, and the body hit the ground with a dull thud.

Just down the hill, another man rampaged through the trees, trampling the grass underfoot, tearing the vines aside. He screamed as he ran. "I'll kill you! Damn cowards, I'll kill you!" Painter. Young Dixon's friend. The man who beat him when Dixon stole his sidearm.

Byrd thought, You crash and yell and we know exactly where you are. We sight on you like you a maddened bear.

Painter ran deeper into the thicket, past Robinson's position. Robinson shot too soon. The bullet sang past Painter and Painter shot toward the sound of rifle fire. There was a cry of pain. Robinson in pain.

Byrd put aside all thought of his own safety. He ducked and ran down the hill, not caring that Painter could hear him. Painter began to fire and the rifle fire followed Byrd as he ran.

Someone else began to fire. Not from a sharpshooter's position. Damn, Byrd thought, another ruffian on the hill. He was in the line of Painter's fire and the stranger's. But no bullet hit him or even came close. It was aimed in the direction of Painter. Painter swiveled, looking for the source of the gunshots, brandishing his rifle. Distracting fire, Byrd thought. Covering for me. One of his own, standing in a spot he hadn't ordered, protecting him as he ran to Robinson's aid.

Who in God's name was it? No time to find out. Painter stopped firing. Byrd ran. He was grinning. Damn fool needs to reload, he thought.

Robinson sat upright, clenching his bloodied sleeve, gritting his teeth against pain. "How bad?" Byrd whispered.

"Hurts like the devil. Can't shoot."

"Hide. Stay quiet."

Byrd edged behind a tree, an old twisted cypress hung with great concealing curtains of Spanish moss. The tree reeked of musk and the dirt stank of rot. The smell of black powder, the smell of battle, hung in the air. Byrd would wait. He knew that Painter would make a sound to give himself away.

Byrd heard footsteps in the wet dirt. The rustle of movement through marsh grass. The creak of cane as someone forced it aside. Painter stopped, turning his head, craning to see through the thicket. He yelled, "Show yourself, you cowardly nigger!"

Byrd felt the sharpshooter's calm flow through him and sighted on the man's chest. He aimed. He fired. Again. And again. The third shot was a fatal bullseye. Painter dropped to the ground, blood gushing from his chest. He was dead.

On the path, the survivors fled down the path in a ragged crowd, screaming in fear: "Damn niggers, they'll kill us all!" Gunfire pursued them as they retreated. A bullet caught a man in the forefront of the melee. When he fell to the ground, the mob behind him trampled the body in their rush to flee the hill. They shoved their way through the opening in the willows and ran for the beach yelling in panic. Byrd recognized young Dixon's voice: "Run, damn you! Before they kill us all!"

On the beach, panicked men shoved each other in their haste to mount their horses. The horses, half of them riderless, jostled each other, nipping and kicking in their haste to bolt. The men on horseback were swept away in retreat as the panicked animals stampeded into the river, taking the survivors with them.

In the midst of the horde was the man on the white horse. Can't command his men, Byrd thought, but they make a fine shield for him. Byrd aimed, sighting on the white hat, but he couldn't get a clear shot. He lowered the rifle. Loveless wasn't dead. Not today.

The sharpshooters watched and listened and waited. Byrd thought, I should look at that position. See who moved there. When it was safe to move, he made his way there.

But no one stood there.

Byrd ran onto the path and whistled as loud as he could. The sharpshooters emerged from the thicket, some laughing in relief, some ashy. Robinson came out on his feet, bare-chested, his shirt torn to make an improvised bandage, sticky with blood. "It were only a graze," he said, trying to sound jaunty, but he looked shaken.

Byrd said, "You did fine. We whupped 'em. Made them turn tail and run."

They nodded, pleased with their commander's praise.

Byrd said, "One thing perplex me. Did one of you change position?"

They shook their heads. Young Glover said, "We stayed put, just like you commanded us."

"Then who was behind the lines covering me when I ran?"

Blank looks.

Byrd said, "Don't mind it. We have the dead to see to."

The path was littered with the dead. Byrd counted them, surprised that only nineteen men could look like a vanquished troop. One of the men was not quiet. He moaned softly, too badly wounded to move.

Byrd bent down and rolled the man over. He had been shot in the gut. He would die slowly, in agony.

The younger Glover said, "Do we take him prisoner?"

Byrd said, "No." He took out his rifle and shot the dying man.

They edged into the thicket, looking for bodies, and dragged them onto the path. They viewed the dead, and for Byrd, the silence was too much like respectful grief. He thought of every white man he had ever hated, his master, his overseer, his adversary Painter. Bile rose into his throat. He nudged the nearest corpse with his muddied boot. "Don't mourn these men. They don't deserve it."

Truehart and the Napoleon crew ran down the path. Glover hugged both of his boys, and all four Willises huddled together in relief that they were unscathed. Out of breath, Truehart asked, "Byrd? How are they?"

"All right except for Robinson."

"How is he?"

"He says it ain't bad."

"How many did we get?"

Byrd gestured towards the corpses. "Counted nineteen."

"Loveless?"

Byrd shook his head.

Truehart said, "We dump them all in the river. And leave their pockets alone! We want everyone to know who they are. How they died."

Byrd said, "We take their guns and their cartridges. We'll need them."

The younger Glover son said, "I don't feel right," and he bent over and puked onto the sand. Byrd went over and put his arm around Glover's shoulders. Glover's face was wet with tears. "Didn't think it would be like that," he said, wiping his face.

The flies had begun to cluster on the corpses and to feed on the blood that had soaked into the dirt of the path. The sharpshooters dragged the bodies of the fallen men onto the beach and dumped them, one at a time, into the river.

Truehart helped Byrd drag Painter's body down to the shore.

He said, "We tell Mr. Levy that Mr. Painter won't be bothering him anymore."

As Painter's corpse splashed into the water, Byrd began to laugh. He couldn't stop; he guffawed until tears ran from his eyes. Truehart asked, "Are you all right, soldier?"

As the exhilaration of battle faded, he felt deeply tired and sick at his stomach. He wiped his face with his sleeve. "I will be."

When the hill and the beach were cleared, the men clustered together. They stood quietly in the hot, humid air that smelled of black powder and spilled blood. Blood plumed in the water as the brown silty current of the river washed the corpses clean. The vultures circled above, waiting for their share. All of them watched as the bodies floated in the muddy water and slowly began their journey down the river.

Miss Louisa screamed when her husband returned with his arm in a bloodied sling, but she didn't faint. Niecy grabbed hold of her husband and cried out, "Tell us what happen!" Danny Willis opened his arms to embrace Miss Carrie and little Isabella both. Next to him, Miss Maggie folded Willis in a tight embrace and a cry of relief. "You all right! You safe!"

Byrd stood aside, watching the women embrace their husbands and sons and sob with the worry they hadn't let themselves feel during the battle. Bernie stood aside, too. He caught her eye and she turned away. Upset.

Jerusha ran to him and hugged him tight, as relieved as any other woman. "You in one piece!"

Byrd broke away. He felt irritated with both of them—Bernie, for sulking, and Jerusha, for carrying on. He said, "It ain't over, not yet."

He went back to his tent, where Buster waited for him. He rubbed the dog's head and said nothing. If he talked to Buster he would do something unbecoming a soldier. He would bust out into something. A puking fit or tears, he didn't know.

Jerusha brought him a plate of food and he nodded and

tried to eat as she talked to him, her voice high and breathy with nerves. She said, "Ambrose, you ain't listening to me."

He wasn't. He was thinking of the odd sharpshooter. Someone who knew the island well enough to sight through the trees and the vines. Someone who had a keen ear and a sharp eye and the skill to shoot through the trees at a man fifty feet away.

Byrd put down the plate, too upset to finish his dinner, and told Jerusha, "Let Buster have it."

Byrd found Bernie, who washed dishes in a tub of water, looking as though she hadn't stirred from kitchen duty all day.

Byrd said, "Step aside with me. We talk quietly, you and I."

Bernie wiped her hands on her apron and followed him to the other side of the hill. They stood near the tree where the shots came from. He said, "Were it you on the hill this morning, standing here?"

Bernie said, "I've been cooking dinner all day. Ask my mama."

"Who covered me when I ran for Robinson?"

She turned away. He grabbed her by the shoulders. "Look at me! Were it you?"

What a strange look on her face. Sick and proud at the same time, just like young Glover. She couldn't contain it any longer. She grinned and said, "Saved your hide, didn't I?"

He shook her. "If you were my soldier, I'd court martial you. Put you in jail! Give you a discharge, and not an honorable one!"

"But you said I was your soldier," she said.

He was too angry to fool with her feelings. The anger rose in him like a tide, that she had put herself in peril against her father's wishes and his own. It took all his self-control not to slap her face. Afraid that he might, he grabbed her wrists. He shouted at her, "Don't want you on that hill, fighting. Do you hear me?"

She tried to step back but his grip was too tight. She couldn't. "Sergeant Byrd, let me go."

"Will you promise me? Lay that rifle down, stay off the hill?"

"Sergeant Byrd, you're hurting me, let me go."

He kept his hands on her wrists, because he was angry enough to hit her in the face. If he held her arms tight, he couldn't. "Promise me."

Now afraid, she cried out, "Let me go!"

Her fear sobered him. Ashamed, he let her go. He couldn't look at her and couldn't speak. She fled.

He searched for a quiet spot to sit. He missed the glade. He missed hunting on the island with the girl who was part of the forest. He missed the daughter he had never had, and the wife he had never had, and the peace he would never find.

He stared at the river, where the gnats danced and the ducks fussed over the ducklings, as though the water had never been a burial ground. He stretched out his legs and realized that he had blood as well as mud on his boots. He wiped the sweat from his face with his sleeve. His shirt had been bloodied, too. He didn't know whether it was Robinson's or a dead man's, and the thought troubled him.

He was a soldier with murder in his heart, and he was angry enough to hurt someone he loved. He felt sick with the thought of it. He hadn't talked to God much in his life, but he wondered if God would forgive him. Back scarred up by slavery and heart hardened by battle. He sat for a long time, thinking, looking out at the water, feeling remorse and regret, hoping that someday he might feel repentant, too.

Not today. He had a battle yet to fight.

Finally he rose to find Truehart. Truehart stood next to the Napoleon, staring over the river with a weary glance. But he roused himself, and with a commander's concern, he said, "You look bothered, Sergeant Byrd."

He said, "Thinking about the battle this morning, how it went."

"We won."

"Won this round. You know it ain't over yet."

"What are you thinking?"

"I wouldn't say this to the men. But it were touch and go on the hill. Don't want another battle like that. Want to be sure next time."

Truehart said, "What are you telling me?"

"Next time they come, we use the Napoleon."

Truehart looked at him in surprise. Byrd said, "We warn the men. When they come, we clear the hill and we use the Napoleon."

"You sure about this."

Finish it. And keep Bernie off the hill, away from battle, safe. "I am."

"Won't get mad and change your mind this evening."

"No, sir, I won't."

Truehart said, "All right. When they come back, we use the Napoleon."

"They come back. Loveless ain't dead yet."

The next day, all four of them—Byrd and Truehart, Willis and Thornton—rested their hands on the cannon as though it were a big, patient mule. Truehart said, "It's time to use the Napoleon."

Willis said, "You been saying that all along." He asked Byrd, "What about you? What do you say?"

Byrd pushed away the thought of Bernie. He said, "I agree."

In astonishment, Willis said, "You been naysaying the Napoleon ever since Jim first mentioned it. Want to hear why you changed your mind."

Byrd said irritably, "Saw the reason of it."

"Thought the battle on the hill went all right."

It was relief to wrap Bernie's secret in a military truth. He said, "It were touch and go on the hill last time, when they only send up twenty men. Don't want to risk the sharpshooters again. We use the Napoleon."

Willis didn't reply. Byrd said, "We use the Napoleon, we get them all. Loveless and his men. We done."

"Hope so," Willis said.

Truehart said, "Don't tell me you naysaying me, too."

"Ain't naysaying." He looked down the hill. "Just figuring. Have to figure it right so it rain down on them."

Byrd asked, "Can you do that?"

Willis looked down the hill again. "Easiest to show you." He gestured with his arm, to show how the canister would fly through the air. "Don't want anyone on that hill. Can't predict just how the shot will scatter when the canister bursts. Don't want your sharpshooters in its path."

"Won't be a difficulty to take everyone off the hill." Except for Bernie, he thought, worried again.

"Man, don't tell me to plan the trajectory and rehearse the crew, just to find out you changed your mind," Willis said.

Truehart said, "We so close. We almost done here. Use the Napoleon and we finished." He looked at Willis. "Don't know. Only God do. But we hope and pray so."

Willis wasn't done yet. "Ain't a matter for prayer. Got to stand on the hill, figure where they might stand, figure how to point the gun. To finish it."

Since Byrd raised his voice to Bernie, she had avoided him. She was afraid of him. It shamed him every time he saw her, to see that bright face turned away from him. But he had to tell her about the Napoleon. He had to warn her off the hill.

He stood a respectful distance from her, his hands clasped together like the Reverend's, his voice low. "Miss Bernie, may I speak with you?"

She found it hard to look at him. She stared somewhere past his head. She nodded.

He said, "Somewhere quiet."

"Quiet enough right here for me to listen to you."

He gestured. "Just down the hill, not far from the Napoleon."

Close enough for the Napoleon crew to hear if he lost his temper. "All right."

Once they were situated on the hill, she stood as far from him as she could and still hear him. She waited.

He didn't know what he wanted to say first. Slowly—it didn't come out easy—he said, "Your daddy and I decided that the next time Loveless' men come, we use the Napoleon."

"I heard," she said.

"We clear the hill to get ready to fire it."

She raised her eyes to his. She didn't seem to need to blink.

"Anyone on the hill in danger of getting hit." He swallowed. "We clear the hill." He implored her. "Keep everyone safe."

Still looking at him. The best shot, and the most disobedient soldier. Not speaking.

"Miss Bernie." The words came out of him like heart's blood. "I regret that I raised my voice to you. That I put my hands on you. It were wrong, and I know it."

Silence.

"I ask for your forgiveness."

Surprise rippled over her face. Now she was too startled to speak. He wanted to reach out to her, to take her hand and hold it softly in his own, but he didn't dare. He broke the silence. "Your daddy and I, we don't oppose you for being able to shoot. Hunting's just fine. Puts food on the table. But shooting a man, that's different. It hurts your soul. That's what we can't bear. That anything would hurt your soul."

Bernie said slowly, "You've been killing men all your life. Has it hurt your soul?"

He couldn't reply. He knew, better than she did, how damaged his soul had become. In silence, he told her so. He couldn't bear to see the feeling on her face and he fled from it. As he returned to the camp, he ached in every part of his body, and he limped like a wounded man.

Chapter 10

Blood on the Sand

As soon as Byrd saw the rowboat, he was instantly alert. But it was oared by a woman, brown of skin. It was Delia, who dropped the oars, waved her arms, and called out, "Don't shoot at me, Sergeant Byrd! Come with news!"

Delia's boat scraped over sand that was still dirtied with the blood of Loveless' dead men. She stepped into a pool that had dried to a rusty brown.

The sharpshooters massed around her, holding their rifles as though she were an invader. She was haggard and sweating like someone sick with fever. "Put them things down," she said. "I have news. And I'd like to see Niecy." Her eyes darted across the beach and up the hill.

Byrd said to young Rice, "Come with me." He marched the boy toward the willows at the edge of the hill and whispered, "Don't want her up the path, seeing the Napoleon." He bent close. "She used to spy for Marse Little and I believe she still do."

As they waited for the Trueharts, Delia's eyes skimmed the river and the beach and the hill like the fluttering flight of gnats.

What do she look for? Byrd thought. Nothing to see but silty water and dirty sand and a mess of weeping willows.

Truehart ran down the hill, followed by Niecy, who panted with the effort. Niecy flung her arms around Delia. She scolded, "You ain't to be here! It's too dangerous!"

Delia said, "Marse Little sent me. Gave me a paper to say so."

Byrd thought, Like a pass! Like in slavery days! Despite all his doubts about Delia he burned in sympathy for her. "Did anyone bother you?"

"Loveless stop me. Read the paper. Tell his men to leave me alone."

Byrd thought, We know how well they obey him. "What do Marse Little want you to find out?"

"I recall what you said to me, Mr. Byrd. How we tell him a bit of the truth to fool him. How we make him look at the right hand when the left hand do what need to be done."

Truehart ordered Delia, "Tell us your news first."

"The bodies washed up down the river. Place called Beulah. And Loveless' men let the word go out. Everyone know you on the island and that you fight for it." She drew a deep breath and it caught in her throat as a sob. "Colonel Loveless go to Marse Little and talk about finding more men. Can't get any. Marse Little mad as can be. Say he don't know why he hire Loveless if he can't frighten a bunch of worthless niggers. Tell him to use the men he got to finish it off." She wiped her ashen face with her apron. "Loveless' men mighty mad, too. They go into town and get drunk and mill about in the street hollering about niggers and people who help them out. They stomp into Mr. Levy's store and threaten him at gunpoint. They tear the place up, shoot at Mr. Levy."

Byrd grabbed Delia's arm. "What happen to Mr. Levy?"

"He shoot back. Then he run off. Safe. Don't know where he went." She cast her eyes upward, through the willows, toward the hill.

"What are you looking at?" Byrd demanded, tightening his grip on Delia's arm.

She shook like a woman with ague. "Nothing. Let go of me, Mr. Byrd, you hurt my arm."

As Bernie had said. Shamed, Byrd let go. She implored Niecy. "I give you my news. Now you give me something to tell Marse Little."

Byrd lay on the ground, worn out but too restless to fall asleep. Buster curled up next to his leg, his warmth soft and heavy in the night's heat. Byrd sighed and stroked the dog's rough flank. Buster whimpered, twitched his ears and his paws, and thumped his tail in his sleep. Buster dreamed, and his rest was not peaceful, either. Finally Byrd fell asleep himself.

Buster's keen ears heard something through his dream and through the nighttime cacophony of the island. He struggled to stand on his arthritic legs and began to bark. Byrd immediately woke. "What is it, boy?" he asked the dog. "What's the matter, Buster?"

Buster barked and barked. Other dogs began to bark in response. People began to wake, angry at being pulled from their own uneasy sleep, recalling the false alarm of Miss Louisa's nightmare. "That damn dog! Rouse me out of a sound sleep! Whatever is he fussing about?"

Byrd bolted upright and grabbed his rifle. He ran to the edge of the camp to hear the boat that splashed and struggled through the cane that grew in the water. The moon cast so little light that he couldn't tell how many men oared the boat.

Byrd cursed himself for not setting up a guard on the swamp side. It was impregnable, he thought, because of the way the shore gave way too abruptly to cane growing in mud. No one could land there. And now Loveless' men were here, trying to.

Buster roused the rest of the dogs in the camp and they growled and barked in response. Men emerged from the tents, half-dressed, rifles in their hands. Women and children crawled out, still in their nightclothes. Byrd ran through the camp, calling out, "Men in a boat! Loveless' men, on the mucky side!"

"Damn you, if it's another nightmare—" Glover growled.

"Get your rifles!" Byrd shouted. The Glover boys ran through the camp, yelling with excitement. "Is it a battle?" the elder asked. "Can we fight?" added the younger.

Byrd cuffed them as he ran by. "Get down! Stay back!"

Louisa Robinson sank to the ground. Her littlest daughter fell into her lap, sobbing. "Is they coming for us?" she asked. Louisa rocked the little girl and closed her eyes. "Dear Lord," she murmured. "Keep us safe. Keep our children safe."

Bernie threw back the flap of her tent, her hair tangled, her eyes puffy with sleep, rifle in hand. She wore a long white nightdress that anyone might sight on. When she rose to her feet, Byrd tackled her and brought her flat to the ground. His mouth pressed to her ear, he said, "Get down and stay down!"

She tried to rise but he pinned her tight. She said fiercely, "Let go of me."

"Stay down." As he gripped her, he was sharply aware of her body under the white cotton. Her green apple scent was strong underneath her sweat of fear. It gave him pleasure to feel her long limbs underneath him and to smell her skin. When he realized how much pleasure he felt, he rolled off her and growled, "What were you thinking?"

Remarkably cool for a girl who had just been covered by a man, she said, "Trying to help."

He didn't bother to be sweet to her. "Stay here! Stay down."

He stood and loped away. He was flushed and riled, and not in the best way for a fight.

The men of Willow Bend, half-dressed, half-awake, ran after Byrd. Glover called out, "Where do you want us to stand? What do you want us to do?"

"Line up so you can see. Even line! Don't hit each other. And fire and fire at them until they dead."

Truehart was on the hill with the Napoleon, as though they'd use it in the middle of the night. No time to run for him. They'd manage without him.

The men arranged themselves like turkeys tripping over each other. Byrd cursed himself again. Never saw this coming, he thought. Never drilled for it. And now we all in danger.

The boat came to a standstill in the heavy muck of the swamp. The smell of rot was at its thickest here, so close to the water. The cypresses grew so near together that they blocked the already-faint moonlight.

The first shot from the boat whistled into the disorganized line. Someone gave a startled cry. Damn, if anyone's hurt, Byrd thought. He raised his rifle and began to shoot in the direction of the boat. "Just fire!" He ordered. "Barrage, like on the hill! Keep firing, and when you out, reload!"

The men in the boat fired through the cane, wild shots that flew past the men, hit the cypress trees, and veered into the camp. A woman screamed, whether wounded or frightened Byrd couldn't tell. A baby bawled. Byrd tried not to think of little Isabella, pressed against Miss Carrie's breast. In a fury, Byrd cried out, "Keep firing and don't hit each other!"

Shots came from the boat in a constant pop of fire. Used to the sound of a hunting rifle, all of the dogs of Willow Bend howled and bayed.

Can't see, Byrd thought, as the men of Willow Bend sent unaimed bullets into the darkness. Can't sight. Can't tell if we hit anything or not. Useless to barrage like we at the siege of Vicksburg.

Miss Bessie entreated, "Save us, Jesus! Save us!" Hell of a time for that, Byrd thought. Another woman screamed without words, and others joined her, in duet with the din of the dogs.

The men in the boat cried out and the boat rocked as they deserted it for the mud of the swamp. Three shadowy figures struggled into the mud and sank into it, waist deep. They kept shooting even as the swamp sucked them under. But they couldn't move, and Willow Bend's bullets began to find their targets. One man screamed and slumped in death. Another yelled out, "Damn you! Damn cowards!" The cry was a better beacon than anything a man could see, and Glover shot at it until the second man fell dead, face down in the swamp. The third man thrashed in the water, sinking deeper into the mud as he struggled. The sound drew a rain of gunfire. When he died he fell into the swamp to join everything rank and rotten and dead within it.

The empty boat broke loose of the swamp. The current caught it to take it from the shore, and it drifted away, out of sight, down the river.

Byrd said raggedly, "We wait. Don't know if there's more to come."

The sharpshooters stayed where they were, kneeling in the mud. Behind them, the screams had subsided to sobs. Byrd reminded them, "Wait! Don't know if there's another boat out there."

"How long?" asked Glover, his voice shaky.

They waited. But there was no splash of oars in the water. No gunshot to break the silence. The swamp resumed its usual nighttime noise, the chirp of the littlest frogs and the booming call of the bullfrogs. In the camp, the dogs quieted, and so did the sound of sobbing.

Byrd said, "Half a dozen men stay here on watch tonight." He positioned them in relative safety. "If you hear anything, if you see anything, yell for the rest of us."

The rest of the men ran back to the camp, but Byrd was too tired to hurry. He let the Glover boys flock to their father, who told them in a ragged voice, "They gone. They dead. It all right now. We all right."

Byrd realized how tired he was. He recalled the lumpy mattress in his lean-to as spacious and easy. He walked painfully back to his tent, where Buster lay on the ground, his head on his paws. He was awake, but he didn't try to rise to his feet when he saw Byrd. He didn't lift his head. He opened his eyes and closed them again. Byrd was so weary that he fell to the ground beside the tired dog. "You all right," he murmured, burying his face in

Buster's flank. Buster licked his face in his relief that Byrd was all right, too.

Byrd crawled into the tent and Buster followed him. The dog sighed and curled up against him.

A few hours later, when the sun rose, Byrd woke. He was stiff and sore. He sat up, feeling an aging man's ache in his back and his legs.

Feeling the familiar weight against him, he reached for the dog's flank and touched it, ready to say, "Buster, time to get up, time for breakfast." He stroked Buster's head. "Buster?" Byrd said softly.

The eyes didn't open. The wiry coat was cool to the touch. No breath stirred the bony ribs. Byrd gently pulled back the eyelid to expose the eye and saw the film of death on it.

Buster was gone.

Byrd pressed his cheek to the dog's head and whispered. "Thought we'd come through this together, old boy." He let the tears come.

Jerusha, who usually brought both of them breakfast, peered inside the tent. "What's wrong, Ambrose?"

Byrd sat up, his face wet. "Buster passed on last night."

She knelt and gently stroked the dog's bony flank. "Oh, Ambrose," she said.

"He died peaceful, in his sleep."

"I hope I pass that way, when it's my time." She clasped Byrd's hand.

Byrd rubbed his face with his sleeve. "He was a good soldier," he said.

"We'll bury him like a soldier." Jerusha hugged him and pressed her cheek to his, her tears mingling with his own.

They buried Buster after breakfast, and everyone, except for the men on watch, stood respectfully as Truehart spoke at the graveside. "He was a good soldier," he said, echoing Byrd. "A hero. We is all sorry that he's gone." Byrd bent down to bid his friend goodbye. He watched as Willis and Glover dug the hole, carefully put Buster into it, and covered him with earth as though they were drawing a blanket over him. They marked the spot with a pile of stones. Truehart laid a comforting hand on Byrd's shoulder. "We'll come back later and mark it proper," he said.

Byrd rubbed his eyes with his sleeve and Truehart said gently, "You stay here a bit, and when you're ready, come to see me."

"Got to figure how to use that Napoleon," Byrd said, throaty.

"Not this moment. Take your time."

Jerusha joined him at Buster's grave. She didn't speak, which he was grateful for. She clasped his hand and rested her head on his shoulder—she was of a height to fit, and she fit as though she belonged there. They stood together in saddened silence.

Byrd drifted up the hill to the glade, where Truehart and Willis hovered over the Napoleon. Byrd was sick of the Napoleon, and he was sick of hearing Truehart and Willis fuss over it like it was a prize horse. Truehart asked anxiously, "You figured the arc? For the beach, and for the hill?"

"For both," Willis said impatiently.

"Is one better than the other?"

"No."

Truehart stared at the barrel of the cannon. "I worry about them canisters. What if they don't explode?"

Willis looked at him with exasperation. "Don't see why."

"If they don't—"

Their voices sounded like the chatter of the birds in the live oaks. Byrd slumped against the carriage, more fatigued than he wanted to admit.

Truehart rested his hand on Byrd's shoulder. "Is you all right?" he asked, with a tenderness he usually reserved for Bernie.

Byrd's eyes stung and he blinked before he straightened. In battle, he never had time to grieve, and he was still in battle. "I'm all right." He surveyed the river and the shore across it, as they all did, anticipating Loveless' men at any moment. "If the Napoleon fail, we sent the sharpshooters back down the hill. Barrage them, like we did last time. And pray to God that we dispatch them all."

The sound of Loveless' horde on the main shore alerted them: the hooves of the horses pounding through the trees; the popping sound of warning gunfire; the hateful sound of the Rebel yell. Byrd snapped to attention at the enemy's call to battle. He raced down the hill, yelling to the guards, "Clear the hill! Fetch the rest and gather in the glade!" He counted as they emerged, all six of them. But he worried. Was Bernie really safe? Or was she defying him, hiding on the hill?

He asked young Glover, "Everyone off the hill?"

"We clear the hill."

"You sure? No one hiding?"

Puzzled, Glover said, "We sure, Sergeant Byrd."

The sharpshooters scrambled to the crest of the hill to stand in safety behind the glade. Byrd addressed them. "We use the Napoleon today. God willing, it do its job, and we won't need sharpshooters. But you stand ready. If I give the signal you run down the hill and take your positions and we barrage, like last time."

Danny Willis asked, "Sergeant Byrd, why wouldn't the Napoleon do its job?"

"Plan for the worst, in battle. Then you ain't surprised when it go right."

Loveless' men landed on the beach, as disorderly as before, a moving throng, with the tall figure in the white hat at its center. We get him, Byrd thought. Then it's over. Cut off a snake's head and it dies.

The white hat gleamed under the morning sun, and rage flooded Byrd. He's mine, Byrd thought. Want to fire the shot that does him in. Want to finish him, today. The smell of blood had gotten into his nose, and he imagined he could taste it, too.

Not the soldier's thought, or the sharpshooter's thought. The killer's thought. We're better than that, Sergeant Shaw's voice whispered inside Byrd's head. Once again, Byrd thought, Perhaps I ain't.

Byrd thought that Loveless' men might come more orderly or more subdued than last time, but again, they were as disorderly as a mob. They spurred their horses into the water and whipped them forward in the river. They held their guns high—they'd learned that much, how to keep a rifle dry—but they yelled and whooped as loud as the Comanches. More hateful than the Comanches. The Rebel yell that boiled the blood of every black soldier. If silence and stealth hadn't mattered, Byrd would have burst into "John Brown's Body" to drown out the sound of former Confederates bent on murdering black men.

They spilled onto the beach, spurring their horses to make them scream and rear. They shouted over the din the horses made. "We're going to kill some niggers today. Kill them all!"

Someone else yelled, "Gals on the back of the hill, boys! Spare them! Got a use for them!"

They erupted into drunken laughter. Byrd surveyed his sharpshooters, who gripped their rifles so hard their knuckles paled. Their faces were as hard as stone.

Truehart and Willis, joined by Thornton, stood by the cannon, readied and loaded with the canister, the gunpowder, and the igniter. All that remained was to pull the lanyard that served as the cannon's trigger. Beside the Napoleon sat the box of canisters, with its extra bags of gunpowder and tubes of igniter, and the tools to reload—the sponge to clean the barrel and the worm to tamp the canister into place. Byrd's gut tightened as he caught Truehart's fears. The canister wouldn't explode. The ruffians would overrun the hill. He stared at the melee on the beach.

Truehart asked, "Is we ready?"

"Let them come up the hill," Willis replied.

They poured through the opening in the willows and streamed onto the path. They shot wild into the thicket, not bothering to aim, whooping in their eagerness. Byrd's nerves tightened.

"Now?" Willis asked.

Truehart nodded. Byrd braced himself, and Willis pulled the lanyard.

The powder ignited in a thick, choking, blinding smoke, booming so loudly that Byrd's ears ached, and for a moment he didn't know if the canister had exploded. Then he saw the grapeshot flying through the air in a deadly rain.

The grapeshot mowed down men like a scythe mowing down grass. The dead toppled to the ground and the wounded fell to their knees, blood blossoming on their shirts. The dying clutched at their wounded chests and grabbed their wounded guts. The air thickened with screaming. The survivors yelled in rage, "Cannon fire! They have a cannon!" Whoever could stand fled down the hill, slipping on the wounded and dead, tripping on the bloodied logs. On the beach, the horses, unused to cannon fire, screamed and bolted into the river.

Among the mass on the hill, Byrd saw no white hat.

Truehart said, "Reload and we shoot another." In the war, an artilleryman swabbed the barrel to prevent fire, but there was no time for it now. Willis rammed the gunpowder and the canister into the barrel and snapped the igniter into the breech. "Stand back," he told Truehart, and he yanked the lanyard.

This time Byrd shielded his ears against the explosion, but he coughed with the smoke and blinked hard against the way it burned his eyes. On the path, the fleeing men fell and mingled with the dying and the dead. The dying writhed and groaned in agony. A high-pitched voice, too young for a battle like this one, shrilled out: "Mama!" The wounded cursed and screamed. "Damn niggers!"

Willis asked, "Do we reload?"

"Yes," Truehart replied. "Want to finish off any man who damns a nigger with his last breath." Willis reloaded and fired. Through the blast and the smoke, Byrd thought, No man live through that.

Fallen men twitched and writhed as their lives slipped away. The screaming faded and all that remained were the sounds of men dying, groaning and gasping for breath and gurgling as blood drowned them from within. The moaning grew fainter and fainter, and the movement weaker and weaker.

Truehart said, "Now we go down the hill."

The sharpshooters bunched together and slowly descended the path, rifles ready. Danny Willis asked, "Like last time? No prisoners?"

Byrd said, "Shoot at anything that makes a sound or moves."

At the base of the path, men were heaped, their limbs twisted, their faces and bodies striated with blood. A sickening, soft plea came from men who looked like corpses, and who quivered with the last breath of life.

At Byrd's feet lay a man whose face was covered with blood. He muttered through a mouth filled with blood. Byrd pointed his rifle at the man's bloodied shirt. "No," the man murmured, too weak to say anything more. Byrd pressed the barrel of his rifle against the man's temple. "No," the man murmured again. Byrd shot him and he was still.

Next to him lay a man who was dead. Byrd shot him too.

"Why shoot a dead man?" Danny Willis asked.

"Make sure he's dead."

Their faces somber, the men of Willow Bend followed Byrd's example, shooting the dying and the dead.

Byrd turned over a man whose hair was clotted with blood. He had been shot in the neck. It was young Dixon.

Byrd nudged him with his foot. Byrd said, "Do you recall me?"

Dixon stared at him through glassy eyes. Byrd aimed his shotgun at Dixon's chest. Unable to speak, Dixon nodded.

Byrd shot young Dixon in the chest—once, twice, three times. Even though Dixon was dead, he shot him in the head, too. He rolled the corpse to hunt for the pistol in Dixon's holster. Truehart said, "What are you doing? Leave their pockets alone!"

Byrd said, "He stole it from me. Taking back what's mine." His hand shook as he brandished it. "Got my name engraved on it." He undid the belt of Dixon's holster, which was smeared with dirt and soaked with blood, and buckled it around his hips.

It was easier to kill a dying man with a pistol than a rifle, and Byrd used every bullet in the revolver, and reloaded it to use it again.

Finally every man on the path was dead.

The island was silent. The smoke and blast had frightened the birds away. The grapeshot so deadly to men had sent the wild creatures deep into the thicket. Byrd recalled the aftermath of the Battle of the Wilderness, finding the blackened corpses of birds and rabbits along with those of horses and men.

On the sullied path lay the white hat, bloodied and dirtied. Loveless might be dead. Byrd hoped not. He had a different death in mind for Loveless.

Truehart picked up the white hat. He asked, "Where's Loveless?"

Byrd said, "We find him when we dump everyone in the river."

One by one, they dragged the corpses over the sand, adding to the blood of the earlier battle, and dumped them in the river. The task stained their hands, soaked their clothes, and filthied their boots with blood, as though they had been as badly wounded as Loveless' men. Byrd dumped the last man in the river and knelt to wash the blood from his hands.

As they watched the bodies float away, Truehart said, "Didn't see Loveless. Or his man, Dixon."

"How could they get away?" Byrd wondered.

"Don't know. But they ain't among the dead." Truehart looked upward. "Is he on the hill?"

They listened for the sound of someone on the hill. Byrd said, "We go up the hill to look."

Warily, slowly, the sharpshooters ascended the path. Byrd said, "Go into the thicket, two at a time. Quiet, like you hunting deer." He and Truehart entered the thicket and combed it, treading softly and peering through the trees, hoping to find Loveless and flush him out. But they found no one.

They gazed at river, where blood plumed in the water and the vultures hissed at the corpses that floated downstream. Loveless wasn't dead yet. Byrd felt his presence still, as though he might reappear to lead one more charge.

Willis said, "We ain't done yet."

"No, we ain't." Byrd said.

When they returned to the camp, Niecy cried out, "You all over blood!" and burst into tears.

"Ain't ours," Truehart said grimly. "Threw a mess of dead bloodied men in the river."

Still sobbing, she asked, "Is it over?"

"Loveless and his man Dixon ain't dead yet," Truehart said.

Niecy cried out in fear, "Where is they?"

Truehart shook his head.

"Slipped away? After this? Slipped through our fingers?"

Bernie stood at the edge of the crowd. Byrd felt her eyes on him. He said to Niecy, "Managed to survive the Napoleon. Probably swam to shore. On the other side of the river somewhere."

"Why are you standing there? Go after him and finish it for good!" Niecy shouted.

Truehart took his wife's arm. "Niecy, honey—"

Byrd couldn't bear it. "I'll go."

"Not alone," Truehart said.

"You need a scout. Not a troop."

"Don't act the fool, not now. We think about it for a moment. Who go with you."

"Ain't time." Byrd's hand stole to the pistol he had just taken back from the thief, young Dixon.

"We go together. Take my boat."

They ran for Truehart's boat. Truehart cried out, "Bernie's little boat. It's gone." He shouted into the camp. "Where's Bernie?"

Niecy screamed, "She ain't anywhere! Where did she go?"

Gone.

Byrd knew. "I go after her." And without waiting for Truehart, he dragged the nearest skiff into the water to follow Bernie. Propelled equally by anger and fear, he went after her in pursuit.

Chapter 11

In Pursuit

When Byrd crossed the river, he saw that Bernie hadn't beached at her usual spot. She'd come aground at the swamp. He landed the skiff and stepped carefully onto the shore, following Bernie's footsteps into the swamp. The air smelled green and dark, half sage and half skunk. The vines twisted around the trees, too much like the snakes that Byrd detested. The cottonmouths.

Bernie was here, and so was Loveless.

Something rustled in the cypresses and his hand went instantly to his rifle.

Whatever was rustling dropped to the ground and began to slither. Byrd couldn't see in the noontime gloom, only hear the whisper of its movement. He watched as it came too close to his feet for comfort and he edged away. The snake opened its mouth wide and hissed. The white lining was startling against the snake's black scaly skin. Cottonmouth.

Byrd controlled his impulse to bolt. He would startle the snake, and he would alert Loveless, if he was nearby.

He backed away quietly. The snake didn't move. He continued to back away. The snake closed its maw and slid into the muddy underbrush. Byrd waited until the snake was gone. He waited.

Something crashed through the thicket, hidden by the gloom of the trees and the web of their vines.

Then he heard the shots. Two shots, one right after the other.

He inched slowly through the thicket, stepping quietly. He couldn't see more than a few feet ahead of him. He controlled his impulse to curse, too.

Something white flashed through the trees. A piece of cloth. No hunter or soldier wore white. But Bernie had run from the island in her apron.

He moved towards her, sighting on the white cloth. Keep quiet. Go slow. He held his rifle ready. Not for her. But for whoever might have shot at her.

He came closer.

And found her, on her feet, her rifle pointed at him.

They regarded each other with equal surprise. She said, "It's you."

"You're all right."

She lowered her rifle. Her hands shook. "I just shot two men dead." And her knees gave way. She sank to the ground and buried her face in her hands as though she were asking God for forgiveness.

He sank to his knees before her. "Bernie," he said softly. She raised her head. In the dim light of the swamp, her face had a ghostly look. He asked, "Where did they fall?"

She pointed. He rose. "I go to look."

"I go with you." She tried to stand, but her legs were too shaky.

He touched her shoulder. "No. You stay here."

He crept through the thicket with a scout's caution. He had been in battle long enough to know that a shot didn't mean a death.

A man lay slumped at his feet, his shirt front stained with

blood. His eyes were open. He was short and stocky, and when he was alive, he had seen fine out of both of them.

Byrd inched through the trees to search the nearby ground. A dying man could stagger through the thicket to die elsewhere. He found footsteps, ragged and uneven. They led into the thicket.

Loveless was still alive. Bernie was alone and unprotected, a few feet away. He couldn't leave her. He edged his way back. She sat unmoving, her rifle slung over her shoulder, her hands resting limply on her knees.

Soldier's heart, they called it in the war. No wound to the flesh, but the heart and mind recalled it over and over, making a hurt worse than the gauge of a bullet or the crater of a minie ball.

He said, "You shot one man." She stared at him. "But he ain't Loveless."

"We go after him."

"No. I take you back to the island."

"We lose him."

"We go find your little boat." He held out his arm.

She stood. Surprised, she said, "I don't feel at all right."

"Lean on me."

They walked slowly back to the shore. She sank against him and he held her tenderly, which she allowed him. He settled her into the canoe and took up the paddle.

As Byrd helped her from the boat, her father came running to meet her. He gathered her into his arms and pressed his cheek to hers. "Bernie, sugar," he said. He held her close, as though she were still a little girl and he could keep her from all hurt by cradling her in strong loving arms.

Love overflowed in Byrd's heart, drowning out the envy. She ain't mine, he thought. She's theirs. He rubbed his face and turned away.

Byrd crossed the river again. He'd start where the dead man still lay. He'd dump him in the river later. Now he needed to find Loveless.

The man had left a trail like a wounded bear, lurching and crashing through the trees, his footprints obvious in the muddy ground. He had been unsteady on his feet. He had fallen, and he had crawled on his hands and knees before rising again. Bernie hadn't killed him, but she had wounded him, and Byrd wondered how far he could go with wounds like that.

The tracks led him toward the road that ran to the Little place. Would he find the mark of a muddied, bloodied boot? He followed the uneven, staggering gait like a hound on a scent until the steps faded, only the scuff of heel and toe on the road, and even those grew faint.

He fell into the long, swift stride of the marching soldier, but he retained the alertness of a scout. He passed the cotton farms of Little's tenants, where the plants grew lush and thick and waist-high. No one chopped in the rows and no one waved from the fields. The sun burned through his shirt and sweat stung his eyes. Water, he thought. He'd ask for water at the next place and find out why Little's tenants were hiding.

He turned at the next dirt path and followed it through the cotton fields until he came to a little house made of weathered, splintered pine. Oilpaper darkened the windows. The door was tightly shut and he saw no living creature: no chicken pecked in the yard, no hog rooted under a tree, and no dog lazed in the dirt.

He knocked on the door and a frightened, muffled voice asked, "Who is it?"

"Ambrose Byrd. From Willow Bend."

The door opened enough to allow a rifle barrel to poke through. Byrd said, "Do you know Jim Truehart? I'm with him on the island."

The door creaked open. A man held the rifle with shaking hands. He asked, "Willow Bend? Willow Island?"

"Yes," Byrd said. The man looked ashen. Byrd asked, "Did you see a tall man with a patch over one eye?"

Trembling, the man said, "Saw him! He put a gun to my head and said he'd shoot me if I didn't give up my horse to him.

Stole my horse from me! Covered with dirt and blood! Looked like he came out of the grave."

"Which way did he go?"

"Tore down the road to the Little place."

Loveless was on horseback and he had the advantage of several miles, maybe more. Byrd asked, "Do anyone else near here have a horse?"

The man was still shaking. He asked, "Did you fight on the island?"

"I did."

"Fought with them ruffians? Killed them all dead?"

"All except this one."

The man's eyes glittered. "That man murdered my relations, ten year ago. We find you a horse."

"I'd be obliged," Byrd said, and a few minutes later, he was on the road on horseback.

From the marks of the hooves in the dirt, Byrd saw that Loveless had forced his horse to a gallop. Wounded or not, he was in a hurry. Byrd urged his own horse to quicken its pace. It was a good horse, a brown gelding, strong of leg and shoulder, a horse that could pull a heavy wagon or carry a man all day. The horse caught Byrd's urgency and broke into a run.

Byrd couldn't shake the habit of vigilance. He was alert for every sound and every movement. He turned his head at the cry of a bird overhead, and he startled at the bray of a mule in a nearby field. He was a scout, sent ahead to look for news of the enemy and to find the best place to fight. He was a soldier, readying himself for battle.

As little as he wanted to, he heard Sergeant Shaw's voice, calm and saddened. "We're soldiers. Fight by the rules of war. We're better than that."

Ain't the same, he told himself. This man served under Forrest and murdered black soldiers. He conspired with Little to murder all of us. He would have killed Bernie, if he had shot first.

He thought of the day he went to find his former overseer. On that day, as today, he had taken his skill as a soldier and put it in service of his murderer's rage.

Soldiers fought. Murderers killed. Soldiers got glory. Murderers went to jail. And then they went to hell.

He thought of the ghosts of Fort Pillow. He thought of the ghosts of the massacre, not far away, still uneasy in their mass grave.

We're better than that.

Byrd thought, Maybe I am. And maybe I ain't.

On the driveway to the Little house, the gravel had been churned by a horse at a furious gallop. Byrd sat up straight and urged on his horse. "Almost there, old boy," he murmured, as he'd once spoken to Buster. "Almost there."

For the first time since he had been on the Little place, Byrd halted at the front door. Today he'd walk past those tall pillars Willis had built. He'd set his boots on those wide fancy steps.

Someone had left the horse untethered. The horse hung its head, lathered, panting, thirsty.

Byrd ran up the stairs and pounded on the door. The butler Sam opened it. Horrified, he said, "You can't come in here!"

Byrd grabbed Sam by the lapel of his butler's coat. "Where is Loveless?"

"Don't go in there," Sam whispered.

Behind Sam, Delia appeared, her face grim, her voice low. "Let him in." Sam flattened himself against the doorframe and Byrd pushed past him. Delia said, "Come with me."

Her pace was deliberate. Like a scout's. They followed the trail of muddied footprints on the carpet. Shards of a vase glittered on the floor. Somewhere in the house, a woman sobbed. Byrd glanced upward. Truehart had told him that Little's ceiling was painted gold. It was, and a bullet hole marred the gilded surface.

In the study, Hiram Little cowered behind his desk, holding up his hands, and a man in a ruined black wool coat, his hair

matted with mud and blood, held out a gun. He shouted, "Your niggers slaughtered my men. Every one. My men are dead. Every one."

Little cried out, "Put the gun down, man. Put the gun down. Sam!"

"If that nigger of yours comes in here I'll shoot him dead."

"What do you want?"

Loveless said, "Can you put it right? The place I lost? The slaves I lost? The mother and father I lost? The honor I lost? Can you put any of that right?"

"Put the gun down, man! You aren't fit to handle a gun!"

Loveless aimed the pistol. Little began to blubber and to beg. "Don't shoot me. What do you want? Don't kill me!"

The hand that held the gun shook.

Little screamed, "Put the gun down! Don't shoot me! I ain't your enemy!"

The pistol shot reverberated so loudly that the windows rattled. Little slumped, his neck spurting blood onto to the mahogany desk that dripped onto the floor and stained the Aubusson rug. He was dead.

Byrd pushed past Delia to rush over the threshold and Loveless swiveled to face him. Loveless' face was crusted over with mud and his goatee was streaked with dried blood. His good eye was wild, the pupil dilated with rage, the white bloodshot. Byrd had seen it before, a man maddened by war, who no longer cared what he did. Byrd's own anger was small compared to this. He was suddenly very cold.

Loveless said, "What are you doing here, nigger?"

Byrd said, "Come to put an end to it."

Loveless tried to raise his pistol to shoot at Byrd, but his arm wouldn't obey him. He couldn't keep it steady.

Byrd trained his gun on Loveless. He had a clear shot to the chest. He could kill him. Put an end to all of it. Was he better than that? Or not?

Loveless raised his arm, but it shook so badly that he couldn't even prop it to still the shaking. He could barely stand. His pistol still trained on Loveless, Byrd said, "Give me your sidearm."

Loveless said hoarsely, "Won't surrender to a nigger," and tried to lift his arm again, and could not.

Byrd held out his hand. "Give me the gun."

Loveless said, "I won't be shot by a nigger, either." He bent his arm, and Byrd was instantly ready, his own pistol drawn.

Loveless said thickly, "Never." He put the gun to his temple, pressing it hard against the flesh to still his shaking hand.

Byrd cried, "No!"

Loveless pulled the trigger and fell to the floor, blood trickling from his temple. He was still.

Byrd stood over Loveless, unable to believe he was dead. He nudged Loveless' body with his foot, too uneasy to touch him.

He stared at the bloodied face, twisted with rage, and the pale blue eye, now filming in death. Byrd recalled his sharpshooters, looking at their dead enemies with an expression close to grief. Sergeant Shaw had never rejoiced in an enemy's death.

We're better than that.

Loveless was eaten up with hatred. He had carried the past with him, the ghosts of all his battles, the ghosts of all his massacres. He had killed people for twenty years, and his soul was damaged beyond repair.

Byrd turned his face away.

Horrified, Delia whispered outside the door, "Sergeant Byrd?"

Byrd returned his sidearm to the holster. "Delia? I need your help." He said, "When the sheriff come, you tell him, you never saw me. I was never here. Colonel Loveless shot Mr. Little, then he shot himself."

She nodded. "Been lying all my life, Sergeant Byrd. I reckon I can tell a lie for you."

All of the wounds of his war, all of the bruises of the latest battle, ached in his body, and Byrd limped to the front door. The smell of battle—the rot of mud, the sulphur of black powder, the iron tang of spilled blood—seemed to linger in the air in Hiram Little's house.

He shut the great door behind him and walked slowly down the steps. The hot summer air was sweet on his face, and the heat sank into his bones like a warm bath.

The battle of Willow Bend was over, and he hoped that the deaths of Little and Loveless would end the fight for good. He wasn't a praying man, but he'd pray for that.

The battle was done, but the ghosts of war and massacre were still with him. He would carry them forever. But his war was over. It might take a long time—it might take forever—but he was ready to put down his rifle and try to live at peace. No, he'd do better than try. For Bernie, for Jerusha, for Willow Bend, he'd do his damnedest.

He heard the cry of a great bird and looked up to see the eagle, its feathers gleaming in the sun. He watched as it circled and swooped for its prey, and then spread its great wings to soar upward and fly free.

Historical Note

This book had a curious beginning. I met my husband in graduate school, as he was writing a dissertation on politics on post-Reconstruction Mississippi. Sad to say, much of black Mississippi history at that time concerned what the 19th century called "outrages," their euphemism for murderous violence.

Years after he finished his dissertation, my husband told me a story he'd found in an obscure Mississippi newspaper, about a group of black Union veterans who stood up to Klan intimidation by fighting a battle so effective that they were never bothered again. But he'd never been able to find the citation. He still hasn't. It remains apocryphal.

Apocryphal or not, the history behind this story—of beleaguered Delta cotton farmers who stood up for themselves and of black Mississippians who founded an all-black town—is solidly based on fact.

The post-Reconstruction 1880s were a difficult time for black Mississippians. Reconstruction had been a time of great hope and great promise for the people who had once been slaves. They saw the possibility of full and equal participation in Mississippi's social, economic, and political life. They elected black officials at every level of government, from Congress to the county sheriff's office; they built schools and fought for state support of black education; they struggled to make a decent living. After Reconstruction ended in Mississippi in 1876, after Lincoln's Republicans were removed from political office, after the nation's attention turned away from the South, the former slaves of Mississippi found themselves fighting the efforts to confine them to a status not so different from slavery.

The black men who had served in the Union army during the war counted their fight for freedom as one of their proudest moments. Former slaves who fought for the Union Army fought for more than an abstraction; they fought for their freedom. During the war, Mississippi contributed more soldiers to the Union Army than the Confederate, and most of them were black. After the war, black veterans in Mississippi saw their political responsibilities, especially the vote, as an extension of their military service, and during Reconstruction, they often went to the polls dressed in their blue Union coats. Insuring that they would "vote the way they shot," the Republican party—the party of Lincoln and the defender of black equality during Reconstruction—printed ballots with the American eagle on one side and the American flag on the other. Despite the obstacles put in their way after 1876, black Mississippians continued to vote until the Black Codes of 1890 ended their participation in political life.

Sharecropping and tenancy arose just after the Civil War, when former planters were cash-poor, but the 1880s boom in the cotton economy, which made so many white planters rich, forced landless black farmers even deeper into the sharecropping system, which kept them in a debt not so different from slavery. Black farmers who wanted to profit from their labor, who wanted to be paid what they had earned, and who tried to do business elsewhere than the company store, where their purchases were added to their debt, were harassed and intimidated. When the Colored Farmers' Alliance came to Mississippi, the organizers were in mortal danger. The massacre that opens this book was based on a real mass murder that occurred in 1889 in Leflore County. A group of black people were gunned down as they listened to a speech given by the man named Oliver Cromwell, who tried to organize Leflore County for the Colored Farmers' Alliance.

Some black Mississippians despaired of life in the South and joined the "Exodusters," the emigration to Kansas that promised a decent livelihood and a life free of racial intimidation. Others, more hopeful, remained in Mississippi. In 1886, about a hundred of them came together to establish the all-black town of Mound Bayou in Bolivar County.

Mound Bayou was the result of a relationship that had begun

before the Civil War—between Joseph Davis, a most unusual planter, and his slave steward, Benjamin Montgomery. Davis, older brother to Confederate president Jefferson Davis, met the utopian thinker Robert Owen and was deeply impressed by his ideas of communal living. He decided to try to apply them on his plantation. While he never created a true commune, he became an unusually open-minded and benevolent master. He educated his slaves, encouraged their enterprise, and provided them with tools for self-government, including their own court.

Benjamin Montgomery, who eventually became Davis' business manager, was able to exercise his considerable talents as an inventor and entrepreneur. He ran the general store on the Davis plantations before the war, and after the war, when Davis was became impoverished, Montgomery bought the Davis plantations from him. Montgomery became a cotton planter, and his cotton-growing enterprise was one of the largest and most successful in Mississippi. He ran the enterprise until 1877, when business reverses and Montgomery's own failing health forced the family to sell the plantation back to the Davises.

For a decade, the Montgomery family were African-American planters, a rarity anywhere in the South, but especially in Mississippi. The family was hard-working and industrious, but they were also wealthy and cultivated. Montgomery educated all of his children—his daughters attended Oberlin College—and encouraged all of them in business. His sons Isaiah and William Thornton both ran their father's general store, and sister Mary worked in the business and served as the postmistress.

Isaiah Montgomery was raised on the utopian ideals of his former master and the entrepreneurial spirit of his father. He cherished the idea of a place where black people could work for themselves, own their homes and businesses, and live independently of white intrusion. In 1886, he bought a tract of land from the Louisville, New Orleans, and Texas Railway and persuaded a group of friends to help him clear the land to make it habitable. By 1888 the town of Mound Bayou had been carved from the Delta swamp. Ten years later, it was incorporated, and

Isaiah Montgomery became its first mayor. With the help of Booker T. Washington, the town rose to prosperity after the First World War. Despite its later decline, it still exists and retains a powerful grip on the hearts and minds of its residents. Decades after Booker T. Washington's visit, the people of Mound Bayou are still fiercely proud of "a town owned by Negroes."

For Further Reading

On the Exodusters, see Nell Painter, *Exodusters: Black Migration to Kansas after Reconstruction*, which paints a vivid portrait of the debt peonage and racial intimidation that drove black Southerners to Kansas. The best source on Mound Bayou remains Janet Sharp Hermann's book, *Pursuit of a Dream*, which covers Joseph Davis and Benjamin Montgomery as well as Isaiah Montgomery. It's fascinating to read the 1904 account written by Booker T. Washington, who helped Montgomery publicize the town to raise money for development. His article, "A Town Owned by Negroes: Mound Bayou, Miss., an Example of Thrift and Self-Government," can be found online at http://www.press.jhu.edu/books/supplemental/booker_t/ch07_02_booker_t_washington_rediscovered.pdf.

Thank you!

Thanks for reading *Freedom's Island*. I hope you enjoyed it.

Would you like to know about upcoming events or be the first to hear about my next book? You can sign up for my newsletter at www.sabrawaldfogel.com or like my Facebook page at https://www.facebook.com/pages/Sabra-Waldfogel-Author/530715473716016?ref=hl.

Reviews help other readers find books. I appreciate all reviews, whether positive or negative.

If you liked this book, you may also like my first, *Slave and Sister*. An excerpt follows. I hope you enjoy it as well.

Prologue

The Union Scouts

On a warm afternoon towards the end of May, three years after the outbreak of the Civil War, a troop of twenty blue-coated men rode warily through the northern Georgia countryside. General Sherman's army was a few miles away, just having tangled with the Confederates at a place called Cassville. The Confederate army was in retreat, so far away that Sherman had lost sight of their position, and these men from the 10th Ohio Cavalry had been sent to find out where they were waiting for the next fight.

Captain Endicott and his second in command, Lieutenant Randolph, rode together. Endicott, slight and pale, with light brown hair and gray eyes, was an Ohio man who had rushed home from Abolitionist Oberlin College to sign up as soon as he heard about the shots fired at Fort Sumter. Randolph, taller, broader, his skin swarthy, his hair dark and wavy, was a New Yorker who had come to the war as a photographer. Once in the Union Army, he learned that a man with a keen eye had greater value as a scout. He was mustered in as a private early in 1863, and after surviving the bloody Battle of Chickamauga last September, he had become a lieutenant.

The road was packed dirt, but it was wide and even. On either side were cotton fields. The plants were choked by weeds, but the crop hadn't been burned to the ground, as they'd seen in the bushwhacked counties along the Tennessee border. They passed a plantation house that looked the worse for wear, the paint peeling and the windows dusty. But it was standing, and whole.

They saw no one on the road and no one in the fields. The fighting at Cassville, which had been close enough to echo here, had frightened the local people into staying in their houses.

Down the road, on the right side, the open fields gave way to a slight hill covered with a thick growth of trees. Randolph said, "I don't like that thicket."

Endicott said, "Neither do I. Can you see anything?"

"No. That's what worries me."

It was a good vantage point, if you were waiting for a battle.

Endicott halted, as did the rest, and he addressed them. "We split up, ten men on the road, ten men behind. Remember, we aren't here to do battle. We're here to draw fire so we know how many there are. After they start shooting, we don't linger." He said to Powell, his second lieutenant, "You and your men approach them from the road. Randolph and I will take the rest and we'll scout them from the rear."

All of these men, with the exception of Randolph, had mustered in together in Ohio in 1862 and had been fighting together ever since. They had all been on scouting and picket duty, both dangerous, in Virginia, Tennessee and Georgia.

Powell and his men rode towards the trees. Randolph,

Endicott and the others left the road, looking for the back of the hill.

Before they were in rifle range, the air began to fill with smoke from black powder and the sulphur smell of powder exploding. The shots came in a steady stream. More than their twenty men. Was it fifty? Or a hundred?

The land behind the hill was heavily wooded, too. There might be a thousand men hidden in the trees. Endicott's men, looking for a way through the growth, were met with a steady stream of fire. They couldn't see through the trees, and the horses were unable to maneuver. One of the horses was hit. It screamed and reared, and a second shot felled it. Unhorsed, its rider was shot before he could run. He dropped to the ground, screaming in pain.

Endicott called out, "Get out of the line of fire!" His men maneuvered their horses through the trees as best they could. They spurred the horses as the shots continued to come at them. In a moment, they were lost in the trees, with only the sound of hooves to tell they were there.

Randolph said, "I'll see to Robson." Before Endicott could stop him, he dismounted, crouched low, and wove his way through the trees toward the man who had fallen. Robson lay on the ground, moaning now, his tunic soaked with blood from the wound in his chest. It was too dangerous to lift him, too dangerous to stand in the rain of fire. Randolph grabbed Robson by the legs and to drag him away. Robson cried out and then he was quiet.

Randolph let go Robson's legs. Still crouching, he looked for Endicott, his vision obscured by black smoke. Keeping as low as he could, Randolph ran through the trees, trying to find a way out of the thicket.

"Randolph! Over here!" It was Endicott.

"Where are the horses?"

"Lost! Follow me!"

Stumbling, they ran together, away from the barrage. Despite the sun, it was dark in the thicket, even darker because of the smoke from the guns. Even here, the air reeked of sulphur.

They ran without getting their bearings, not knowing where they were, until they could hear the shots but were out of their reach. They slowed. Panting, Randolph said, "I see a break in the trees." It was a path. "Let's hope it leads to a road," Endicott said.

They followed it, and came onto a dirt road, narrower than the one they had left. They could see beyond the trees to cotton fields again.

When they stopped, Randolph asked, "Are you all right?"

Endicott looked down to see the hole in his right sleeve. He moved his arm and groaned in pain. Randolph said, "Take off the tunic and let me see."

The sleeve of Endicott's blouse was streaked with blood. Underneath, there was a graze, ugly but not deep, in his upper arm near the shoulder. Endicott said, "Nothing serious."

Randolph poured whiskey into the wound and bound it with his handkerchief. Endicott said, "That should hold it." He reached for his rifle and groaned in pain again.

"Can you shoot like that?"

Gritting his teeth, Endicott said, "I'll have to."

They walked slowly, doubly vigilant now that they knew that the Confederates were nearby. There could be an army in the next thicket and just beyond it.

They had walked less than a mile when they saw it.

"I'll be damned," Randolph said. He was looking at a flagpole, and atop it flew the Stars and Stripes, which fluttered prettily in the slight breeze. Next to the flagpole was a sign that said "Kaltenbach," and a driveway.

In surprise, Endicott said, "Is there another regiment already here? Holding this place? I thought we were the advance troop."

"Let's find out."

Endicott held his rifle ready, despite the pain in his arm, and they walked slowly down the driveway.

The gravel of the driveway had been recently raked and smoothed. There were shrubs planted on either side, magnolias as tall as young trees, intensely fragrant, which had been recently pruned. As the driveway curved, they saw flower beds, which had been kept free of weeds. There was an expanse of lawn, which looked as though it had been tended.

Even in his apprehension, Endicott thought of his family farm, where his mother took good care of the front yard. He had not seen a Georgia plantation that looked house-proud, like a Northern homestead.

It looked peaceful. But both men had been soldiers long enough to know that peace was deceptive, and could be shattered with a single shot.

On the steps of the house stood a group of about ten black people, women and children clustered in the center. They were flanked by four men armed with rifles, who held them ready. A voice came from the center of the group. "Who are you?" she asked, and when she pushed back her straw hat they both saw that she was white.

Randolph and Endicott didn't lower their rifles. Endicott asked, "Are there Union men here?"

"No," she said. "Just you."

"Who put up the Union flag?"

The woman to her right spoke. She said calmly, "We did." Her face was the color the former slaves called medium brown, and even a glimpse of it showed that she was pretty, with a rounded face and a dimple in each cheek. She wore a neat calico dress, and over it, a clean apron. Her hair was hidden by a white kerchief. Despite her slave's attire, she stood very straight. If she were a soldier, her commander would be proud of her bearing.

Endicott asked, "Are you for the Union?"

"We all are."

Endicott's right arm ached unbearably. "Then put your rifles down."

She nodded to the four armed men, who lowered their rifles and laid them on the ground at their feet. Randolph and Endicott lowered their guns. When Endicott slung the gun over his unwounded left shoulder, he gritted his teeth against the pain.

Endicott said, "My name is Captain John Endicott. This man is Lieutenant Thomas Randolph. We're both attached to the 10th

Ohio Cavalry, and we've just skirmished with the Confederates not far from here." He looked at the white woman. "Who are you, ma'am?"

"I'm Mrs. Adelaide Kaltenbach. My husband owns this place." She turned to the pretty ex-slave. Mrs. Kaltenbach said, "This is Rachel Mannheim, who manages it."

Randolph and Endicott looked at each other in surprise at the surname. Most slaves—or recently freed slaves—referred to themselves by only a Christian name.

"How do you do, sir," Rachel said. Her speech was clear and grammatical, not at all like someone born a slave.

Mrs. Kaltenbach gestured to one of the men who had been holding a rifle, who stepped forward. He was darker than Rachel, with broad shoulders and muscled arms. He wore a cotton shirt, plain blue trousers, and boots dirty with the mud of the field. She said, "This is Miss Mannheim's cousin, Charles Mannheim, who looks after the crop."

Endicott asked Adelaide Kaltenbach, "Where is your husband?"

She said, "He's away, fighting."

Endicott asked, "For the Confederacy?"

"Yes, to his regret. He's with the 18th Georgia in Virginia, God help him."

"Is he a Union man, too?"

Rachel was the one to reply. "Mr. Kaltenbach has always been a Union man, since before the war."

More and more surprised, Endicott asked, "Do you people know about the Emancipation Proclamation? That you're free?"

Another of the former riflemen, a short, sturdy man, said, "Miss Rachel read us the Emancipation Proclamation when it came out last year, and she and Miss Adelaide explained it so we could understand it."

So Miss Rachel Mannheim could read, too. Endicott, who had borne the news of freedom to many slaves in Georgia and Tennessee, asked, "What did you make of it?"

To his surprise, the sturdy man answered. "It said that we're forever free, and we can come and go as we please, and get paid wages for the work we do, and defend ourselves, and join the Union Army to fight for freedom."

Randolph said, "That's as neat a summary as I've heard from anyone."

Adelaide said, "May we offer you some refreshment? Even if it's only water?"

Endicott swallowed hard at the thought of fresh water. "Lieutenant Randolph and I would be greatly obliged."

Rachel turned to a woman who was so small that both men thought she was a child until they saw her face. She was very dark, African black, and her eyes were wide with apprehension. She held a small white boy, about five years old, tightly by the hand. Rachel said to Endicott, "This is Mrs. Minerva Davis, who looks after the house." Endicott nodded. Rachel said, "It's much too hot to stand in the sun. Please, wait on the piazza. Minnie, would you get these men a drink of water?"

When Minnie brought them water, she watched them drink it gratefully, and she said to Endicott, "Sir, are you wounded?"

Endicott said, "It's not serious."

"But it pains you."

Randolph said, "You can't ride or shoot like that." He asked Adelaide, "Might we stay for a day on your land? So Captain Endicott can rest?"

Between the two women, Adelaide Kaltenbach and Rachel Mannheim, passed the easy look of people who knew each other well. Adelaide nodded, and Rachel said, "I think we can do better than that. There's plenty of room in the house. We can make up the bedrooms, and we can give you dinner, too. And tend to that wound of yours."

Endicott was so startled at this courtesy from an ex-slave and her former mistress that he blushed. "We don't mean to trouble you."

The complicit look, and the nod. Adelaide said, "It's no trouble at all. Please come into the house."

Both men had been on grand plantations in Tennessee—

they'd been headquartered in the home of one of the biggest planters in Marion County, outside Chattanooga—and they knew right away that this was the house of a small planter. The walls were painted a plain white, and the floors were a plain varnished oak. Like the grounds, the house was well-kept. The Turkey carpet in the hallway wasn't new, but it had been lightly used, and the colors were bright. Someone took care to beat the carpet and sweep the floor.

As they stood in the entryway, Endicott murmured to Randolph, "What do you make of it?"

Randolph looked at the pleasant house, which seemed untouched by the war, but he was thinking about the Union flag and the ex-slaves who understood so well that they were free. "Damnedest place I ever saw," he said.